ACHIEVING
POWER

ACHIEVING POWER

Practice and policy in social welfare

Stuart Rees

ALLEN & UNWIN

First published 1991
Allen & Unwin Pty Ltd
8 Napier Street, North Sydney NSW 2059 Australia

National Library of Australia
Cataloguing-in-Publication entry:

Rees, Stuart, 1939—
    Achieving power: practice and policy in social welfare

    Bibliography.
    Includes index.
    ISBN 0 04 442335 7.
    1. Social policy.   2. Public welfare.   3. Poor. I. Title.

361.61

Set in 10/11 Plantin by Times Graphics, Singapore
Printed by Dah Hua Printers, Hong Kong

Contents

Figures

Acknowledgments

A book with a title like this represents a collective effort. In this respect, during a year in which I was preoccupied with this task, the encouragement and support of Ragnhild has been indispensable.

Students and staff at Sydney University have provided the atmosphere in which one can conjure ideas and I am particularly grateful to those colleagues who have commented on specific chapters. Michael Horsburgh and Robert van Krieken are excellent editors. Alec Pemberton has always been a significant source of scholarship and a creative commentator on anyone's first draft. With reference to writing about skills and the politics of organisations, I have leaned heavily on Lindsey Napier's and Mary Lane's knack of always making one take stock, find space and think again.

Zita Mullaly and John Usher have been the generous marathon runners who read the manuscript from beginning to end. Their questions kept the discussion flowing and their ideas, about connections between one source and another, were crucial in achieving any continuity of argument. The responsibility for any inconsistencies and discontinuity is however entirely mine.

My largest debt of gratitude goes to this department's exceptional secretary Janice Whittington. Janice has the unfailing good humour and the well-honed skills required to type and retype drafts; and even after all that she could still summon the stamina to produce the final version.

Stuart Rees
Department of Social Work and Social Policy
Sydney University

Various works of poetry have been used to illustrate the text. In all cases the works have been fully attributed and the author has used his best endeavours to inform copyright owners.

I Issues and prospectus

1 The issues

As an antidote to the promotion by leading politicians and economists in the 1980s of the values of self-interest, this book proposes an optimistic and realisable practice for welfare in the 1990s. It also presents a challenge to the preoccupation with control that has been a priority of governments and bureaucratic organisations, including those representing welfare interests.

Responses to these issues of economic self-interest and control have been fragmented. *Achieving Power* therefore identifies some consequences of separating people and ideas; for example when policy makers have little to do with practitioners, when welfare is discussed as though it has little to do with economics, when art is kept distinct from science, and when politics is seen only as a rather grubby business engaged in by politicians.

These forms of separation are disempowering and compound other forms of powerlessness. The solution to this puzzle lies not in some generalist account of welfare but in a political literacy, drawing ideas from numerous sources to debate common goals, developing social analysis and skills to implement decisions which have been carefully argued by citizens of all kinds.

The advocacy of these ideals is concerned with means of empowerment which would be personally encouraging and politically astute, emphasising the value of equity and the politics of mutual education. To begin the steps towards that goal requires recognition that even the word 'empowerment' has been and is being used as a term of convenience, to justify the maintenance of disempowering policies and practices rather than to achieve their elimination.

Some common usages of 'empowerment'

In social welfare circles and among politicians, the word empowerment has become common. Right-wing politicians use it to stress the merits of economic independence at all costs; somewhat ingenuously, they have argued that citizens have a right to fend for themselves. In specific contexts, for example in education, the same politicans have emphasised the values of competition and diversity of educational opportunity in preference to the ethos of equity and cooperation. The word empowerment has been used to camouflage this set of values and priorities.

A more predictable use of the term by teachers of all kinds, in schools, colleges and universities, includes the claim that their methods are aimed at empowering students. In the same vein social workers contend 'I'm empowering people' or, 'the empowerment process is old hat'. When asked to explain what they mean, they fall back on clichés about people taking control of their affairs through casework, or about staff developing indigenous resources from the bottom up through community development. A relatively new concept is being substituted for old ones without the political nature of empowerment being developed, with little indication of the way power is being defined or exercised, and with no reference to evidence about the interdependence of policy and practice.

Unless the meaning of politics and power and the interdependence of policy and practice are addressed, social workers and those who work in community development and in other human service organisations will be adrift, confronting neither the constraints which affect the direction of the welfare state nor the reasons why some forms of practice are encouraged while others are actively discouraged. Without a critique of politics and power as they are applied in different contexts, education to address the various tasks in social work and social welfare will once again reproduce mirror images oblivious of shifting political alignments (Bitensky 1973). Even among serious-minded commentators, rhetoric about empowerment has given the term an aspirin-like quality, as though it is a pill for all seasons, to 'reverse the process of disempowerment or oppression' (Reisch et al. 1983), or to say 'no' to agency demands (Smith 1975). These examples belie a tradition which has avoided claims about immediate cures.

Social work with oppressed groups and communities has been described as a form of empowerment. The groups and communities have included powerless black people in the United States (Solomon 1976), poor families of different racial origins (Pinderhughes 1983) and newly arrived immigrants who were unfamiliar with the language and culture of the host country (Hirayama and Cetingok 1988). Specific vulnerable groups have included the elderly in nursing homes (McDermott 1989), elderly women (Settlerlund 1988), vulnerable children, not just those in institutions or living with foster parents (Hegar 1989), people with disabilities (Safilios-Rothschild 1976) and ex-psychiatric patients (Rose and Black 1985).

Inherent in these descriptions is the belief that if empowerment is achieved, it can have significant effects on people's physical and mental health and on their attitude towards powerful people and institutions. The process in achieving these goals involves an improvement in people's image of themselves, the acquisition of tangible resources such as money or shelter and intangible resources such as information and the creation of supportive social networks.

The story that follows

The following approach to practice and policy in welfare can be applied by staff with different goals and responsibilities, including work with individuals and groups, campaigns to achieve policy outcomes and in community-oriented projects. It applies to educators, students, clients and practitioners.

Although most examples will refer to education and practice in social work, including community work, the pattern of values and skills outlined here should be seen as relevant to all human service workers interested in promoting social change and empowerment. For that reason, the arguments will often use the generic term 'human service organisations' and will sometimes refer to different groups, perhaps nurses, teachers or other educators, as well as community workers, welfare and residential staff or volunteers, and a range of social workers, from practitioners in health settings to those in social security, from those in youth refuges and other residential care settings to those working in the fields of probation and parole. Despite differences in the education and employment conditions of those various practitioners, each has been affected by dominant trends of the 1980s, such as governments' uncritical reverence for the values of business management and the scant attention given to the contribution of human services in the development of any culture. In response to those trends a narrowly conceived professional literature, particularly one that is apolitical and ignores the constraints of practice, will not produce the coherent ideology, the language, theories and skills for the 1990s and beyond.

The eighteen chapters of this text are organised into five parts. Part I, which includes this introduction, identifies the issues with which this text is concerned. These include people's feelings of powerlessness and the need to maximise the sources of inspiration, perhaps by drawing on music as well as literature, dance and art as well as the social sciences and different disciplines and cultural perspectives in order to overcome such a condition. With that in mind the following chapter discusses significant traditions in the writings about empowerment and explains the key concepts in any political literacy about welfare: biography, authority and power, politics, skills, and the interdependence of policy and practice.

Part II begins with 'the promise of biography': an examination of the perspectives of students, clients, migrants, poets and prisoners who have addressed and often overcome experiences of powerlessness. That consideration of biography is a significant part of the overall context in which the discussion of political literacy, social analysis and personal skills occurs. Other parts of this context include an appraisal of theories about the exercise of power, interpretations of politics and discussion of the connotation of language. That last issue will include consideration of discourse about the human condition and thereby an appraisal of what societies value most. Part II concludes with the reminder that commitment to empowerment has to take notice not only of the conflict between economic rationalism and campaigns to achieve social justice but also of the controversy as to who defines social justice. In addition to that issue, conflict between people engaged in the same social movements but who differ as to how goals can be achieved, will not be overlooked.

Part III examines processes in effecting change. It begins with a discussion of the meaning of social justice and of the moral and professional justifications for the goals of empowerment. Subsequent analysis of the relationship between empowerment and the smorgasbord of other offerings in the conflict-consensus traditions of social work theory indicates how different students and practitioners could respond to these ideas. An emphasis on implementation continues, in chapter 8, with an account of the significance of recording small victories at almost any stage of dialogue and partnership. A similar process, described in chapter 9, is applied to staff who want to overcome disempowering conditions at work.

Part IV describes the interactive and political skills in almost constant use in any form of practice. It also identifies specific task-oriented skills in evaluation, assessment, administration and planning, formal negotiation and advocacy. Although skills are linked to an overriding ideology and theory, their separate treatment is intended to highlight their importance in taking decisions, and in giving individuals the confidence that they can do things and do them well.

In Part V, the social and economic policy issues which have virtually enveloped all the previous discussions of problems, objectives, theory and skills, are addressed, beginning with the disempowering consequences of theorising about policy as though it is always separate from practice. The need for practitioners to take steps towards achieving some degree of economic literacy is seen as a crucial process of empowerment. Without such literacy, economic forecasters can continue to bamboozle and economists of a particular persuasion will continue to promote the view that only further cutbacks in welfare programs will revive national economies.

2 The prospectus

The prospectus which explains key concepts derives partly from a tradition of writing about empowerment and addresses the question: what is new in the thesis being offered here? In that tradition two sources of ideas should be acknowledged. The first derives from the work of Paulo Freire and the second from the women's movement.

Two sources of ideas

Freire aimed to create self-awareness among illiterate Brazilian peasants whom he described as having few ways of knowing the sources of their oppression. In spite of criticism that his work displayed a patronising attitude, a 'we know what is good for you', or a 'you don't know what is good for yourselves' approach to education (Berger 1974), his methods did emphasise the value of teaching literacy by broadening people's intellectual horizons.

The idea of people learning to read and write around topics that related to their everyday experiences did not have to mean a patronising and hierarchical interpretation of consciousness, and Freire's optimism could be applied to people in all walks of life. He wrote: 'In order for the oppressed to be able to wage the struggle for their liberation they must perceive the reality of oppression, not as a closed world from which there is no exit, but as a limited situation which they can transform' (Freire 1972 p.34).

Freire described a dialogue between educators and their subjects to challenge the banking method of education which had prevented people from being active witnesses and protagonists in their own interests. Domination was the major theme, liberation his objective and an educational process of 'thematic investigation' the means of achieving that objective. (Some of these ideas are developed further in Chapter 8.) The flavour of the educational process was captured in his recommendation that if dialogue was to represent 'the practice of freedom', it required 'love, humility, faith in man's power to make and remake, hope and critical thinking' (Freire 1972 p.63).

Writers in several traditions of feminism have much in common with a philosophy of education as a means of liberation. They have identified the restricted world of women who are child-carers, housekeepers, husband-minders, unpaid voluntary workers or lowly paid employees. They have exposed the history of women's oppression as a product of social structure and have shown how some form of liberation could be achieved by examining the political implications of personal lives. Liberation was possible from restrictive thought processes, from dominating relationships in the world of work, including the home, and from compliance with influential professionals who have been unable or unwilling to see the political issues affecting women's powerlessness.

Any brief description of feminist perspectives will inevitably gloss over very real differences in ideologies and theories (Wearing 1986; Nes and Iadicola 1989). Liberal feminists, for example, have emphasised the importance of equality of opportunity as a path to equality between the sexes whereas Marxist feminists have concentrated their efforts on exposing capitalism and resulting class differences as the source of women's oppression. Radical feminists have identified gender as the source of women's oppression and have seen men as an opposing class. In their analyses, 'the seat of power has been moved from the economic to the sexual dimensions' (Wearing 1986 p.45).

Socialist feminists have rejected the idea that all women have similar problems. They have highlighted the specific difficulties of working-class and third-world women and have also given attention to variables such as race, ethnicity and age. A potential divisiveness in these perspectives is coupled to a promise to be realised, in the sense that 'no theoretical approach has all the answers; each has a particular focus and is more useful for certain aspects of certain aspects of practice than for others' (Wearing 1986 p.52).

The contribution of feminist perspectives to empowerment seems to lie in analyses of experiences of privilege and oppression which show gender and class-related differences in the power of different women, as well as between men and women (Curthoys 1988). A perspective which depicts all men as the enemy and which is blind to the social contexts of sexism, seems equivalent to using Freire's notion of consciousness raising as though the better educated will always have a superior view of reality. On the basis of such superiority they will be entitled to encourage others to adopt their point of view. That exercise of power would probably be experienced as disempowering by women as well as by men.

Significant achievements of feminist perspectives in social work have included a focus on the victimisation of women and the location of this problem not in the female psyche but in patriarchy-inspired values and institutions (Berlin and Kravetz 1981). Pressure for social, legal and economic reforms, initiatives in using networks of support among women and the development of alternative social services have been other outcomes of feminist-inspired practice (Brook and Davis 1985; Collins 1986).

The application of such perspectives has emphasised the value not only of opportunities for women to discover why and how they have been kept in subordinate positions, but also for men to learn about equity in relationships and about the creative and constructive exercise of power generally. To this end, in education and practice, feminist perspectives have successfully challenged the content of curricula and influenced teaching methods (McCleod and Dominelli 1982). They have also shown how personal biography can be used as valid evidence of the conditions affecting women's image of themselves and their control over their lives (McCleod and Dominelli 1982; Setterlund 1988).

However, if an analysis of 'achieving power' required only an elaboration of the ideas of Freire and some feminist writers, no new treatise would be necessary. In the following prospectus, a list of ambit claims extends their perspectives by discussing how the architects of social policies, including middle managers and front-line practitioners, must not be coopted by the undue influence of a particular brand of economics. That prospectus also redefines politics, confronts the neglected issue of the relationship between policy and practice, and emphasises the need to acquire personal skills.

The interest that an investment in this package might yield cannot be predicted but the prospectus does not disguise what is being offered, or the possible costs of becoming a shareholder in the exercise (Figure 2.1). Based on conflict analyses of society and social institutions, the 'essential ideas and concepts' of this approach to practice are located in the left-hand column of the figure. Each can be described briefly, though at this point, considerable space will be given to discussing the first two concepts, biography and power. With regard to the latter topic, key issues will include the nature of the relationship between authority and power as well as the different interpretations of power.

Biography

Biography refers to individuals' experiences and to the careers of movements and organisations. It is a beginning and end point in empowerment, a possible source of misgivings about the risks of breaking new ground but also the means of coherence which comes from fitting together those things which may have remained separate. In this respect the individual or collective biographies of students, practitioners, clients or others could be used.

Figure 2.1   What's new? The empowerment prospectus

Essential ideas and concepts	Rationale for inclusion	Possible costs of emphasising the value of these concepts
Biography	Provides a familiar basis for analysis and encourages the application of ideas and theories from numerous sources.	May be threatening, because it requires frankness, yet might be seen as apolitical: precludes consideration of wider issues.
Power	Has to be seen as a multidimensional concept: the exercise of power can be liberating or restricting.	Many people happier with using the term glibly and in a conservative one-dimensional fashion.
Politics	Political understanding is essential in a practice which addresses numerous constraints and opportunities.	Requires a redefinition of practice to reflect a constant examination of power and the way it is exercised.
Skills	Empowerment can derive from skills. Attaining objectives depends on a mixture of interactive and political skills of evaluation, administration, negotiation and advocacy.	Not too many costs for students and practitioners but theoreticians might object to this emphasis on experiencing power through the possession and use of skills.
Policy and practice: their inter-dependence	The separation of policy from practice serves interests of status quo. Policy may reflect pratitioners' use of discretion.	Means casting aside the educational and agency tradition of separating policy from practice. This change may threaten investment in the separation.

Sharing ideas from various sources to express the relationship between personal context and the dominant values in a culture represents the promise of biography. Those sources could include artists and scientists, colleagues or clients, novelists or poets. Even under the most distressing conditions, the unravelling of biography could realise a power in being creative, perhaps by developing the potential for everyone to become an artist with respect to their own lives. The Irish poet W.B. Yeats explained this point by saying that to find the energy to take responsibility for wider social issues in the world of his time, he first had to rediscover and remotivate himself.

> The fools that have it I do wrong
> Whenever I remake a song
> Should know what issue is at stake
> It is myself that I remake
> (in Rubinoff 1968 p.207)

Yeats' point about the potentiality of everyone to be an artist was the equivalent of Mathew Arnold's notion that all individuals possess the seed of Socrates. This potential was expanded by Antonio Gramsci who claimed that everyone is a philosopher 'who contributes to sustain a conception of the world or to modify it, that is, to bring into being new modes of thought' (Entwistle 1979 p.118).

The influence and unfolding of biography is never likely to be a story of individuals alone. To understand biography demands a lot more than self-referencing although, as in Yeats' verse, that is where we might start. Given that 'the promise of biography' stands at the gateway to the rest of this book, the theory as to how this promise might be realised should be made explicit. There are three points. The first concerns the struggle to make sense of individual circumstances in relation to the dominant constraints and opportunities of a specific issue and time, a matter of struggle in context. The second point is an acknowledgment of the continuous and ongoing process of trying to comprehend and influence the world around one. The third point concerns the growth of freedom and the exercising of power in a spontaneous and creative way.

The writings of Gramsci and Erich Fromm help elaborate these points. Gramsci, in his search for the ideal of using literacy to attain a unity in theory and practice in education and in politics, was a kindred spirit to Freire. Fromm's insights into the mechanisms which enable people to escape freedom highlighted the central issues of authority and power in the unfolding of biography (Fromm 1960). Put another way, Fromm identified spontaneity as the creative expression of power and was absorbed with unmasking what it was that inhibited the realisation of people's emotional and intellectual potentialities.

Now we can return to the three issues that incorporate and explain the promise of biography: struggle in context, continuity of experience, and factors inhibiting spontaneity. Struggle in context refers to the ability to question major issues in relation to a set of constraints. It implies the value of encouraging anyone, student, worker or client, to raise questions and to seek answers, whether by conversation, by reading or writing. This notion of struggle and questioning was evident in Gramsci's own life in which 'everything was presented as uncertain' with a recurrence of phrases like 'I have not yet decided what to think', 'in general I think' (Entwistle 1979 p.5). The reference to context is intended as a reminder that historical and contemporary forces need to be addressed in people's questions and doubts. For example, this book about the ends and means of empowerment is written in response to the apolitical nature of much of the writing about welfare practice and to the deadening yet dominating effects of a particular economic creed. This creed, described here as economic rationalism, has attained the influence, in Fromm's terms, of anonymous authority; it remains disguised yet is so well promoted as to be taken for granted, perhaps as a form of science, as a representation of normality or as being almost synonymous with sensible public opinion. In the 1980s and into the 1990s such anonymous authority influenced the priorities for debate in political, policy and media circles, and affected people's aspirations; it therefore could hardly be ignored in any unravelling of the content and direction of biography.

The second step in this tracing of the promise of biography concerns the value of developing questions over time, as part of a disciplined approach to personal and professional development. A student can be encouraged to develop questions about the present, not merely to solve an immediate problem but as a means of developing a philosophy for practice, and skills in so doing. Gramsci had this in mind when he spoke of schooling as a continuous experience. It is not an extravagant step to extrapolate from this that biography could be grasped as a continuous educational experience, perhaps in the way that disadvantaged people are enabled to overcome their predicaments, or, in more commonplace terms, in the way that we may 'understand the news, engage with works of imagination, become involved in conversation with workmates and friends and make sense of daily experience' (Entwistle 1979 p.90). Gramsci himself was concerned that his writings and other forms of practice should produce a political philosophy which committed people to the pursuit of social change.

The third point in this account of the promise of biography concerns a focus on the factors which inhibit the freedom to express thoughts and feelings. Fromm identified the earliest training of a child, restrictions in formal education and the absence of the experience of loving and being loved as among the strongest forces which suppressed spontaneity and thereby encouraged hostility, dominance and the growth of authoritarianism.

In community activities or in any human service organisations, numerous psychological, social and other material forces will affect individuals' development of their own sense of freedom and their ability to exercise power creatively. To know what forces hinder that freedom requires skills in assessing obstacles to growth and spontaneity, a claim to be developed when we discuss the nature of authority and power. Suffice to say here that in ruminating on the forces which hinder spontaneity, it will be important to go beyond questions about childhood development and formal education.

Wider forces constrain lives by rendering people powerless to comprehend, make challenges or develop alternatives. With regard to all sorts of practitioners in human service organisations, such forces could include the rhetoric of economists or the managerial emphasis in the language of administration, or, more specifically, the problem of organisational overload. Each, or a combination of such forces, would hinder spontaneity in the workplace.

Power

At this point we should identify controversies over the meanings of power and authority, and say how such terms will be used in this text. A key premise in claims about empowerment is that a clarification of terms facilitates people's ability to communicate and to cooperate. With that premise in mind, it will be important to spend time discussing the meaning of power and authority, and the relationship between them.

In the discourse of this book, analysis of the exercise of power provides a recurring theme. Yet it is authority which first requires clarification, in part because this is the reference point for the exercise of power: action by individuals or groups can be justified by reference to some view of authority. In dictionary definitions, authority refers to a power or right to command, to act, to enforce obedience or make final decisions. In Erich Fromm's analysis, authority referred to 'an interpersonal relation' in which one person looks upon another as somebody superior to him (Fromm 1960 p.141). Dictionary definitions indicate that authority in an interrelationship is invested by one person in another by virtue of opinion, respect or esteem or by the influence of character or office.

We should still postpone the consideration of the meaning of power by exploring further the different forms of authority which provide people with the permission, the incentive or the justification to act. In this regard Fromm identified three types of authority. External authority was derived from a person or institution. In contemporary human service organisations preoccupied with hierarchies as the means of control, employees' freedom to use any discretion is curtailed by emphasis on higher or external authority. Such emphasis is often made by the people who represent the rules which identify what it is administratively or legally possible to do.

Internal authority, in Fromm's terms, could appear 'under the name of duty, conscience, or super-ego' (Fromm 1960 p.143). From that surmise he explored the sense of integrity and conviction which individuals' inner authority could represent. Translated to human service organisations, it could mean that the positive use of discretion in association with, or on behalf of others, would be more likely if practitioners possessed their own inner sense of authority, notwithstanding external constraints. They could justify their use of discretion by reference to such authority. They could transcend the limits of the organisation, or at least not be always overawed by what they could not do.

A third form of authority was described by Fromm as 'anonymous . . . It does not demand anything except the self-evident. It seems to use no pressure but only mild persuasion' (Fromm 1960 p.144). The point about anonymous authority was that it was and is disguised, difficult to fight against, yet pervasive in its influence. For example, in subsequent discussion about welfare or justice and the means of achieving such states, the anonymous authority of a certain recycled form of economics will be addressed. That recycling usually crops up in references to goals of efficiency, productivity and accountability for such goals. That these terms may have been borrowed uncritically from a set of business-oriented values is not made explicit, neither is any admission made that the relevance of these goals to ideals of welfare and justice has not been evaluated. The anonymous authority is there to be unmasked and challenged. Without challenge, such 'authority' (as in a particular view of the primacy of economic management in the conduct of human affairs) comes to be taken for granted.

These forms of authority are not mutually exclusive. External and anonymous forms of authority may be internalised so that individuals use these reference points as their philosophy, providing justification for their actions. It is as though they have been submerged by the organisation in which they work, or absorbed by the culture or religion by which they live. They have little separate identity. Where and when that submerging and absorption constrains the freedom of individuals and groups, the process of empowerment is pertinent. The struggle is to replace reliance on external, or anonymous, authority by reference to inner authority and control, albeit without that pursuit of selfishness so apparent in the desire to dominate others.

The issue of overlap between one form of authority and another is not to be pondered at length here, but another issue merits attention. It is important to recognise the characteristic of authority evident in a relationship. For every person who exercises authority another person responds or complies. This was the issue exposed so forcefully by the experiments of Stanley Milgram when he depicted various habits of obedience and the lengths to which people would go in order to be seen to conform to some external or higher authority (Milgram 1974). These lengths included being very cruel to experimental subjects, apparently because the desire to conform to orders was stronger than the influence of any principles concerned with being reasonable or fair. The Milgram experiments remind us that compliance is a dimension of authority: as evident in the unquestioning student, the conforming practitioner or the passively accepting client or patient. That reference to compliance introduces discussion about the meaning of power and the way it is going to be used in this text.

In dictionary definitions, power usually refers to the capacity to act, to a capability of performing or producing. Prompted by, or in response to some form of authority, power is usually described as being of two kinds: that which is potentially creative and liberating and its opposite, such as thought and action which limit and constrict. Fromm, for example, saw power as meaning 'one of two things, domination or potency' (Fromm 1960 p.139). The two experiences of power were mutually exclusive. The domination of others might be an expression of material strength but in a psychological sense it was probably evidence of weakness. By contrast, the individual who is creative and enabling, or 'potent' in Fromm's terms, is someone able to realise their emotional, intellectual, artistic or political qualities without interfering with the freedom of others to do likewise. It is that form of power which captures the spirit and the objective of empowerment. By contrast, 'power, in the sense of domination, is the perversion of potency, just as sexual sadism is the perversion of love' (Fromm 1960 p. 140).

This distinction between power over people, and power to achieve goals which are liberating for others and which provide a sense of self-enhancing creativity for the actor or actors, will be explored by focusing on the exercise of power in different contexts. At this stage of introducing the key concepts in the discussion I merely want to emphasise that the meaning of power has been contested by various social theorists and is a concept which should never be used glibly . In chapter 4, the nature of this contest and controversy will be discussed. The focus here, and throughout the rest of this book, is on the different meanings and uses of power. To achieve that objective, the distinction will be made between one, two and three-dimensional ways of exercising power (Lukes 1974).

That significant sociological analysis of the exercise of power will show that the meaning of power looks and feels different according to the experience of different professionals or ordinary citizens. To achieve goals of empowerment, the exercise of power would seldom if ever be one-dimensional, because to act in that way would involve a preoccupation with compliance to official authority and that usually involves thoughtless control of others. By contrast, three-dimensional exercise of power would eschew control. It would be evident in policies to achieve justice, or in projects concerned with equity, as in the promotion of the interests of the most vulnerable groups in a population. The applicability of Lukes' scheme to human service organisations is discussed in chapter 4.

Politics

A critical analysis of the exercise of power presupposes a view of politics as activity which is concerned with defining the public good and reconciling conflicts between individuals with a view to achieving that goal (Marquand 1988 ch.8). This view of politics implies the articulation of values which support community interests over individual gain. It emphasises the struggle to achieve welfare as appropriate political activity which will occur in familiar contexts of interpersonal exchanges, in deliberations over the way an agency conducts its business and in debates over the significance of any policies which affect justice. For example, it will be argued that because the peace and environment movements address issues of social justice, they have much in common with empowerment objectives in welfare. An implication in this last statement is that someone has already decided on the choice of purposes for others and to do that puts at risk the value of tolerance. The politics of open discussion can be inspirational, and criticism should be valued as long as it never merely expresses intolerance. This point about criticism being compatible with empowerment will be discussed briefly with reference to the popularity of systems theories.

Definitions of empowerment which have relied on the consensus-oriented language of systems theories (Pinderhughes 1983; Solomon 1987; Brown 1988) do not appear to have paid much attention to ideology and politics, or to practitioners' involvement in economic and social policies. In that respect they are too simple. The use of theories about social systems has produced consensus-oriented goals for people and societies: namely to achieve balance, homeostasis or equilibrium (De Hoyos and Jensen 1985; De Hoyos 1989).

It would be inflexible education and foolish politics to suggest that the creative use of power is only exercised by those who reject such consensus-type views. It is not known with any certainty whether practitioners who claim to be 'radical' pursue radical practices, or fall back on consensus-type actions. Or the other way around. That is another reason why subsequent discussion of different levels of theorising encourages the development of ideas from people located at any point on the continuum of values from consensus to conflict.

Related to this point about the usefulness of ideas from numerous sources is another disclaimer. The thesis mounted here is not a repeat of radical treatises, though it has something in common with some of them. The notion of 'achieving power' highlights a practical orientation to taking decisions and implementing them. A focus on doing even small things well is also intended as a guard against some interpretations of radical ideologies, based on which claims about liberation are expressed with dogmatism, or with that distressing lack of humour which always seems to accompany certainty. There is neither skill nor sensitivity in talk about the transformation of society which is accompanied by a disregard for the politics of conflict between powerful interests, and for the caution of those who want to take risks but are fearful of doing so.

Skills

Practitioners' skills in achieving objectives concerned with equity and justice are intended to address their own and others' powerlessness. They are part of a challenge to the preoccupation of policies which have emphasised financial accountability and individual power as criteria to measure the performance of welfare agencies, as though they were commercial concerns.

This prospectus rejects the idea that skills can be acquired only in field work and insists that the links between theories and skills be made explicit. Students' and practitioners' confidence to take risks comes from knowing that they possess skills which give them credibility in their own and others' eyes, and which enable them to implement administrative and policy goals and so test claims about the politics of practice.

Skills are not an end in themselves. If they were they could be taught as though practice in social welfare was some technical task. On the other hand, a sophisticated analysis of social problems without the skills to administer a program or to negotiate with those who do not share your views, would be tantamount to a conductor lecturing on the theory of composition who was unable to get the orchestra to perform. For this reason, disicussion of skills and exercises to acquire skills are given special prominence.

Policy and practice

A view of empowerment as a bridging concept to span different interpretations of policies was developed by Rapoport (1981) with respect to children. The tension between a policy which stressed that state's role in protecting children's needs and a liberation-oriented policy which emphasised their rights, was to be resolved by practitioners. They could enable children to exercise autonomy by helping them to learn from others, to gain confidence in themselves and to do so by giving attention, in association with adults, to needs and to rights (Hegar 1989). Practitioners' resolution of the difference between conflicting policies could be empowering or disempowering.

Lack of coherence in comprehending the policy–practice relationship has occurred when students, educators and practitioners have been taught to perceive these topics in ways which denoted separate areas of enquiry, dealt with by different scholars and by practitioners with different levels of responsibility. Such teaching has amounted to a 'separation game' with predictable outcomes. In particular with regard to the discretion of front-line practitioners, it could be as disempowering to treat policy as separate from practice as to behave as though the inspiration derived from the arts could contribute nothing to progress in science, or vice versa.

The proposition that students and practitioners should become confident in analysing the political nature of exchanges in different forums is intended to enhance their ability to assess the relationship between policy and practice. That task would include an appraisal of some aspects of economic policies with a view to overcoming some fears and illiteracy in economic matters. Discussion of economic policy will concentrate on arguments about the costs and benefits of the welfare state but will also address differences in men and women's financial control and management.

However, we will start with biography, by unfolding activities which individuals cherish, to show how coherence and the basis of achieving power can begin to be realised. The promise contained in that claim will be addressed in the next chapter.

II Contexts of empowerment

3 The promise of biography

Biography refers to the life course of a living being but does not have to mean only the unravelling of the story of one individual, though at first sight that may be its most obvious use. The term 'biography' could also be used to describe the process of depicting the life of a group of individuals with something in common or the activities of an organisation over time.

The unravelling of biography requires the bringing together of past and present events and the making of projections about the future. In that 'bringing together', individuals' interpretations of the causes of past events usually depict key aspects of their lives and affect their ability to move into new roles. The story which unmasks choices made in the past can suggest opportunities for the freedom to choose in the future.

The promise of biography is in the telling of a story with a view to participating in a different way in future events. In this respect social workers' clients and students can be both participants in and surveyors of the flow of events, and characters in and tellers of stories constituted by those events (Carr 1986). Through such participation, powerlessness can be replaced with some sense of power, confusion can give way to a feeling of coherence.

The telling of a story will contribute to empowerment if the listeners as well as the storytellers recognise the importance of coherence: the relationship between points in a cross-section. Coherence connotes the value of joining ideas and activities which usually remain separate. The student studying the academic literature on power may regard this study and such literature as separate from her domestic life, yet discussion of her interpretation of power also reveals the value which she places on writing, finishing and posting a letter to a friend. The connection between writing and power is made. Fragmentation has been replaced by a feeling of coherence and understanding, the experience of putting things together has contributed to a sense of well-being and direction.

Coherence as a goal also characterises the experience of those who are applying scientific procedures in research. Their task is not only to make observations but also to make a connection between observations. People say, 'Ah, I see, I can connect, now I understand.' This making of a connection provides the 'a-hah' pleasure and direction referred to earlier. The skilful use of observations involves making connections and achieving coherence.

Bits of biography may be revealed without reference to context but to do this not only limits discussion but also reproduces a sort of psychological determinism, divorced from the cues and constraints that prompt behaviour and give meaning to it. For example, when youths in custody challenge authority, officials and politicians responsible for their custody have a habit of explaining that such angry and often violent behaviour is caused by inadequate parenting and bad backgrounds. The relatively violent nature of institutional authority, which is also part of the story, is often ignored. One-sided assessments are made because the biography of young people in custody, or at least some part of it, has overlooked the contribution of the gaolers, and has talked only of the gaoled. In compiling an assessment, a picture or a story, connections are best made in context and with reference to context: to historical record, tensions and contradictions, resources for fulfilment and the constraints in the lives of individuals and organisations.

In Part I, three concepts were suggested as a means of enabling people to participate in discussing their own biographies and the way they were affected by contemporary social, political and economic events. These three concepts or ideas were: struggle in context, continuity of experience and factors inhibiting spontaneity. Gramsci's writings about the value of continuous schooling, as embodied in the notion that everyone could be an intellectual, was one way of assembling these ideas. These three concepts suggest how students, clients, practitioners and educators could reflect their experiences of the exercise of power. Yet the promise of biography will not be realised if that is where they begin and end. Otherwise we will finish up with self-indulgent storytelling which enables neither the teller nor the listener to develop any wider discourse.

If the unravelling of people's stories focuses on experiences of power and powerlessness, that should open the flow of ideas to a realisation of events unfolding and to an analysis of obstacles to empowerment. This thesis has an application for students, for clients, for educators and for practitioners. The students study topics such as welfare, justice, practice and policy with reference to their own lives as well as to the lives of others and to the dominant issues of their time. In the course of their education and training they will have some responsibility to make assessments of people in different contexts: perhaps a court, a hospital, a youth refuge or with reference to a group of staff and volunteers engaged in a community project. In these respects the concept 'biography' will have value as a focus in assessment, provided the associated theories concerning context, continuity and factors inhibiting spontaneity are applied. Such theories are intended to provide the questions to stimulate appraisal of experiences of power and powerlessness.

The relevance of the concept of biography to people in the predicament of being clients or patients, or perhaps detainees or prisoners of other kinds, can also be clarified. They can be enabled to tell their stories in such a way that they learn to make their own assessments and do not remain dependent on others for so doing. From confidence acquired in making assessments, in context and with reference to a continuity of events, they also participate in and contribute to a wider discourse about issues such as justice and welfare. The opportunity to take part in such discourse is not limited to students, to educators or to practitioners.

With a view to analysing aspects of biographies to show that far more is to be made of people's stories than a repeat of the past, the balance of this chapter will record the accounts of some students, and examine the predicament of different clients, with reference to their reported habits for solving problems. It will also pay attention to the experiences of migrants and make use of the writings of poets, activists and prisoners, all with a view to obtaining answers about the means of empowering people, materially, psychologically, spiritually and politically.

The importance of practitioners' biographies has not been overlooked but will not be addressed immediately. The way in which the huge demands and scant resources of agencies affect the feelings, the health and the careers of practitioners merits separate treatment of its own, in chapter 9. Besides, today's students are tomorrow's practitioners and students' stories have something in common with current practitioners' own dilemmas.

Students

The awareness required to enable anyone to examine issues of choice and control in their lives can be developed in students by encouraging them to record their interpretations of power and powerlessness. These first person accounts can also be a significant form of experiential learning, paving the way for subsequent discussion of the considerable differences in the ways power may be exercised. Students' accounts of powerlessness usually imply but do not always make explicit the means of overcoming such a condition. But the exercise of asking them to say something about themselves by describing powerlessness in their terms does denote aspects of the context of their lives and almost always depicts common problems which they had seldom known they shared with one another.

Students' perceptions of powerlessness have included their difficulty in expressing feelings, the undue influence of religion, the social and financial constraints of family background and the influence of social class. This latter 'influence' is not always perceived at first sight as a matter of class. It is more likely to be implied in accounts of conflict between parents' expectations and their children's aspirations: the dismay that a son or daughter should display social pretensions by going to a college or university, or the disappointment that they might not show any ambitions to pursue tertiary education. In each of those examples, there is pressure even on adult children 'to do the right thing'. This 'right thing' may be narrowly defined.

Personal statements about powerlessness portray tensions as students struggle with the objectives of practice and the curriculum which describes it. If that curriculum concentrates on analyses of social class and social inequalities, students are faced with a challenge to values which had influenced their early childhood and adolescent socialisation. For example, a middle-aged woman described as a tightrope experience her conflict of loyalties between a curriculum which she quickly grasped and a family whom she had left but to whom she felt bound to return. She explained:

> Issues about class and inequality were never heard of in my family. 'Courteous' and 'proper' was what we were supposed to be, especially the girls. People concerned with welfare were long-haired, left-wing radicals, people you never met. Now I'm confronted by the inequalities of class and I accept the explanations but I still have to live with my family. I'm having a tightrope experience.

As in this example, students' references to their powerlessness and their power may also show problems associated with gender and sexuality. Women refer to their experience of not being taken seriously in education, employment or in family circles and to their fear of physical violence. Such 'fear' could be a limit to social life and affect personal development, a constraint on spontaneity in Fromm's terms. In one year at Sydney University, female students said that the major issue which illustrated their powerlessness and coloured so many other aspects of their lives was fear for their own safety. A 23-year-old said it wasn't exactly 'fear', but: 'The thought of not being able to go out at night alone annoys rather than frightens me. The realisation that it's difficult to go out after dark without the prospect of being molested is hardly ever off my mind. It's as though you have to plan each week around that expectation.'

In other observations about powerlessness and their sense of having had limited choices, students have described constraints within family, school and religion. These constraints have been highlighted in accounts of the difficulties experienced by the children of migrants and the value conflicts between the mores of the host country and the culture left behind. An account of several events affecting the biography of a young Catholic man in multicultural Australia in the 1980s was given by Lou, who said:

Having Italian parents I was aware of cultural differences between my
peers and myself from an early age. Not having English as a first
language made life difficult for my parents. They only felt confident
speaking to other Italians. My brother and myself were interpreters. This
gave us some power but it meant having a foot in both cultures ... I
went to a very regimented, conservative Catholic school. This gave one a
fear of authority which I'm slowly overcoming ... I've abandoned all
institutionalised religions since experiencing hell, fire and brimstone
sermons. I still feel nervous and powerless in speaking in public and I'm
impressed by people who have no qualms in this area.

The potential to learn from the powerlessness expressed by Lou is not
always realised. Instead, students feel confused over the relationship
between their own experiences and curriculum objectives as in the
following example from a group discussion among students in a British
polytechnic. A mature-age student, who already had years of welfare
work experience, summarised her view of the lack of links between
students' personal experiences, social theories and social conditions in
Britain:

> There's so many theories in these social work books and our staff like
> to talk about the ones that mean something to them, irrespective of
> whether anyone uses them. 'Systems theories one week, the radicals the
> next.' They talk about integration but they leave that to us. Meanwhile
> 'Mrs T' is screwing the health services and cutting back drastically on
> social work.

A curriculum which she expected to be empowering was having the
opposite effect.

Although easy to describe, the process of empowerment may be
difficult to sustain because various conditions hinder even the ideal of
the freedom to criticise and the freedom to learn. The undue weight
given to the values of economic rationalism has produced an irony in
the social and economic context of higher education. In many countries,
participation in higher education has been regarded as desirable for as
many prospective students as possible, yet it has also been made more
expensive. The user has to pay. Students argue that their feelings of
powerlessness reflect a combination of events: having little or no money,
being faced with a curriculum which is too crowded, and having
conflicting roles in their family, at college or university and in part-time
employment.

Attention to biography would uncover the resources and constraints
in the contexts of students' lives. They are searching for a sense of
coherence, though this sometimes comes across as treading water,
trying to survive. That 'trying to survive' is just as apparent in the lives
of people dubbed clients.

Clients

There is nothing homogeneous about people who have contact with
social and welfare workers; their orientation to solving problems, their
resources for doing so and their interpretations of appropriate or
inappropriate help vary. For example, those who seek solutions to their
problems and are able to explore various avenues of help have been
described as 'copers' (McCaughey and Chew 1977), 'circumspect' (Rees
1978), 'problem solvers' (Perlman 1975) and 'rational' (Silverman
1969). Such people might feel temporarily powerless if they were faced
with the unknown circumstances of a crisis, but usually they have the
optimism and skills to take their own initiatives to combat such
powerlessness.

Slightly less able to take initiatives to help themselves are people who
have been described as 'vulnerable' (McCaughey and Chew 1977), the
'resource seekers' (Perlman 1975), the 'magical' (Silverman 1969) and
the 'assertive' (Rees 1978). Common to these groups is a sense of
grievance and anger. In seeking solutions to problems, the group with
this orientation are not as effective as the 'copers' and they often finish
up with a sense of pessimism about themselves, their entitlements and
their relationships with agencies.

The group whose powerlessness is most deeply entrenched and for
whom the step-by-step process of empowerment could have special
relevance are those whose 'problems have usually existed for a long time
and [whose] life is felt to be a never ending struggle against forces
largely out of their control' (Rees and Wallace 1982 p.147). They
include people who have had long experience of poverty, unemployment, being a single parent, or dependence on welfare benefits and
whose financial difficulties have been compounded by other problems
in the areas of health, family, welfare and relationships. This group have
been identified by researchers and described as 'defeated' (Silverman
1969), 'buffeted' (Perlman 1975) and 'passive' (McCaughey and Chew
1977; Rees 1978).

In pondering the promise of biography with reference to clients,
it is the group who have shown themselves passive in their
orientation to solving problems who merit most attention. It is not
so difficult to talk about achieving power with those who have
personal and other resources, and who have already experienced
some success in protecting and developing their own interests.
Fatalism and resignation is more difficult to address. These are
attributes of those who have probably never planned much in their
lives because they have seldom had the means of doing so, including
that chink of optimism which encourages people to feel that the
future is worth thinking about.

People who say that they know almost nothing about officials and
officialdom are usually reflecting a long experience of pessimistic

expectations and compliance. Ignorance about services is coupled with a fear of finding out, as though integrity could only be maintained by some form of social isolation. For example, at a time of winter when she was living with no heating fuel and little food, a single mother explained why a family welfare agency was not relevant to her circumstances: 'Oh, I thought they were just "the welfare" giving out blankets and coal but not to people like me' (Rees 1978 p.12).

Stigma associated with welfare is often a barrier to finding out about services. An elderly widow, a respondent in the same Scottish study referred to above, explained her ignorance of her entitlement to rent assistance from the central government's Department of Social Security: 'I didn't know about getting any help from that place. I thought they were just for charity types, not for people who have paid their taxes, not for people like me who do not like being dependent on anyone' (Rees 1978 p.14).

Pride in keeping themselves to themselves may reflect passivity rather then assertiveness. This 'pride' may be coupled to a lack of confidence and be expressed in anxiety, fear and numerous examples of compliance. Michael Lerner made an exhaustive examination of this issue and concluded:

> When we feel powerless for any extended length of time, we tend to become more willing to accept parts of the world we would otherwise reject. We act in ways that run counter to our best visions of who we are and who we can and want to be ... if we want to change things, we first need to understand why people have come to believe that nothing can or will be different (Lerner 1986 p.2–3).

Such pessimism occurs when political, social and economic constraints are internalised: objectively, people have had few positive experiences; subjectively, they have adopted the view that these discouraging past experiences are their own fault. The landlessness and illiteracy of poor people in Brazil, said Freire, did not necessarily mean that the oppressed were unaware that they were downtrodden, 'but their perception of themselves as oppressed is impaired by their submission to the reality of oppression' (Freire 1972 p.30).

Compliance as a product of economic, social and political constraints has also been described with regard to the family life of Afro-Americans who are going it alone; they are fatalistic, have high spirituality and live for today (Pinderhughes 1982). These are not surprising reactions because the powerlessness created by structural forces 'undermines the very skills that are so necessary for coping with them' (Pinderhughes 1983 p.332).

Passive compliance is also a response to the experience of long years spent in an institution. Rose and Black observed that the process of being and becoming a good mental patient meant that the skills and orientation necessary for doing well in the world outside were lost. They contended that the 'social being' or 'personhood' of ex-psychiatric patients:

> ... is overwhelmed by their patienthood; their active participation in and consciousness of historical/social reality is overwhelmed by their passive acquiescence or functional adaptation to and acknowledgement of their own invalid state. They have been disconnected from ongoing social existence, almost as if their capacity to engage in the process of struggling to live meaningfully has been surgically severed (Rose and Black 1985 p.31).

The unravelling of bits of biography is a way of beginning the process of empowerment with those people who have felt powerless for a long time. In that process, a marking of small victories can combat a history of defeats. Some of the small victories will include the replacement of ignorance with information, and fear with a willingness to challenge authority.

There will be numerous other people, adults and children, who have seldom felt that events were always beyond their control. Yet the feeling of ignorance when faced with new events can be a confusing, disempowering experience. For example, children faced with a court system have been described as being mystified and fearful of the procedures and the professionals. They had little idea of their rights, they could not distinguish between the police prosecutor, the duty lawyer, the social worker (a child welfare officer) or the clerk of the court (O'Connor and Sweetapple 1988).

Migrants

Confusion is a predictable response to unfamiliar events, such as children's experience of being assessed by a court (O'Connor and Sweetapple 1988), a sudden death and the experience of bereavement (Marris 1974) or parents having to manage the news of the birth of a handicapped child (Rees and Emerson 1984). It is also a response which characterises the experience of migrants, in particular where the language and the culture of the host country are unfamiliar (Mc-Caughey 1987). Such new citizens can be encouraged to explain, perhaps through an interpreter, why their language and their assumptions about services are at odds with the new culture.

The decision to migrate, the initial difficulties of settlement and the conflicts associated with adaptation or integration are part of an unfolding story which affects family members differently 'depending on the life-cycle phase they are in at the time of the transition' (McGoldrick 1982 p.17). Even the first part of this story, the decision to migrate, could reveal differences in the power of family members: the decision to migrate may be made by a husband irrespective of a wife's wishes, or by parents without reference to their children or 'even by adults neglecting to allow their parents the right to choose freely' (Cox 1989 p.104).

When the decision to migrate has been involuntary, often in response to difficult political and economic conditions at home, all the family members may be vulnerable to a transition period of unemployment, low pay, low status and discrimination at work. The only immediate option for families in such situations may be for the women to work even though they come from families where mothers have traditionally played the unpaid caring role.

In Australia, where disproportionate numbers of migrant women finish up in lowly paid positions in the work force (Department of Immigration and Ethnic Affairs 1984 p.12), the individual decision for a woman to seek work may reflect a financial necessity but it also produces other predicaments, such as the conflict of values inherent in such a role change. The means of solving such problems frequently involves a shift in power and authority from husband to wife and from parents to children.

Faced with such a shift, the process of empowerment in social work with Asian migrants in the United States has seen these migrants being encouraged to become 'bicultural', by taking lessons in assertion, persuasion, negotiation, compromise, the creation of alliances and the building of coalitions. These skills were difficult to learn for those whose normative behaviour had emphasised the values of obedience, acceptance, loyalty and cooperation (Hirayama and Cetingok 1988).

Accounts of powerlessness and descriptions of ways to overcome this predicament vary from one ethnic group to another and between the generations within different groups. The manner in which groups comprehend features of the dominant culture such as the organisation of housing, education, health and welfare services, seems likely to depend on a flexible attitude to authority and a capacity to learn and compromise. In this respect children have a distinct advantage over their parents, in particular where those children quickly overcome language barriers and enjoy the support and influence of peers, and where their parents may still adhere rigidly to their old values and may appear to be living in another world.

However, the promise of biography is unlikely to be realised merely by encouraging clients to speak, or students and practitioners to make sense of what the interviewees say, though such staff do have a major responsibility to communicate meaning and to do so accurately. To fulfil this responsibility they can be encouraged to make connections between the demands of their work and the inspiration to be derived from others, from poets, activists and prisoners who have depicted powerlessness and highlighted the qualities required to achieve a sense of power.

Such connections could be invaluable for several reasons. Not only have such writers opened up the discourse about the meaning of welfare, justice and freedom but they have done so in a variety of ways which can appeal to different people. One person may be inspired by poems about the holocaust, another may like the contemporary feminist poet Alice Walker, while some students have found the writings of Gramsci of particular value in their thinking about the links between biography and the ends and means of empowerment. The point is that all may be relevant and all may be used. They each enable the users to go beyond the boundaries of their agencies, their professions, or other immediate personal concerns.

Poets, activists and prisoners

A tension in social work and social welfare education and practice lies in the relationship between science and art, between the systematic collection of information on the one hand and the imaginative use of self on the other. This distinction is blurred. To maintain it is to play into the hands of those who believe that scientific endeavour is the discipline which practitioners should follow whereas to see their work as art is to encourage a pleasant but peripheral pastime.

In a scholarly appraisal of this issue, subtitled 'Making sense for good practice', England has shown that implicit questions about welfare and explicit questions about the interdependence of society and the individual have preoccupied novelists and critics as well as social scientists (England 1986). It would be disempowering to ignore the work of creative artists intent on comprehending and communicating the biography of people in their times. England argued the role of the social worker as artist, not merely making observations about others' behaviour but giving expression to those observations in ways which others would value. Such artistry could be evident in written reports, such as those for courts, but was just as important in the conduct of interviews, or in the development of agency policies and in working relationships with colleagues. Each context provided an opportunity 'for a constant attention to the understanding and expressive ability of the individual social worker' (England 1986 p.132).

In Australia, Aboriginal writers and artists appear to be an obvious source of ideas and ideals for the development of a political literacy in welfare practice; perhaps not so obvious, given that their writing has seldom affected the mainstream of dominant white values and attitudes. It is not too late to explore Aboriginal writers' interpretations of their past and their current struggle to move from a preoccupation with survival to an assertion of independence.

Insights from Aboriginal poets, painters and storytellers should not produce merely romantic appreciation divorced from factors which will influence empowerment. With this premise in mind the leader of the Aboriginal Lands Council in New South Wales, Tiga Bayles, insisted that power could be derived from the maintenance of dignity but he has criticised assumptions that mere celebrations of the past will result in political leverage in the present or change in the future. At a seminar conducted to consider a treaty between the federal government and all Aboriginal people, Bayles observed: 'We can hang on to our sovereignty, you can't take that away from us. Sovereignty cannot be changed by invasion. But don't get me wrong. We are not deluded. We cannot negotiate a treaty from a position of weakness' (Bayles 1988).

Aboriginal people's explanation of aspects of powerlessness is coupled to caveats of political realism. Their anger about the past is apparent in conversations, in the campaign for land rights and in their poetry.

> He left me and the kids
> to be something in the world
> said he was sick of being
> black, poor and laughed at,

wrote Charmaine Papertalk-Green (Gilbert 1988 p.74). Her lines were echoed by Mary Duronx who wrote of the self-respect and control inherent in the possession and use of a lauguage. Such self-respect was difficult to maintain when a language became obsolete. In 'Lament for a Dialect' she wrote:

> O beautiful words that were softly spoken,
>   Now lay in the past, all shattered and broken
> We forgot it somehow when English began,
>   The sweet sounding dialect of Dyirringan
> If we're to be civilized whom can we blame,
>   To have lost you, my language, is my greatest shame
> (Gilbert 1988 p.28)

Poets' pictures of power and powerlessness convey a struggle for meaning in other than obvious forms. Good poetry has, potentially at least, more depth and dimensions to it than good prose. To say this is not to start a tangential discussion of what is good poetry, but to recall that in many cultures, poetry and poets play a larger role in the protest for basic human rights than in the white Anglo-Saxon parts of the world. The non-conformist Indonesian poet Rendra performs his work to audiences of 12 000 people, an experience, says Janet Hawley, which is 'like watching a Javanese melange of Yevtushenko, Mick Jagger, Baryshnikov and Marcel Marceau' (Hawley 1988 p.71). Rendra speaks of the inevitability of conflict with governments if change is even to be proposed. That inevitability occurs because 'I am not in accord with their [the government's] harmony of power' (Hawley 1988 p.71).

As artist and activist, Rendra uses many expressions of feeling in his performances: compassion and satire, humour and emotion, eroticism and self-restraint. He also argues that it is an artist's duty to be alert, to criticise, to warn when things are out of balance in society, government and nature. He is pursuing a tradition of creativity and courage, which was also followed by that somewhat forgotten American community activist Saul Alinksy and by the current Indian social work educator Armity Desai. Alinsky insisted that new ideas emerged from conflict. Powerlessness, he argued, could be challenged through organisation and the sense of personal fulfilment that came from being creative. He exhorted community workers to be curious, irreverent and imaginative, to develop and maintain a sense of humour, an open mind and a respect for the relativity of values. The irreverence of such 'radicals' was, paradoxically, to be rooted in a reverence for democracy, for a free and open society. The work of organising to achieve such a society was to be driven by the belief that people's dignity, security and peace could not be achieved by economic considerations alone but would require opportunities for all people to be creative, to realise their potentialities. Alinsky's recurring theme about creativity was expressed in challenges to intolerance and by asking people to question repetitive and unchanging practices in employment, or in family, social and religious life. He wanted the creative thinkers and activists to take risks in 'a quest for uncertainty, for that continuing change which is life' (Alinsky 1969 p.xvii).

In conversation with social work students and practitioners in Bombay, Dr Armity Desai refers to the giant challenges involved in working with the rural poor, with small and marginal farmers and with severely exploited women. Such social work requires creativity, including toleration of uncertainty, even rejection and failure. She challenges the students, 'be angry . . . develop your potential for leadership, for risk taking and liberation from the bondage of traditionality, even superstition and an attitude of playing safe' (Desai 1988).

Poets and other writers in the white and Western traditions have also tried to avoid 'playing safe'. The Irish poet Louis MacNeice wrote in the 1930s 'Prayer Before Birth':

> I am not yet born; O fill me
> With strength against those who would freeze my
> humanity, would dragoon me into a lethal automaton,
> would make me a cog in a machine, a thing with one
> face . . .
>
> (Allott 1959 p.167)

The eccentric genius, the American poet Marian Moore, wrote in the 1950s: 'blessed is the author who favours what the supercilious do not favour—who will not comply. Blessed, the unaccommodating man' (Moore 1981 p.173).

On 15 December 1989, immediately following the death in Moscow of the Nobel Prize-winning physicist and human rights campaigner Dr Andrei Sakharov, the poet Yevgeni Yevtushenko wrote a eulogy which included the following stanzas.

> It was not vindictiveness or personal offence that
> led him, but his brain, his will to save the country

from petty tyranny, from self-genocide, which had long
ago grown into a war against itself . . .

Could we manage, having avoided indifference,
not to sacrifice our conscience or spirit,
and preserve the freedom of sovereignty
where everyone has power
and conscience is the only power?

(Yevtushenko 1989)

The influence of Sakharov's courage and Yevtushenko's eloquence can
grow beyond the pages of history, if their protests are maximised by
sharing sources of inspiration. Students can share their appreciation
of the novelists and poets, the dancers and musicians or other artists
whose work they value. Such exchange sometimes becomes a celebra-
tion and produces an unexpected experience of solidarity.

Although the promise of biography begins to be achieved by
encouraging people to tell their story with reference to power and
powerlessness, the educators and poets already quoted were also making
statements about the growth of self through writing. They were
expressing resistance and achieving coherence. Communication by
writing can be an artistic experience and a significant aspect of personal
development and self-fulfilment. The general value of completing a
letter to a friend, or the specific purpose of enabling someone who has
had a stroke, or experienced some other debilitating illness to begin to
write again, demonstrate the pleasure of creativity and present a
challenge to powerlessness. There are other experiences in which
writing is the only way to maintain sanity and integrity, and simultaneously resist oppression. Prisoners deprived of freedom for long
periods and subject within that imprisonment to solitary confinement
have described the lifeline effect of recording how they felt and
describing the conditions in which they were kept.

To make the connection between the day-to-day chores of employment in human service organisations and the imprisoned leaders of
resistance movements may appear like moving from the ridiculous to
the sublime but the messages from contributors to resistance literature
are germane. Power in the act of writing emerges as an indelible lesson
from the experiences of those imprisoned by the authoritarian regimes
which control what people write or which prohibit writing altogether.
In these circumstances, writing becomes a process in the redefinition
of self, part of a collective struggle and often the only form of
resistance.

The Kenyan diarist Ngugi remembered another prisoner telling him
how writing could contribute to survival: 'The thing is . . . just watch
your mind . . . don't let them break you and you will be all right even
if they keep you for life . . . but you must try . . . you have to, for us,
for the ones you left behind' (Harlow 1987 p.131).

The writer in prison sustains the self-respect of fellow detainees by questioning the relationships between gaolers and gaoled, between coercive governments and their victims. The writer also in this way empowers himself or herself. At one point during his many years in South African gaols, Breyten Breytenbach recorded, in *True Confessions of an Albino Terrorist*:

> In the dark I am not in the way. There is nobody to look over my shoulder. I am relieved! Then, like an irrepressible urge, there would be the need to write. In the dark I can just perceive the faintly pale outline of a sheet of paper. And I would start writing. Like launching a black ship on a dark sea. I write: I am the writer (in Harlow 1987 p.131).

The energy in these statements is a reminder that physical containment does not necessarily imprison either spirit or intellect, whereas imprisonment of a capacity for criticism and vision may occur even when a human being is not constrained by four walls. The closed mind of the influential senior executive staff, the resistance to change of the conservative bureaucrat, the acceptance of the status quo by the fearful student, the debilitating grind of poverty or of stigma, also have stifling effects. By unravelling the biography which reveals these other forms of imprisonment, expressions of powerlessness become the means of achieving change.

The courageous Christopher Nolan, who suffered cerebral palsy and who, with the support of parents and friends wrote to abolish his particular form of slavery, showed how struggle to change the assumptions of others about the plight of a person with a severe disability could simultaneously reduce some of the powerlessness in that individual's life. Through that process came an acquisition of power which, when publicised, could change the aspirations of others, with and without disabilities. Nolan described not only his own life but also that history of neglect and cruel labelling which guaranteed the powerlessness of people with a disability. 'Century upon century saw crass crippled man dashed, branded and treated as dross in a world offended by their appearance, and cracked asunder in their belittlement by having to resemble venial human specimens offering nothing and pondering less in their life of mindless normality' (Nolan 1988 p.18).

As educators, students and practitioners confront oppressive displays of power they are asked to develop their sense of self by being critical, by recording their observations, analysing the links between them, and by identifying the factors which inhibit their own and others' spontaneity. The alternative holds no promise. It is indifferent and apolitical. It involves 'offering nothing and pondering less'.

4 Power, politics and language

Chapter 3, 'The promise of biography', recorded the observations of students, clients, poets and writers in prison about powerlessness and discussed the means of combating such a condition. Some sense of power was experienced in the coherence that came from understanding, the confidence that derived from making choices and the control that was inherent in solving problems. These accounts told something of individuals' emotions, their relationships with significant others, the context which affected their interpretations and included comments on the culture which influenced the meaning they attached to their words.

Time spent considering the meanings of power is intended as preparation for subsequent analysis of the objectives and theories of empowerment (chapters 6 and 7), the steps in the process of achieving power and the agency contexts in which such steps may be taken (chapters 8 and 9). In this discourse, it will be important to consider the dominant economic and political influences of the past decade. Without such discussion it is difficult to see how educators and practitioners can develop goals to share with a wider public, or acquire the expertise to achieve such goals. Such expertise will include a familiarity with the theories used to explain the exercise of power. That field of enquiry should not only focus on major social trends but should also consider the ways in which language and everyday usage reflect people's self-image, their psychological and political understanding. But we need to begin with a reminder of the dominant ideology and language against which *achieving power* is a protest and with which it is in competition.

The economically inspired values which have influenced so many countries' policy priorities in the past decade have seldom reflected matters of context, culture and the complexities of individuals' lifestyles. A critique of the policies of economic rationalism and of the neo-classical theories from which it emerged shows how complex matters, such as the effect of power differentials on individuals' choices and on the exercise of preferences in a community, have been ignored (Etzioni 1988). In consequence, this dominant economic perspective has produced prescriptions for conduct with a simple but strong behaviourist flavour, implying that people were socially isolated, emotionless and rationally calculating individuals, nothing more. To counter such a narrow perspective, even in a study of small-scale financial transactions, the influence of individuals and social collectivities on shifts in priorities and choice among alternatives would have to be addressed (Etzioni 1988).

In this plea for a new socio-economics, Etzioni echoed the thesis that the nature and meaning of power was a central issue in any account of social order and human relationships. It affected men and women's interactions with their environment, within themselves, with and within interpersonal, group and international relationships; it permeated every aspect of human life and was unavoidable (Clarke 1974). With slightly less flourish, in an account of social work in oppressed communities, Barbara Solomon spoke of power, as 'a bridging concept which described aspects of interpersonal relations at family, small group, organisational or community levels' (Solomon 1987 p.79).

In a theory of motivation to overcome feelings of inferiority, the multidimensional idea of power as a life force contained within the individual but related to the characteristics of social forces did not escape Alfred Adler. In his terms, a striving for power was rooted not only in the psychodynamic feelings of inferiority emerging from the impediments of childhood dependence on adults but also in the social issues which compounded an individual's experiences. Although an originator of child guidance clinics, and an innovator in psychotherapy, he could hardly avoid the multidimensional view of power which came from experiencing the politics of everyday life. The Nazi regime eventually closed down all his psychiatric units.

Interpretations of power

Interpretations of the meaning of power which have a bearing on social work and social welfare have included Offe's focus on the opposing tasks in a capitalist state. On the one hand power is being used by the state's representatives to manage people and resources as efficiently as possible and on the other those same representatives are called on to provide communities with a service. Social work and other social welfare practitioners are caught between these two forms of power, the one concerned, in Offe's terms, with accumulation, the other with legitimation (Offe 1984). Their response to conflicting demands at work, and their reflections on the satisfactions or dissatisfactions of their own careers, would be affected by such conflicting expressions of power.

In relation to different forms of authority, external, internal and anonymous (discussed in Part I), Fromm's point about the power to dominate, or to effect liberation, is also germane to the ends and means of empowerment. Creative, liberating expressions of power were the opposite of domination. Fromm argued that power over people, when it expressed a lust for power, was not rooted in strength but in weakness.

'It is the expression of the inability of the individual self to stand alone and live. It is the desperate attempt to gain secondary strength where genuine strength is lacking' (Fromm 1960 p.139). These dual interpretations of power, accumulation versus legitimation, domination versus liberation, may be helpful as far as they go, but they camouflage other differences in the nature of power and its consequences for different people. In social work literature, several distinctions have been made in discussions of the bases or sources of power. Reisch et al (1983) discussed legal, information control, expert, coalitional and negative bases. (The latter was a reference to the ability of employees to make an agency look bad.) Lee (1983) adopted the classification of French and Raven (1959) and referred to coercive, reward, legitimate, expert and referent bases of power. (The latter was illustrated by the achievement of positive feelings between individuals.)

These are important distinctions but they do not describe what people do and what consequences follow. The bases of power may provide the opportunity to act but a critical perspective on the exercise of power will affect what people ask, see and do. A 'critical perspective' includes consideration of what the exercise of power feels like to people in dominant or subordinate positions. On that there may be no agreement. Actions which a practitioner considers creative may seem stifling to a client, requests which a teacher feels are liberating may be experienced by the pupils as constraining. The meaning of power and interpretations of its consequences will remain in dispute and in this respect Foucault's point that some of the most creative expressions of power occur in disputes over the meaning and justification of actions, has relevance for our purposes (Foucault 1974).

For Foucault the appropriate way to understand power was to focus not on the mechanics of control exercised by central or sovereign authorities but on the experiences of the subjects of such control. However, he also insisted that power should not be perceived as a fixed phenomenon which some people possessed and others did not, but rather as circulating through a net-like organisation in which individuals could be both subject to the effects of power and the vehicles for its articulation. Key features in that circulation were the instruments for the formation and accumulation of knowledge and for studying techniques and tactics of domination. Those techniques and tactics were and are apparent in the disciplines of discussions as to what we think is appropriate and normal behaviour, and how we should conform to such normality. Foucault argued that it was the discipline of conformity inherent in language which made individuals accept what was normal through 'those continuous and uninterrupted processes which subject our bodies, govern our gestures, dictate our behaviours etc' (Foucault 1986 p.233).

The exercise of power in the name of welfare, equity or justice may not always reflect such noble goals, in particular if different interpretations of behaviour are compared in face to face exchanges, or in correspondence. Individuals as individuals, or as members of a group, are usually concerned about their presentation to others and how those others will respond. The motives of the more openly assertive may have to do with their office, their pomposity or egocentricity and with years of failure to understand how their behaviour affects others. Whatever the content of an exchange, or the overlapping contexts which affect conduct, individuals have expressed power and been affected by it.

In personal relationships, in controversies within organisations and in the body politic at large, the essence of power, Foucault has argued, is to participate in, to influence or even to take control of discourse. That discourse will be concerned with determining facts, priorities and responsibilities, hence the need to examine who participates in such determinations and to contest the language by which power and powerlessness is expressed. At this point, however, Lukes' analysis of the exercise of power, which has avoided dual either/or explanations and which has direct application to practice and policy in community work, in social work and social welfare, needs to be developed (Lukes 1974).

One, two and three dimensions

At first, as with so many sociological theses, Lukes' work comes across as one of the 'it's all right for you to talk' variety (Cohen 1975). Fascinating ideas are thrown up that leave the practitioner wondering how such interesting concepts might be applied. Lukes' portrayal of power from three different perspectives does show why power is a concept never to be taken for granted, and what is likely to be occurring if it is neglected.

In Lukes' terms, a one-dimensional or conservative view of power adopts the bias of a political system by assuming that the focus of enquiry into power relationships is observable conflict. Thus, the absence of conflict, as in the lack of complaints by people in subordinate positions, is used to claim that all is well. This conservative view ignores more issues than it confronts. For example, a social worker interviewing elderly people in an old people's home merely hears and recalls what they say: a repeat of the subservient views of themselves in relation to more influential officials. That has been the story of their lives.

In a prolonged doctors' dispute in Australia, in which social workers as researchers documented the experiences of patients in need of urgent treatment in public hospitals, accounts of what was occurring varied according to different analyses of power (Rees and Gibbons 1986). The one-dimensional view came in the story which dramatised the virtues of powerful medical specialists. Public expectations that patients were being treated according to Hippocratic principles governing medical conduct were promoted. The bias of this point of view in favour of the surgeons and their supporters, and against the interests of patients without private health insurance was sustained by acceptance of a normative conception of interests: a take it or leave it attitude by officials in positions of power, a grudging acceptance by subordinates and a lack of enquiry by investigators and interviewers.

A two-dimensional view of power Lukes equated with a reformist conception of interests, a perspective which would examine which topics do not get on to political agendas as well as those which do. This exposes the bias inherent in the one-dimensional view yet is still preoccupied with the behaviour of key personnel. The influences of ideology and social structure on setting agendas and on the suppression of conflict are still not examined.

The reformist social worker, i.e. one operating with a two-dimensional view of power, is capable of responding to what inter-viewees do not say as well as to what they do. For example, in interviews with elderly people in an old people's home, this practitioner would be aware of the fatalism and fear characteristic of vulnerable people who do not like to offend anyone let alone make complaints. This social worker would say, 'I want to hear several points of view.' She would ask herself what do these elderly people mean by what they say and what are the constraints which hinder them from asking questions or from expressing spontaneously what they feel.

Returning to the investigation into the doctors' dispute, a two-dimensional view enabled the social worker researchers to probe beyond official accounts portraying the surgeons as doing their best under difficult circumstances. This more critical approach to the way in which power was being exercised, raised questions about the roles of all health professionals in stopping certain patients from being treated. It revealed the absence of any moderate medical leadership, the reluctance of politicians to defend the interests of patients (apparently out of fear of offending the powerful doctors' leaders) and the failure of other occupations to insist on unselfish behaviour from doctors and principles of fairness in the treatment of all patients. The exercise of power as a result of the political–economic interests in the national organisation of health services was not examined.

The three-dimensional or radical view of power involves a thorough appraisal of the behavioural focus of the first two views. Applied to social work it would expose the political dimensions of practice, from arenas where policies and politics are discussed explicitly to those in which an understanding of power is implied, as in unravelling the uses of authority in interpersonal relationships. This three-dimensional view focuses not only on the behaviour of decision makers but also on the way in which people's interests may be defined by a system which works against them. For example, the practitioner using this interpretation of power responds not only to what people say and do not say, but also to what might be in their best interests if they were able to make the choice. The social worker interviewing respondents in an old people's home can relate their answers to policies regarding the care of elderly people, including consideration of ageist attitudes and the unequal access to resources which mirrors social class differences.

In the investigation into the doctors' dispute, the social worker researchers were capable of a serious sociological analysis based on a conflict view of the way that health institutions were funded and how various political interests affected the distribution of resources. When the concept of power was used in this way, it was incumbent on them to analyse the operation of vested interests and so avoid a preoccupation with the idiosyncracies of individuals and groups.

The three-dimensional view claims far more than an analysis of people's interests. It also raises questions as to what might be in their interests under different socio-political constraints and this implies the creative exercise of power to produce possibilities which might never have been anticipated, either by the parties who are defending existing interests, or by those who are demanding change. The agency manager who has the vision to say to the staff, 'let's suspend our assumptions about hierarchy and programs and existing use of resources and work together to see if there are far better ways to provide a service', is, arguably, creating a conducive climate in which to think of new possibilities. The front-line practitioners who look on their discretionary power imaginatively, and who are determined to enhance other people's freedom instead of taking the easy way out by always conforming to official expectations, are also likely to realise new possibilities.

This three-dimensional conception of power embodies the spirit and objectives of empowerment. It also contributes to a fascination with the politics of social work and social policy in their varied contexts. A redefinition of politics goes hand in hand with a critical appraisal of the meaning and uses of power.

Defining politics

An effective way of controlling the ideas, questions and activities of different individuals within families and organisations is to insist on a narrow view of politics: that perhaps such activity is best left to politicians. For example, a common response to those who challenge authority within organisations is that they are being unprofessional, dabbling in politics which is none of their business. Such responses derive from a conservative stance: controlling agendas and people, maintaining relationships of domination and subordination, ensuring that social workers should be confined to some intellectual backwater which precludes an examination of the exercise of power and its consequences.

That separation of professional from political activity which is maintained so that consideration of one does not contaminate the conduct of the other, derives from those explanations and pictures of over-arching social control inherent in a consensus-oriented, positivist tradition in social theory. It is evident in the conduct of government, and in the management of organisations. It is apparent in those explanations of feminine behaviour which refer to human nature but ignore sexual politics and social structure.

Prescriptions for uncritical conformity in the family, the school, the agency, the college or university derive from certain assumptions about politics and human nature and leave little room for contesting these definitions. This is the same point of view which says that educators' consideration of ideology is a dangerous activity because objectivity demands that students, teachers and practitioners should be non-ideological. Such a view of ideology sleeps with the assumptions that politics should be conducted at a distance from everyday life.

The definition of politics which was foreshadowed in this book's introductory prospectus rested on the assumption that political activity included participation in debates about personal and collective interests and about the determination of programs and policies (Altman 1980). A view of politics as mutual education, as the means of influencing choices through the constant process of communication with others from all walks of life with a view to defining the public good, also matches the purpose and the spirit of deliberations about empowerment. Such deliberations should not be left to those who control economic markets because they limit participation and in consequence pursue a narrow set of values, but it could be achieved by a respect for argument and debate which would virtually enable 'the polis [to be] writ large' in the household (Bell 1979 in Marquand 1988 p.216).

'Politics' has also been defined as the exercise of influence where there is a conflict of interests (Banfield 1961) and denotes processes by which resources are obtained, conflict is settled and always involves the use of or the struggle for power. Politics is involved in any critique of social order and in any challenge to domination in relationships. These definitions predate the feminist premise that the personal is the political (Gilbert 1980; Collins 1986), though this familiar expression does not mean that any action is justifiable as long as its goal could be regarded as political. That premise and the view of politics as mutual education do recognise that struggles to define the common good are conducted in political arenas. In those struggles, agreement may be reached to exercise power equitably, or disagreement may continue but with a realisation that the expansion of the influence of one group might involve an erosion in the influence of another.

Political decisions in social work and related activities are apparent in attitudes which suppress or address conflict. In an account of the politics of therapy, Halleck observed that whatever a psychiatrist did would always involve encouraging a patient either to accept the existing distributions of power in the world or to change them (Halleck 1971), hence the argument that every encounter with a psychiatrist would have political implications. This contention had already been developed in R.D. Laing's thesis that some forms of psychiatric treatment were best viewed as repressive political acts (Laing 1967).

In settings where social work is not the primary function, practitioners pay attention to politics to effect survival as well as influence. For example, in a hospital, unless they wanted to merely do other people's bidding, it was incumbent on medical social workers to achieve influence in handling relationships between different staff. Credibility in the eyes of medical personnel did not necessarily mean compliance, but unless the question of the status of the different groups was addressed and the validity of social work established, the objectives of empowerment were unlikely to be attained (Murdach 1982).

Social work in schools required an awareness of various audiences—teachers, pupils, parents, pressure groups and politicians. The social worker was often caught in the middle of the conflicting interests of these audiences, for instance concerning the issue of whether education policy should address the different interests of deviant children and high achievers in the school environment (Lee 1983).

Facilitating the least influential kids' progress in a competitive system was likely to be aided by viewing the school as a political environment and social work in schools as a political endeavour. Being political in such a context meant defining the social work task so that it was understood by other employees. This understanding was achieved by compiling information about educational issues, maintaining credibility in the eyes of others, making connections between social work and educational objectives, and effecting alliances with interested constituencies, such as parents, students and key pressure groups (Lee 1983 pp.303–305).

Within organisations it may be obvious to practitioners that to help other people achieve power, they need to consolidate their own positions through political understanding and skills. Even if that point seems obvious, its implications need to be developed by examining how changes in the exercise of power and awareness of such changes can influence people's sense of identity.

Acquiring political identity

Attention to politics hints at the process of enabling people to replace powerlessness with some feeling of control. Such a change, usually gradual and painstaking, occasionally sudden and dramatic, occurs when people act in association with others and in this way begin to sense their political identity. The experience of being a participant in events that affect the quality of one's own or other people's lives involves a transformation from being passive to being active, from being a receiver of goods and services to being someone who develops a capacity for self-expression, a confidence in making choices and taking decisions. These activities have challenged the 'nothing can be done' fatalistic view, as in the case of the development of 'identity politics' which occurred when disabled people became involved in planning their own affairs (Anspach 1983).

Acquiring political identity is a process and an outcome which has little in common with the experience of being a consumer, a role of choosing from a range of objects determined by others. Such activity does not encourage questions because it implies that the mere act of consuming may be sufficient to ensure people's interests. By contrast the process of achieving a political identity, through doing something creative, is the opposite of consumerism.

In human services, if professionals maintain control, patients or clients, as consumers, can at best express gratitude. The very consuming may equip them only to consume again, whereas the struggle to achieve political identity through empowerment should encourage people to resist being treated as consumers. Empowerment presupposes critical questions and analysis. Consumerism is characterised by an acceptance of problems and services defined by someone else. In their account of advocacy and empowerment in mental health after-care, Rose and Black observed that the power imbalance in conventional user–provider relationships left little room for challenge and change. 'What we want to stress here is that the process of consuming the service consumes the person. . . The likelihood of the consumer transcending or transforming the given universe of meaning established by the provider is very little . . .' (Rose and Black 1985 p.38).

The promise of biography showed the association between personal and political identity through a process of change, from feeling unworthy or incapable, to exerting a measure of choice and control. This topic has been discussed by several writers, from Freire (1972) to Lerner (1979), from Blun (1982) to Rose and Black (1985). Each used different terms to illustrate challenges to individuals' acceptance of their powerlessness. Blun referred to 'animation', Freire to 'conscientization', Lerner to 'a challenge to surplus powerlessness', Rose and Black to 'the objective world of oppression and the need for subjective validation'. The latter writers acknowledge their debt to Freire. Their goal in working with ex-psychiatric patients was to transfer those people from the status of being known and acted upon to having the experience of knowing and acting. Such a transfer captured the meaning of empowerment and was reflected in ex-patients' new self-image.

Rose and Black's ideas have much in common with Lerner, who applied his analysis to unequal power in the organisation of work and to the predicament of people on the shop floor of industry. Such employees had long experience of feeling that they could not effect changes in their working conditions. This added burden of defeatism dominated their thoughts and was surplus to other obstacles which confronted them. Supporting workers by enabling them to achieve personal confidence in solidarity with others helped to change their views of themselves and of their relationships with employers (Lerner 1986 ch.3).

Freire's educational goals, in common with Gramsci's, did not stop at teaching people to read and write but included political literacy to demand dignity, justice and meaningful participation in the politics of everyday life. Such literacy was effected by the development of critical consciousness to enable individuals to comprehend their conditions by acting upon them. In their terms, people could acquire political identity by questioning the sources of their oppression and, in solidarity with others, working to change those conditions.

For Brun, using the French concept of 'animation', the object was to enable social groups to express themselves and to promote programs addressed to needs defined by them. 'Animation' emphasised human relations techniques 'to encourage autonomous group development, promote consciousness in shaping the group's own priorities and stimulating group action [towards] controlling the environment that shapes the group's development' (Brun 1982 p.69). In examining their experiences of domination and submission, group members could link their sense of individual identity to political structures, thus enabling the processes of political education and empowerment to run in tandem.

Whether people are encouraged to practice animation and conscientization, or challenge surplus powerlessness and take steps to avoid being a consumer, the objective is to offer a choice between similar goals and processes. The language is slightly different, the process the same. Each contributes to a political literacy. Each demands some feeling for the ways in which language reflects the exercise of power through illustrating individuals' views of their worlds and their links to wider social and political structures.

Language

The promise of biography has been posed as a goal to encourage questions about the connotation of a word like 'choice' by reflecting on experiences of power and powerlessness. In discussing their lives the storytellers could make connections between issues of choice and control, between personal problems and wider events. They could discover the novelty of struggling to change their views and actions, or they might stick with the limited and limiting notions of choice inherent in descriptions of adjustment and acceptance.

These points about language as a carrier of ideology and thereby a creator of aspirations apply to practitioners as well as clients, to educators as well as students. Each can develop confidence in the language of empowerment by examining the different meanings of power and each would then be ready to search for the different connotations of a word like choice. Or they might examine their experience of choice as a way of redefining what they understand by power and politics.

The process of learning new language and pondering the meaning of words and how they are interpreted by different people is an essential feature of self development. Command over vocabulary contributes to people's capacity for reflective thought and should sharpen their awareness of themselves in relation to others. This process can have an empowering effect on individuals if it enables them to anticipate the responses of others, to play new roles and respond to the political cues in the world around them. These points are embedded in the theory of symbolic interactionism which explains how the constructing of meaning affects power plays in different interpersonal exchanges including those in various contexts of social work and social welfare (Knott 1974; Edelman 1974).

The association of language and other symbols with specific roles may be taken for granted on a stage but is just as evident in the theatre of everyday life. People in subordinate positions: school children, patients, defendants, prisoners and women who do not expect equality in relationships with male counterparts such as their husbands or employers, have been described as using a language of submissiveness, of acceptance, apology and non-assertiveness. By contrast those who are used to filling powerful positions are experienced at projecting themselves as cool, dispassionate, task-oriented, independent and even objective. Theirs is the language of certainty: imposing definitions, exposing few signs of weakness.

This contrast in the roles and language of superiors and subordinates has been assumed to be the difference between masculine and feminine words and style. It is not. Female speech, says Kotker, is not the speech of women at all; it is the speech of the powerless, depicted in the demeaning question and the silent reply: 'Whadja say, lady?' (Kotker 1980).

The language of powerlessness can be expressed in the fatalism produced and maintained by years of subordination in an inflexible hierarchy. For example, in a discussion with mostly non-medical personnel in a psychiatric hospital, the goals and language of empowerment were approved yet discussed as unrealistic: 'You're an idealist and an optimist, we can't all be powerful.'

This response rested on assumptions that power was some finite phenomenon always in limited supply and that being powerful involved an assertion of control and strength over others. Subsequent discussions with the staff encouraged a redefinition of power, starting with reference to the achievement of something done well and the sense of coherence which derived from that experience. Still the expressions of subordination, in terms of deference to hospital hierarchies and relative ignorance about the Health Department's policies, kept coming. 'People like their powerlessness' said a nurse about her colleagues and her patients. 'They're happy with it.'

This nurse and her colleagues exhibited some discomfort with their lowly positions and with frustrating characteristics of their jobs but at that time they possessed neither the language, the confidence nor the skills to empower themselves even by examining the nature of the conflicts between different occupations. A new arrival, an occupational therapist, did offer a political analysis of the quality of work in the hospital. 'This business of powerlessness and politics to control discussions describes this place completely. The morale is low. No one knows about closures. No one is asking. We work in the dark. That makes it difficult to do a good job.' Her association of feelings with policies being made elsewhere seemed hopeful, but a put-down was at hand. A glimmer of political appraisal in her assessment of staff morale was snuffed out. Another staff member, a social worker, advised: 'I've been here for three years. You think it's bad now. It's been worse than this. We're on an upward curve at the moment.' With a look of puzzled gratitude the relatively new occupational therapist nodded acceptance of the advice and said no more.

The context of work conditions workers' attitudes and aspirations, but these effects pale beside the language and other constraints characteristic of social class. For example, families who approached a large Catholic relief organisation in western Sydney in the late 1970s came expecting counselling for their inability to cope with poverty. They were blaming themselves. They reported their experience of domestic violence, alcoholism and problems with children in terms of personal faults. Causes of poverty and related difficulties were explained via a one-dimensional understanding of power: depending on your own or someone else's behaviour you made it—or you did not. 'My husband is an alcoholic.' 'I'm a very poor father because I don't earn enough money.' 'My husband hates me because I'm not attractive enough.' 'I've failed as a wife and I make my husband so angry that he bashes me around a lot.'

At the beginning of contact with that agency, the author of this study observed: 'Not one of the 22 families had any sense that their "failure" could be attributed to a structure outside their immediate nuclear family' (Usher 1988 p.27). The process of empowerment began via engagement with like-minded families in seminars aimed at examining the causes of poverty. Steps in this process included keeping in touch with one another and learning to listen, obtaining and exchanging information about Social Security, health, welfare and legal services. The beginnings of critical analysis about welfare, health and legal systems were conducted in an atmosphere of mutual support aimed at understanding and solidarity.

A process of change occurred in the families' movement from fatalism to a recognition of the value of being a participant in a struggle. The powerlessness and fatalism appeared in familiar glimpses of biography. One mother explained: 'As a teenage girl I was a victim of incest. I married Ken because I knew nothing of men except violence and exploitation. He was the same as my father and I believed in marriage and the needs of my kids demanded that I stay married and shut up about the violence' (Usher 1988 p.63).

Later this mother and other families were seeing themselves in a different light. Freed of self-blame, they made critical appraisals of the housing market, of helping professions and hire-purchase companies. One mother explained that she used words and raised questions which had been uncharacteristic of her when she was tolerating everything. 'Today we struggle to understand more about the social and political system which makes it so difficult for young kids to have a home of their own ... we understand how cruel powerful institutions can be to marginal people like us.'

Of his exploitation by finance companies, a father explained the confidence he gained from distinguishing himself from a great blob of life which had just carried him along:

> At the seminars I was challenged constantly for the reasons for my behaviour...to look for reasons outside myself. Constantly being challenged helped myself and my wife to understand what hire-purchase companies were doing to people like us. Fancy owing [X Company] $7000 and buying more off them because they convinced us we were good customers. At 20 per cent interest we were very good customers.

Uncritical dependence on professionals such as doctors also merited critical appraisal. The special language of some members of the medical profession was replaced by families' own appraisals of the association between their health and their social and economic environment. A widow who had felt uninformed about the effects of her husband's medical treatment for diabetes, and uninvolved in decisions about his health care, resolved that her sense of victimisation inherent in false dependence on a doctor who did not speak to her would not recur:

> (The seminars) were a profound learning experience over four years. After Bernie died I was able to hold the family together, even though we had nothing but the pension. I was determined to keep in control of my life. Never again would I let professionals control my thinking and add to my fears (Usher 1988 p.72).

Two specific points are apparent from this mother's comments. The first concerns the significance of struggling with interpretation and meaning. The second concerns the circumstances which facilitate education to develop political identity, to achieve some sense of power. The mother no longer accepted others' descriptions of what words meant or denoted. The difference between what words denote and connote is a distinction between logical, one-dimensional versions of events handed down by others and a struggle to attach meaning by reflecting on current feelings, living conditions and wider economic and political events. Imposing definitions is an exercise of power which mystifies and hinders people's thinking for themselves. Resisting others' definitions by searching for the connotation of words is to insist on the importance of demystifying things and thereby developing political awareness. That awareness is seldom acquired by acting alone. On the other hand, mere expression of solidarity among people in similar states of powerlessness may only lead to drowning in common despair.

In the examples taken from the account of families at the seminars run by the Catholic relief organisation, enthusiasm for the ideals, language and goals of empowerment contributed to a sense of solidarity. Armed with the language and encouraged by mutual support, people changed their image of themselves and felt confident in unravelling the relationship between political order and personal experience. Political literacy emerged from the chemistry of heightened consciousness in association with others. Usher concluded: 'as their sense of belonging in solidarity with like-minded people increased, so the ability to use an accurate language to describe their world emerged' (Usher 1988 p.80).

This last comment heralds the need to spell out in some detail the steps and stages by which people change their views of themselves, gain in knowledge and confidence and so achieve some semblance of power. But it is premature and limiting to proceed to that task without reference to the historical precedents which have influenced this current discussion of empowerment.

Seeking easy answers presupposes simple questions. If people do not question social and economic issues, including past social policy trends, they will have forfeited the opportunity to be taken seriously in debates about social objectives and the means of attaining them. The significant historical precedents which have influenced current practice in social welfare are the influence of economic rationalism and various campaigns to achieve social justice.

5 Economic rationalism and social justice

Practitioners may feel that time spent thinking about major social and economic trends is wasted. On the contrary, it is well spent. In a river of accumulating personal and social problems the source of pressures is often located upstream, and hence it is proposed that an examination of external issues can equip people to handle what they perceive as internal or personal difficulties. Conversely a political literacy to enable people to make connections in their lives and obtain tangible resources will equip them to address wider social issues.

In chapter 4, an objective in discussing different explanations of power and various interpretations of politics was to enhance the political literacy of students, practitioners, clients and educators. That literacy should give people confidence in analysing issues of powerlessness and thereby participating in finding solutions to such problems. But the issues discussed so far have only hinted at their wider context. In the 1980s and into the 1990s two characteristics of this wider context have been apparent and one of those has been more dominant than the other. On the one hand pressures for efficiency and effectiveness in human services have been influenced by market principles and by the economically inspired values of managers and administrators. On the other, the language and values which underpin pleas for greater democracy and for more equitable administration can still be heard. These pressures and pleas are not mutually exclusive. Efficiency can contribute to equity. Effectiveness can be facilitated by greater democracy in all levels of government. Yet these pressures have not been complementary. They have led, in Yeatman's view, 'in different and conflicting directions' (Yeatman 1990 p.6). The emphasis on justice through equity has raised aspirations concerning the politics of community representation and consultation, whereas the economic efficiency drive has emphasised 'rationalized techniques of controlling human and material resources within strict and centrally provided guidelines' (Yeatman 1990 p.6).

As a final prelude to more direct discussion (in Part III) of the process of empowerment, the two conflicting demands will be elaborated upon by reference to social justice and the influence of economic rationalism.

The concept of social justice as a panacea has been bandied around almost as loosely as empowerment. The very looseness has played into the hands of those market-oriented politicians and managers who have enjoyed stereotyping welfare and justice as sloppily conceived and therefore incapable of being implemented. In the balance of this text justice will be equated with goals of equity in social policies, in the conduct of human relationships generally and as an outcome in the provision of services. But these goals and outcomes are easier spoken of than achieved. Answers to the question 'What is justice?' may involve a struggle as dramatic as a campaign to have people released from prison who have been imprisoned unjustly, or as apparently mundane as controversy over fair treatment of a child or student. Whatever the examples, the question of justice is significant for everyone. Society, through its representatives, needs ethically grounded standards of conduct to be associated with just outcomes. The less powerful participants need to be reassured that their powerlessness will not be compounded by the refusal of superiors to reconsider evidence and points of view. Debates about what is just need to be open and constant.

In relation to social policies, different interpretations of social justice will be considered later. For practitioners concerned with empowerment in relation to social justice, the immediate issue to which they need to respond is the influence of economic rationalist ideologies and their implicit strategy of the containment of social change.

The influence of economic rationalism

Governments in the 1980s made considerable use of catchphrases such as effective management, economic efficiency, cost-effectiveness and productivity. Economists of a particular persuasion and their disciples the economic forecasters, some journalists and some management consultants used this language to set the terms for debate about national priorities. In countries such as Canada, the United States, Britain, New Zealand and Australia, the values of economic rationalism have not only produced specific economic strategies such as the deregulation of economies and the facilitation of growth by reliance on the invisible hand of market forces, but they have also influenced policies on social issues. Rationalist views of order and discipline have been developed gratefully by governments and their servants and by the leaders of private industry who in turn have encouraged governments to adopt their business aspirations.

Born as a theory of eighteenth century neo-classical economics, its twentieth century inheritors emphasised that goals of economic policies—such as the tightening of monetary control, regulation of budgets, and cutbacks on public sector investment—would demand a disciplined populace. That discipline was evident in people talking tough, being tough and not tolerating dissent from those who did not share their visions of the future.

In these views of social order, the equations were simple and contained an apparent logic and an unashamed moralism. The simplicity proved anaesthetising and made it difficult to question such obvious 'rational' uses of power. Mrs Thatcher's speech to the General Assembly of the Church of Scotland in May 1988 emphasised that social and economic arrangements which were not founded on acceptance of individual responsibility would be harmful and that welfare, 'the exercise of mercy and generosity', should not necessarily be a public responsibility (*Guardian* 12 May, 1988 p.12).

In this watershed speech about Christianity and politics, individual responsibility, hard work and thrift were used to justify the revival of charity and its associated messages of prestige to the givers and the subordination of recipients. A new responsible world could be attained by the erosion of the welfare state and its alleged encouragement of dependence. In this new world, unless weak people could be perceived as morally deserving, they would be classified as undesirable deviants. Social workers could be depicted as wet and irresponsible if they identified with such deviants.

Simple prescriptions, beguiling moralism and increasing inequality were also a legacy of the Reagan years in the USA. That president's projection of a folksy image of intimate concern for the country's welfare belied his indifference to the conditions of powerless people. In the language of that presidency, work incentives had high priority and welfare was to be stigmatised because it was automatically seen as contributing to dependency. This simple message said that almost everyone could be independent. Some could be far more independent than others. The Reagan administration, said Robert Lekachman, 'would foreclose a widow's mortgage to stimulate work incentives and eliminate a Social Security pensioner's maximum benefits to restore his self-respect and alleviate his guilt at collecting unearned subsidies' (Lekachman 1982 p.180).

The overall plan inherent in such rationalism was evident in increasing central government control over key factors in the moral equation. Reagan's concerns included public school prayers, abortion bans, and limitations of court jurisdiction over school integration (Lekachman 1982). In spite of the alleged Christian compassion in such policies, they were to reward whites far more than blacks. The racism in rationalism was not easily disguised. The Economic Report of the People concluded that blacks and other people of colour had disproportionately borne the brunt of high levels of unemployment, as in the gutting of fair employment practices, abolition of the Civil Rights Commission and cuts in social programs (Centre for Popular Economics 1986).

In Australia in the 1980s, politicians in power rushed to promote policies of tough economic management. It was as though many of them had no other values and no other words. What else could they think and say? State governments claimed that they should behave and be judged as business corporations. State premiers wanted to be known as efficient managing directors of New South Wales Inc. or Western Australia Inc.

Foundations for such events had been consolidating for years. In Australia, in the seclusion of the nation's capital, a majority of senior public servants had been educated in a narrow band of econometrics and had little experience of social and economic life in other parts of the country. Socially and professionally they practised their theories by meeting almost exclusively with those of similar educational background whose common mission was to promote such views (Pusey 1991). In the 1980s their influence had grown because the rhetoric of such rationalism was seldom challenged or unmasked (Beilharz 1987) and because Friedman and his followers had successfully sold the false view that the welfare state had aimed to achieve equality—rather than security—and in the process had destroyed individual freedom (Beilharz and Watts 1986).

In the drive to imitate the entrepreneurial values of the business community, a user pays philosophy was inevitably going to clash with an ideology about entitlement to services irrespective of the ability to pay. If a service could be labelled economically inefficient, that would also carry the connotation morally unjustifiable. For example, it was not just in remote areas of countries like Australia and Canada that the closing of welfare offices was to show the clash between different ideologies about welfare and the role of social workers. In such areas, the conflict between business goals and the ideals of giving a service were highlighted. Cost-effectiveness in country districts could mean that individuals and families in crisis would be denied a service or wait days for assistance. By one set of criteria, from the point of view of rural residents, a social worker could be shown to be an effective practitioner, despite the travel time required to cover long distances. Such practice could also be considered inefficient if the policy makers were intent on cutting back on local services by retaining only their economically 'rationalised', centralised urban locations.

Rhetoric about the value of the market and the associated respect for unbridled individualism gave new meaning to empowerment. Emphasis on families being totally responsible for all their dependants meant that previous government policies could be judged an unnecessary interference. Public money to fund health and welfare services would be assigned reluctantly, or regarded as wasteful because individuals should be encouraged to demonstrate personal responsibility through financial independence. The heroes and heroines of the age of monetarism were stockbrokers, merchant bankers, financial speculators and their legion of advisers, the lawyers, accountants, business managers and the multipurpose persons of the 1980s, the consultants.

In their ability to manage financial information and manipulate the markets, the young and upwardly mobile yuppies of the 1980s represented a new form of power. Yet it was the ubiquitous consultants whose activities symbolised the very obverse of the goals of social justice. They tendered for almost any project to do with reorganisation, rationalisation, regionalisation or rejuvenation. They were willing to borrow and repackage information and claim the reports were their own—but they never owned up to the consequences. They were supremely confident of their versatility and could immerse themselves in efficiency and productivity enquiries whether they were into education, welfare, health services or the administration of the court system.

Yet this tribe left people disempowered and dispossessed. Solutions to problems were once again imposed from the top down. The consultants contributed little to knowledge, and almost nothing to the understanding of the people whose activities they were examining. The idea of coherence had nothing in common with the consultants' ad hoc reports and recommendations. A culture of sharing and teaching, of collective struggle and consolidation, was largely discarded in favour of the values of the marketplace.

However selfish the policies which nurtured the work of the consultants, they could always be justified by the appearance of efficiency and economic durability. In applying the smooth surface of firm and rational government, the painters and decorators were to be a new breed of managers whose ability to exercise control over people and events would be a test of their effectiveness.

Management and control

Before focusing on practitioners' experience of managers' intolerance of dissent, it is salutary to emphasise that such control from the centre has not been peculiar to capitalism. Handa, for example, showed that both Marxist and liberal forms of government have had similar influences on world order. Both have produced a 'highly managed and centralized violent world of antagonistic nation states' (Handa 1985 p.193). In both, the technology and management of work conditions have been intended to extract from the individual the maximum amount of output and have not been intended to develop human life. In both systems education has been concerned to teach skills and attitudes which 'prepare the individual to adjust and contribute to the continuation of a violent social order' (Handa 1985 p.194).

The flip side of these forms of centralism in the management of economies and in the exercise of power in organisations is the experience of oppression of those who have neither economic resources, political clout nor professional influence. This refers in many countries to the material and political powerlessness of masses of people, yet other disempowering experiences have occurred in the very organisations which should have had precisely the opposite effect.

In health, welfare and other government bureaucracies, a new breed of managers has reinstituted goals once discredited and now back in favour. An ideology of managerialism has provided the incentives to exercise control, the language to express it and the criteria by which it is to be assessed.

Considine has summarised the recent history of changing styles of management, from right elitist forms to pluralist modes and to those which have incorporated historical and structural perspectives on the conduct of human relationships (Considine 1988a). The elitist versions of management derived from studies of private corporations and the military. These studies also depicted the relationship between the production of rules for public service bureaucracies and the values of dominant people. Crozier showed how the rules to bolster the values of leaders in French bureaucracies existed to protect the dominant values in French society (Crozier 1964). In the United States, Lerner argued that private corporations relied on control through hierarchies as the principle for efficient management and were successful in having such a model imitated in non-business contexts (Lerner 1986).

By contrast, a period of history which witnessed enthusiasm for community development and participation was characterised by an emphasis, within bureaucracies, on negotiation, mediation and adjustment. Such a pluralist model of management included attempts to recognise the role in decision making of employees, clients, client organisations and other public and private institutions.

Those perspectives which emphasised historical forces and the need for structural change addressed questions about the labour force, the need to harness new technology and the importance of having wider social movements represented in management deliberations. For example, in Australia the recognition of the value of women's, ethnic and Aboriginal groups led to positive discrimination in employment programs; and community representation became a measure by which to judge management policies.

The managerialism of the 1980s was built on political platforms which discredited the pluralist and social movement influences, but it is virtually impossible to attribute the revival of the elite model of central control to a particular political party. Politicians of different political persuasions were impressed by the language of rational instrumentalism and by corporate management structures. Reagan in the US, Thatcher in Britain, and Labor governments in Australia and New Zealand were all keen to be seen as striving for businesslike efficiency, even though, in the case of New Zealand, this policy resulted in the closing of post offices, the undermining of jobs, careers, families and the viability of whole towns (Considine 1988b).

A means of achieving such economic efficiency policies was apparent in the arrival in organisations of managers with neither specific qualifications nor knowledge of the activities—perhaps nursing, education, community development or social work—for which they were to have executive responsibility. They were managers who were to manage. This would not necessarily require a particular view of education or nursing or welfare because too much thought about the meaning of these specific issues would hinder their priorities. Such managers were likely to be 'executives recruited from fields which have a quite different organisational culture to that formerly shared by social service professionals and community group representatives' (Considine 1988a p.24).

In her study of the behaviour of senior managers in Australian public sector bureaucracies, Yeatman showed how a reverence for the phenomenon called management constrained the influence of professionals with specific expertise. 'These professional engineers, doctors, social workers, lawyers and so on in the public sector may find that the discretionary authority they require to interpret their task and to respond to needs has been seriously circumscribed by the requirements placed on them by professional managers' (Yeatman 1990 p.25).

The means by which the managers tried to achieve efficiency were also the ends by which their own performance was assessed. Program budgeting might appear to have ignored the personal and political tensions in providing services but it did push staff towards a concern with some artificial consistency, as in judging how many objectives had been achieved and at what cost. From these indicators of costs flowed a proliferation of other measures: a record of numbers of interviews, visits, telephone calls and training sessions.

Conflicting values of respect for autonomy and for control were not easily reconciled. Not all of those managers were anti-intellectual, but questioning and debate had little place in their ideas about good administration. The jargon of management included prescriptions such as 'mainstreaming human management systems' which could mean cutting back on the money previously invested in so-called 'non-productive' welfare services. That the cutbacks might be as indiscriminate as the alleged wasteful expenditure merited little attention if the goal was to be seen to take tough decisions and ensure their rapid implementation.

In the process of achieving these objectives, dissenters such as practitioners with ideas, let alone members of unions, could be brushed aside. In a description of Rambo-style management practices, Clare Burton, the director of the Equal Employment Office in New South

Wales, depicted the determined, obedient managers as almost always men whose mission was to do more with less. Policies of fair play and equal opportunity were of little interest unless they could be used to suppress dissent and could be fitted into an image of efficient management. Burton attributes to her typical macho manager lines like: 'Show me a disabled woman who can have a go at the unions and cut back on staff, and I'll have ramps built into all the entrances to this building' (Burton 1989).

The association of strong management with effective control has had its effect in many areas of social welfare policy. Any deviants, not just in subordinate and disrespectful staff, must be dealt with resolutely. Juvenile and adult law breakers must not be treated leniently. Social workers, such as probation officers, were to be more explicit about their punishment role. A British enquiry into the supervision of young offenders called for 'a more concerted and purposeful approach, "less drift"' (Home Office 1987). Determined and prompt actions were to be taken with juvenile offenders, school truants and parents suspected of child abuse. Intervention and resolute use of statutory authority were to be the hallmarks of good social work. Such a view was promoted in policies which reflected a respect for authoritarian populism (Thomas 1988). These policies were justified by reference to the values of control which were claimed to characterise majority opinion and which should therefore, it was argued, be the priority of governments. Such reverence for control, as in the emphasis on the social police role of social workers, was also sustained by an obsession with keeping social welfare controversies off the radio waves, television screens and the front pages of newspapers.

Claims about efficiency through management by control display linear, over-simplified attitudes to the complexities of human relationships. Such characteristics are also a strength. These rules of management are easily learned and imitated. They offer the security and predictability inherent in simple solutions.

Struggles for social justice, however, have survived because of and not in spite of the selfishness of economic rationalism and the new managerialism's preoccupation with control.

Some traditions of social justice

An analysis of how to achieve different forms of power has to be far more than another technique in a professional merry-go-round of methodologies. It emerges from a long tradition of social policies to protect the most vulnerable citizens, the long-term unemployed, poor children or the frail elderly. Although those policies might be lumped together as representing goals of social justice, such a term could represent different theories and traditions. In Sweden it would reflect policies to expand social democracy through economic and social policies operating in tandem, and in Germany justice has been equated with high levels of employment. In the UK social justice has covered a history of central planning to produce some universal services and in Australia, federal policies for welfare, employment and other support were intended mostly to provide protection for wage earners (Beilharz 1989).

From these traditions can be discerned a common thread of goals, to provide security and equity in the implementation of social and economic policies. These goals do not include any obvious explanation of the means of attaining them. Nevertheless, the thread identifies the historical precedents and the philosophical rationale for the objectives of empowerment (see chapter 6).

When the great depression of the 1930s highlighted the disastrous effects of long term unemployment and exposed other indications of massive social and economic inequalities, the intervention of governments was expanded to attain some universal services for all citizens. Tawney (1931) and Beveridge (1944) in the UK, Coombs in Australian postwar reconstruction (see Watts 1987) and the architects of the New Deal in the US depicted the predicament of citizens who were powerless through no fault of their own. They emphasised that social justice demanded government responsibility to ensure freedom from hunger, homelessness, ignorance, sickness and unemployment. Galbraith was reflecting on these goals when he identified society's highest task: 'to reflect on its pursuit of happiness and harmony and its success in expelling pain, tension, sorrow and the ubiquitous curse of ignorance' (1970 p.280); and Titmuss saw the welfare state as a perpetual struggle to achieve social justice by building into national cultures assumptions about collective responsibility to meet states of dependency (Titmuss 1958).

These ideals were resuscitated in the late 1960s and 1970s by the rediscovery of poverty and the realisation that even in affluent countries, large proportions of the population remained poor and powerless. This 'rediscovery' led to various wars on poverty, in the Great Society programs of the Johnson administration in the US, the urban community development projects of the Wilson governments in Britain and Assistance plans of the Whitlam government from 1972–75 in Australia.

These programs referred to empowerment in a series of familiar objectives: giving power back to people, effecting reform from the grass roots, creating and using indigenous resources. Always these processes aimed at greater equality in power sharing, either by the consensus-oriented gradual process of community development or by the conflict-oriented swifter skirmishes of community action and its concern with enemies, targets and the achievement of specific objectives within a short time frame. This period also witnessed the re-emergence of the women's movement, which emphasised the interdependence of the personal and political as the intellectual and ideological hub of ideas and projects to achieve liberation.

As argued above, a poorly disguised backlash against these ideals arrived in the late 1970s and early 1980s. The dominance of the language and values of right-wing economics emphasised accountability for public money, and produced arguments that welfare state policies had not only failed to help people in need but had also undermined national economies. The alleged failure of social welfare and community projects to achieve social reform via a lasting redistribution of resources led to a view that their ideals were misplaced and their ideas out of date. The architects of those reformist policies were dismissed as yesterday's men and women and these dismissals became the overture to the age of economic rationalism.

In this age of reverence for the value of the market, success in life could be measured in terms of individual gain and an accumulation of power at other people's expense. However, protest was made against political leaders' adoption of corporate management's preoccupation with financial criteria to assess performance, for instance in Stretton's (1987) critique of the cult of selfishness, Lekachman's (1982) warning that infinite greed produced endless cruelty and Marquand's dubbing of ten years of Thatcherism as an exercise in producing an unprincipled society in which there was not much room even for enlightened self-interest (1988). Running parallel to these critiques have been the peace and environment movements and their twin lessons that new policies can emerge from the success of pressure group politics.

The peace and environment movements

In so many countries, the search for a just peace has been the priority in the struggle for welfare. In the middle of wars and faced with the threat of war, ordinary people have felt victimised and helpless, unable to overcome the widespread feeling that they did not count in terms of affecting the use of power in the world (Nader in Macy 1983).

Before the apparent rapprochement between the United States and the Soviet Union, the threat of nuclear war had produced a despair that little could be done. The anti-war and peace movements were motivated to overcome such attitudes by challenging military priorities within their own societies and by working to change the hostile relationships between peoples. Macy argued that in the United States people felt afraid and their fear was maintained by the illusion of their separateness from one another. To remedy such a 'planetary crisis', projects were developed to enable people to share their common energy for humanity, to develop self-confidence by finding out about issues and acting on them (Macy 1983 ch.3).

Macy described the projects and exercises to combat powerlessness under the threat of nuclear war as 'empowerment work'. This description shares with the thesis developed in this book the emphasis on solidarity through the personal experience of shared learning and the practice of political and communication skills.

While it is valuable to recognise the despair felt about nuclear war and to applaud Macy's emphasis on encouraging love and compassion between people, her goals could have been enhanced by some appraisal of the relationship between violence and the imbalances of power in different contexts. A preoccupation with techniques to deal with personal despair precluded any consideration of the link between massive social inequalities and harmful conflict. The lessons for social work in the activities of the peace movement are not merely about individual powerlessness and the means of stopping war. They concern the purposes and priorities of societies which would no longer be arming themselves for war.

Deconstruction of military institutions and assumptions about the growth of the armaments industry and powerblocs and wars requires answers to the questions, what do we mean by welfare and can welfare in different contexts be achieved? The environmental movement has been confronting those issues. The greens and the peace movements are both opposed to abuses of power. They have raised the plight of any object or person who is powerless—from the most precious commodity, spaceship earth, to the poorest of the poor in countries ravaged by war or denuded of natural resources.

In th eyes of the greens, the degradation of the environment is a self-defeating abuse of power with uneven consequences. When economic and ecological crises occur, it is the already disadvantaged countries and people of the world who suffer most. The value of the greens' objectives is the adoption of a global perspective which international commissions (Brandt 1980) and biologists have urged for years (Ehrlich et al. 1976). In the pursuit of this perspective, Schumacher's questioning of the disastrous consequences of growth for growth's sake (1973) has been incorporated into a political platform which advocates a technology compatible with people's need to be creative and the need to avoid activities which detract from their humanity.

This platform focuses on the consequences of economic growth and disputes unquestioned assumptions about the contribution of science and technology to progress and welfare. But an ecology-before-economics argument would severely test adherence to other principles of justice. Even if there was a consensus about the value of protecting the environment for the benefit of all the world's people and as an investment for future generations, that would still leave controversy over the issue of fair redistribution of resources.

In a steady state economy, or one where there is negative economic growth, policies to take away resources from those in the top wealth-owning and income-earning brackets in order to increase the resources of the poorer section of a population have usually provoked violent opposition from those who want to maintain their positions and defend their own interests. This shows the considerable difficulty in achieving justice. Yet inequality has been increasing in growth-producing economies and there is no evidence that such growth makes the attainment of justice any easier. Of the need for strategies to achieve justice and of the obstacles hindering their attainment, Thurow concluded about the United States that 'our society has reached the point where it must start to make explicit equity decisions if it is to advance . . . if we cannot learn to make, impose, and defend equity decisions, we are not going to solve any of our economic problems' (Thurow 1988 p.194).

If the problems of justice and equity are presented as a large zero sum equation (i.e. where one group gains, another loses) few will have direct means of influencing a solution, except perhaps by making larger donations to charity. The economic and social justice equation is more complex and the opportunity does exist to pose the problem in a way that enables most people to contribute towards solutions. Steps towards empowerment (see chapter 8) provide just one opportunity for different colleagues, clients and volunteers to consider local issues in relation to goals of economic and social justice. And in places of work, staff can strive to achieve equity in relationships, in part by ensuring that they keep themselves informed about the distribution and use of financial resources (see chapter 9).

In national policies as well as in local initiatives, an overall goal would be to balance ecological considerations with economic ones and vice versa. Strategies to achieve economic justice would also involve recognition of the economic inefficiency of maintaining social inequalities and the importance of a fair tax system as the means to redistribute resources. In addition, given the significance of jobs for people's financial and psychological well-being, the creation of valuable employment opportunities is a central and indispensable feature of any program for justice. With reference to such goals, Thurow argued that equity and economic efficiency could be achieved if all sections of the population had the employment prospects and related financial incentives that were enjoyed by all fully employed white males (Thurow 1988 p.204).

Challenging abuses of power carries with it the responsibility to develop liberating conditions for human relationships, a task which the greens have shouldered in their emphasis on quality of life issues such as the promotion and conservation of peace, personal well-being, beauty, tranquillity, wilderness, the survival of endangered species, a sense of community, friendship, cooperation, personal safety, security and clean air (Brown 1989; Ife 1989). Each of these topics are value statements which imply struggles to overcome forms of powerlessness: endangered species are enabled to survive, previously isolated people find strength in a sense of community. The diffusion of power and responsibility by decentralisation, by emphasising local forms of democracy and cooperation are the means of simultaneously empowering people and preserving the key resources of the environment.

The greens' agenda and ideology is sceptical of reliance on a particular version of science. To them and to this thesis about empowerment, the empiricist tradition in science represents a practice which has avoided questions about the political purposes of knowledge. To put this point in another way, that tradition has maintained the myth that scientific enquiry never has been and never should be contaminated by value judgments. Yet in social work and other social science research, the tension will persist between allegedly objective statements of what is and value judgments about what ought to be. To pretend otherwise is to collude with a cosy consensus view of the world. In the thesis of empowerment, that tradition represents a one-dimensional exercise of power, supporting the status quo and leaving people mystified and ignorant, distant from certain forms of knowledge and deferential to the scientists who promote it.

The environmentalists' scrutiny of the claims of scientists and other experts that they are developing technology for human betterment is part of a philosophy which says that unnecessary dependence on experts is disempowering. The same school of thought sees uncritical acceptance of professionalisation in an occupation such as social work as the virtual equivalent of saying that the concentration of power in hierarchies and at the centre of organisations is both inevitable and desirable. Yet the task of enabling even the most powerless of people to achieve some semblance of power requires social workers to reject professionalisation when it discourages political analysis and to always evaluate what this process means and in whose interests it is maintained. To complete that evaluation is not as easy as it seems, though some critics would immediately dismiss all aspects of professionalisation. A more cautious response is possible.

It is not being implied here, or in the ideology of the greens, that professionals such as social workers should not strive to be as competent as possible, to attain the highest standards in their work. Without such demonstration of competence and high standards, no practitioner is entitled to be taken seriously. However, if professionalisation means the protection of one group at the expense of ordinary citizens, or involves keeping community groups in the dark over social issues, that process would be alien to ideas about the creative and liberating exercise of power.

The growth of interest in the greens' advocacy of harmony between human beings and dwindling natural resources should blind no one to the difficulty of maintaining cooperation between loose coalitions of environmental groups, each of which wants some element of power and control. The dilemma of how to share responsibility between people in a constructive way always becomes apparent when the challenge to governments and other concentrations of power is successful. To question the dominant exercise of power is one thing: to provide and implement alternatives is another. To harness the values of social justice in the development of a social work and social welfare practice for the next decade will involve controversy, not just over the personalities of the people involved but also over any attempt to explain and justify the specific objectives of empowerment.

III The process and politics of change

6 Explaining objectives

The objectives of empowerment should contribute to social justice, a crucial goal which has been discussed with reference to social policies designed to give people security and to achieve greater political and social equality. For example, a valuable definition of justice was developed at great length by Rawls from a rank order of principles: equality in basic liberties, equality of opportunity for advancement, and positive discrimination in favour of the underprivileged to ensure equity (Rawls 1972 pp.302–3).

Basic liberties would include rights such as protection against arbitrary arrest, against imprisonment without trial, against other forms of harm such as discrimination on the basis of race, or any unnecessary interference with individual freedom. In exploring the difference between positive discrimination to achieve equity and the guarantee of basic liberties, Kathleen Jones described equity as a second order concept which followed primary principles of social justice (Jones et al. 1978).

With responsibilities to implement social policies and to assess their relevance and consequences, social workers and community workers are well placed to work for justice. They can observe that wasteful and unjust use of human resources caused by gross social and economic inequalities and by the discrimination evident in racism, sexism and ageism (Moreau 1979). They also have tasks which affect the administration of justice, housing, health and welfare and which provide them with opportunities to advocate fair play and equity, although the determination of what is equitable will almost always be a matter of dispute. For example, although altruism is regarded as a laudable goal in social policies and a desirable trait in the conduct of relationships, it could reflect a permanent imbalance of power which would be inequitable. This criticism has been articulated by influential feminist scholars who say that some forms of altruism, as in a sick and poor mother's care for all the dependents in her family, are not only unequal but virtually compulsory because the weaker person 'is required to give in a continuous way more practical and emotional help than she receives' (Land and Rose 1985 p.90). Other expressions of altruism, 'support between friends of approximately equal social power, in which practical and emotional help is offered and received on a mutual basis' would represent a form of 'generalized reciprocity' and would be equitable (Land and Rose 1985 p.90).

Social justice and equity are as interdependent as social policies and social work practice, but the point about achievable goals is that the practitioners and the people they work with need the reward and encouragement that comes from knowing that something has been done well, that some progress has been made. In the development of political understanding, those small achievements will be indispensable, even if they do not lead immediately to the abolition of the injustice experienced by the people in question. Overcoming injustice is part of a process based on mutual support, teaching and learning in which day-to-day practice plays an important part.

The achievement of small goals is a building block in the process of enabling people to think and act for themselves, to become confident participants in addressing those social issues which affect them and which are linked to social justice generally. Encouraging people to believe in themselves by undertaking tasks which produce progress is an antidote to a decade preoccupied with rewards to powerful competitors. Praise and huge financial returns for the successful managers, executives and consultants have promoted selfishness based on the virtues of individual enterprise while those endeavouring to promote the equity inherent in fostering community interests have largely been disregarded.

The process of empowerment addresses two related objectives: the achievement of the more equitable distribution of resources and non-exploitative relationships between people and the enabling of people to achieve a creative sense of power through enhanced self-respect, confidence, knowledge and skills. It is important to emphasise the interrelatedness of these objectives. For example, some people might feel 'a creative sense of power' in exploiting others, but such a goal would be in conflict with the first objective's concern with non-exploitative relationships and thus have nothing in common with empowerment.

These objectives could refer to relationships between members of different social classes, people of different cultural or ethnic backgrounds or between men and women. They could address relationships between individual family members or the behaviour of officials towards subordinates, for example, a warder's response to an inmate of an institution, or a clerical officer's attitude towards an applicant for a social security benefit.

In this statement of objectives, the ideals of social justice and equity are associated with the experience of social and personal power. In chapter 4, distinctions have already been made between conservative and innovative ways of exercising power. At this point, the creative exercise of power will be discussed as an outcome and as part of a process, as a quality of work in achieving non-exploitative relationships and in terms of equity as a desirable end product. Such an outcome is often discussed in debates about administrative and policy priorities which revolve around questions of fairness in the distribution of resources. It is also a daily topic in personal relations, whether implicitly, as in conflict between children and their parents, or explicitly, as in formal mediation of disputes.

Justifying these objectives

Any statement of objectives runs the risk of sounding lofty, but to avoid such an explanation or such a justification of its merits is to slump into pragmatism. Besides, the culture of economic rationalism and the demise of the values associated with social justice underline the need to articulate such objectives. It might also be argued that there is no more justification for 'empowerment' than there is for the privatisation of every welfare agency or the introduction of a scheme to pay social workers by results. Why should staff employed in community projects or in any human service organisations embrace the goals of empowerment and why should anyone agree to be empowered?

Part of the justification for empowerment lies in the consequences that would occur if special people such as social workers did not act to achieve what might be equitable and just. Those groups whose encounters with officials have been characterised by passivity and other features of powerlessness needed encouragement and support before they could begin to revise their view of themselves, let alone take effective action on their own behalf. Left to the freedom of everyone for themselves, such vulnerable people had few means of protection and were ill-equipped to compete, unless of course they were prepared to confirm once again that they were losers. Therefore, argues Goodin, a goal of social justice is to protect the vulnerable, to 'stop those with overwhelming market power from exploiting those without it' (1989 p.8).

Implementing a commitment to vulnerable people involves a distinction between negative duties to protect them, or not to harm them (the issue of basic civil liberties) and positive duties to help them (Goodin 1985 p.18). Social welfare agencies and the architects of social policies have a responsibility to protect the vulnerable in specific quality of life issues such as the provision of food, clothing, shelter, self-respect and civil liberties. Statutes and social policy guidelines already give instructions to fulfil those duties, so that vulnerable adults and children stand some chance of experiencing both choice and a semblance of control over decisions. Universal health insurance which should ensure that people are not financially penalised for being sick, child protection to facilitate healthy growth and development without undue interference from adults, and positive discrimination to enable people with a disability to enjoy resources such as housing and educational and job opportunities are examples of policies which incorporate goals of social justice. Without such policies, it is difficult to see how poor people who are sick, children at risk of abuse and individuals who are socially marooned because of their disabilities could expect to have access to important material and other resources.

The specific goals of empowerment are positive duties to help and should be familiar to individuals with a strong commitment to improve the quality of the lives of those for whom they have special responsibilities. The questions of not only how to help but why to help, remain. Practitioners who identify with vulnerable community groups and are committed to doing their best for them will know the moral conundrums which affect the interpretation of their responsibilities. Even if they overlooked some of the old chestnut arguments about the principles of self-determination, they do not rush around using 'empowerment' to justify any kind of intervention. On the other hand, these practitioners do not have to wait for a child at risk to be killed before they practice child protection. They do not have to wait for evidence of the inhabitants of an old people's home being ill through boredom before they enable those individuals to start making choices and reasserting control.

References to individual freedom to justify inaction and non-intervention are the relics of the ideology which says that everyone can be responsible for the quality of their lives. The positive duties of social workers to help does not mean 'taking the care of people's lives out of their own hands, and relieving them from the disagreeable consequences of their own acts' (Mill 1848, in Goodin 1985 pp. 127–128). To take over from people, to make decisions for them, to allow them choice only on predetermined terms has nothing in common with empowerment. Such intervention, said Berlin, promotes coercion and enslavement not liberty (Berlin 1969). The same point, in another era, was made by Mill when he said that unenlightened and short-sighted benevolence 'saps the very foundations of the self-respect, self-help and self-control which are the essential conditions both of individual prosperity and of social virtue' (Mill 1848, in Goodin 1985 p.128).

The Siamese-twin nature of the objectives of empowerment shows not only cherished values but also the goals which are excluded. Acquiring power through exploitation in relationships is an example of the enjoyment of power for its own sake. Such a 'pornographic' use of power (Rubinoff 1967) was evident in the objectives of the 1984 character O'Brien in 'tearing human minds to pieces and putting them together in new shapes of your own choosing' (Orwell 1965 pp.202–203). The presence in almost any organisation of those who seem preoccupied with their own importance and are intensely opportunistic in their mission to consolidate that importance and enlarge their power, means that we should not have to reflect on Orwellian characters to make the point about lack of generosity to others and the pursuit of power for its own sake. It is not the objective of empowerment to make everyone millionaires or dominating managers of agencies or preoccupied-with-their-own-interests academics, or bankers, lawyers, accountants, financial or property speculators, or the here today, gone tomorrow consultants. Those successful people may show flashes of altruism but their self-image and professional agendas seem mostly preoccupied with the production of good consequences for themselves. The positive tasks in empowerment include the process by which practitioners achieve self-respect for themselves and in relation to the interests of others, or a community. That statement is a repeat of Rawls' notion that the good society is to be defined in terms of what is good for all individuals, especially the most vulnerable such as the poorest. Self-respect is a valuable means of achieving a sense of personal well-being but does not exist in isolation from notions of social well-being. In the goals of empowerment, the personal will be important but the social will be critical.

That is easily said but belies a process which may involve a lot of people and take a long time. Before describing the steps and techniques which contribute to such a process of change, it should be valuable to consider some interpretations of these objectives. What do they mean?

Interpreting those objectives

Social workers and the people they work with can seldom control the outcome of services, at least not immediately. Yet almost any exchange could be liberating and creative, conveying support for the ideals of freedom to think, to evaluate and to act. Conveying respect and treating people with dignity can create the happiness which an individual feels, even for a moment, because they are not totally dependent on others. This feeling gives people control over some temporary feature of their lives, a self-space which, said de Bono, can provide for dignity if that space enables a person to be at ease with himself and his circumstances. 'Dignity is being happy with oneself. Without that foundation happiness can at best be a fleeting pleasure' (De Bono 1979 p.131).

A similar point was made by Bertrand Russell when he observed that while it was crucial through democracy to seek justice in society at large, 'by means of elaborate systems', this was not enough if it overlooked individuals' daily need for satisfaction. 'Daily joys, times of liberation from care, adventure, and opportunity for creative activity, are at least as important as justice in bringing about a life that men can feel to be worth living' (Russell 1977 p.93). And that contention is valuable encouragement for practitioners who want to feel that something worthwhile, some sense of dignity if not happiness, can be achieved even though the people they are working with may appear to start out from a position of powerlessness.

This theme, about dignity and happiness, is present in stories of people's desperate attempts to realise control over 'self-space'. In April 1830 Jane Eastwood, the 30-year-old wife of a transported Manchester bootmaker, was asking for more than the need to be treated with dignity by a social worker. She wrote to the Home Secretary of the time, Sir Robert Peel, that her husband had written requesting her to apply to the government so that she could join him in the convict settlement in Sidney Island, Australia. 'I am determined to go out to my husband even at the risk of my life ... Put it in my power of becoming happy, by uniting me again to the Best of Husbands' (Hughes 1988 p.133). The government agreed to her request.

This example of one happy ending shows the enhancement in the 'power' of one person being effected by the release of constraints previously exercised by another. But in much of social work, the first steps towards empowerment do not always revolve around the simple making of a decision such as to give someone something, to release them from prison or allow them entry to another country. The art of using power creatively is subtle and demanding. For example, a social worker meets with the parents of a child who is suspected of being abused. Anxious to avoid losing control of even one interview, the practitioner becomes preoccupied with her agenda. Neither parent nor child feel able to express their feelings. On another occasion but in a similar case, the same social worker acts differently. She provides space for each participant to express a view, when together or in private. She treats them with dignity and is sensitive to the likelihood that both mother and father are likely to view her as just another representative of authority or as some anonymous expert. She confounds this expectation by giving them a sense of personal space. It is a matter of judgment whether this is easier to achieve within the privacy of someone's own home or in the apparent anonymity of an office, but whatever the location, the process of empowerment begins within a time frame of no more than a couple of hours.

There is a paradox inherent in the goals of empowerment in this situation. The possibly destructive use of power by one of the parties (the reason for the intervention and enquiry), may be constrained by the practitioner's aim to give both parents and child a chance to express their views. Instead of saying 'I don't like what appears to have been going on here' and so polarising the exchange, the practitioner says 'It would be helpful if we found time for each person present to express their point of view. Where would be the best place to do this?' This latter approach defuses a potentially volatile situation and begins the process of questioning and perhaps changing the exercise of power in that home. However, a focus on the exercise of power in that home includes an appraisal of the social and economic conditions which reflect the family's social class position and hence their resources for exercising choice and control in society at large. Assessment in the empowerment tradition always includes an appraisal of the exercise of power in linked but different contexts.

In another lay—professional exchange, the social worker is a witness. A doctor explains his objectives for rehabilitation to a young man recently disabled in car accident. The doctor is preoccupied with his medical model of treatment and with his own importance. The patient is invited to respond but only in terms of the doctor's agenda. The social worker's participation is encouraged only if she accepts the walking-on role that this medical director—producer has in mind. The exchanges are characterised by an inequality which is disempowering for the patient and the social worker, though the doctor does not see it that way.

Conversely, the doctor, social worker and patient participate in an exchange about the nature of disability and thereby the nature of normality. This sets the tone for a mutually valuable educational experience, characterised by a sense of reciprocity and sharing. Therein lies the ideal, that each party can lay claim to expertise by learning from the other. In this and other examples, the business of demystifying some claims of professional expertise is a means of empowerment and we have identified another paradox. The objectives of empowerment imply that expertise is attained by some denial of its existence. Expertise can be exerted by loosening the reins of control, by refusing to be mysterious and by achieving some sense of equality and partnership.

In each of these examples the objective is to respond to people with the respect and dignity which enables them to feel that they are fairly treated, or that some attempt is being made to treat them fairly. That response may reflect a well-thought out ideology about the pursuit of equity as the priority for practice but it says little about the theories and the difficult questions which such theories pose. The ways of analysing society, assessing people and their circumstances and explaining relationships and conditions depend on the questions asked by practitioners or researchers. Those questions flow from theoretical perspectives. Although claims about empowerment were identified in chapter 2 as coming from the conflict tradition in social theory, the meaning and implications of such conflict theory need clarification and discussion.

7 Developing theory

In an earlier comment on the place of empowerment in the smorgasbord of social work theories, as much was said about the values which this thesis challenges as was declared about the one it elaborates. For example, those explanations of social work which use the language of consensus—systems, interlocking parts, homeostasis and levels of equilibrium—have little in common with an approach which concentrates on the means of maintaining unfairness in societies and the consequences of doing so. Nevertheless empowerment presupposes that in practice there may be no strict dividing line between the use of insights derived from one theoretical tradition rather than another.

In four sections, this chapter examines the sources which influence the development of a theory about achieving power and shows how such a theory coexists with other social work theories. The first section discusses the nature of theory and ways of distinguishing one level of theorising from another. The second discusses the distinction between conflict and consensus explanations of society and of practice. The third identifies characteristics of empowerment theory and a final section discusses the adaptability of this approach by students and practitioners holding different values, from consensus to conflict, from conservative to radical.

Theory and theorising

Given that empowerment is concerned with implementation, with the theory–practice, policy–practice relationship, it would be sensible to consider difficulties in acknowledging the value of any specific theory. For example, practitioners have been reported as unable to say what theories they used in their practice (Young 1979) and some have denied that they were using theory 'to any significant extent' (Carew 1979). A pejorative view of theory has seen it as separate from practice, 'the sort of thing people talk about when they forget the pressures of doing the job', explained a disgruntled practitioner.

The claim that theory is separate from practice is also a familiar retort of some students in field work placements. 'Theory is something you have to do for academic reasons, like essays, it has nothing to do with what I'm doing here. I'm too busy to even think about theory,' was the response of a student who was expressing her disenchantment with years of study and her relief at the chance at last to be seen to do things. An anecdote about two universities' schools of Social Work in the same Australian city also illustrates some stereotypes of the theory–practice distinction. In one of the universities, students had a reputation for being able to do things but without thinking. In the other the students were reputed to be able to think but were incapable of doing anything. The one university supposedly taught students skills but little about the society in which they lived. The other course was allegedly strong on theoretical analysis but ignored practical things such as learning skills.

In an effort to address the false theory–practice distinction, as embodied in the insistence of some practitioners that they did not use theory, Curnock and Hardiker (1979) developed the notions 'practice theory' and 'theory of practice'. Practice theory, they said, was implicit in what social workers did and included imagination, intuition, cognition and affective experience. Theory of practice covered knowledge from social and behavioural sciences as well as specific theories from social work. This distinction between two types of theory has been justifiably criticised as being far too simple. 'Practice theory' included many things which were 'too unsystematic and unconscious to be dignified with the name "theory"' (Smid and van Krieken 1984 p.15). Theories of practice fused theories of intervention, as described in social work texts, with more general social scientific explanations of social life.

This criticism of the practice theory and theory for practice distinction was aimed at encouraging students and practitioners to recognise that some type of theorising went on all the time but in various ways and at different levels (Smid and van Krieken 1984). This point having been grasped, students should be able to make connections between their reading and their assessments of people and problems, their studies and their practice. With such goals in mind these authors developed a typology of three theoretical fields, or three levels of theorising: materialist social theory, strategic practice theory, and working concepts.

Materialist social theory included those consensus or conflict explanations of society which provided an overarching view, a general picture which could address the question whether the organisation of society was efficient or equitable and if not, why not. Conflict theories of social order represented a level of theorising whose major purpose was to analyse the political and economic structure of society and the purpose of social institutions.

The second level of theory developed methods of social work intervention and was dubbed strategic because it confronted questions about how to do things. As long as it was not divorced from social and historical theory, i.e. the materialist level of theorising, it was unlikely to be regarded and used just as a technology. However, the danger is that practitioners and educators become so fascinated with their methods, perhaps casework or community development, crisis intervention or group work, that they cease to ask questions about ideology and drift into thinking that practice can occur in some political and economic vacuum. In this regard Simpkin observed that there was nothing wrong with casework as a method but he objected when casework became an ideology, when problems were explained only in individual terms and an establishment view, namely a consensus explanation of society, was implied but not acknowledged (Simpkin 1979).

The third level of theory was defined as 'the totality of a worker's political standpoints, experiences, theoretical knowledge, their self-image, experience of their training and practice, their guidelines for action—in short their practice ideologies . . .' (Smid and van Krieken 1984 p.16). This reference to concepts in everyday use was a reminder that one way to consider the use of theory was to ask how people were using their experience. In the language of empowerment it would be relevant to ask whether the concept 'biography' was being used to raise questions about the exercise of power and the experience of powerlessness, and whether answers to those questions were transforming the thinking of the student, practitioner or client.

However, these specific questions only follow from one tradition or another within overarching or materialist theory. At that level, a significant way to sift theories is to distinguish between those which derive from a social conflict or social consensus perspective.

Conflict or consensus

Social work practice informed by social conflict analysis has been labelled structural (Moreau 1979), critical and radical (Findlay 1978; McIntyre 1982; Bailey and Brake 1975) and has included works which set out to develop explicit feminist (Marchant and Wearing 1988) and socialist (Corrigan and Leonard 1978; Galper 1980) perspectives.

The nub of these authors' scholarship concerned the goal of analysing society in terms of conflicting interests and ensuring that social work would not be allied with forces which maintained social inequality. They perceived social order as sustained by conflict between capital and labour, between powerful institutions and ordinary citizens, between influential groups and their opponents, or between influential groups and their clientele (Corrigan and Leonard 1978; Galper 1980; Walker and Beaumont 1981). They drew their inspiration from analyses of social problems which covered the influence on people's lives and lifestyles of economic organisation, culture and agencies. Instead of being preoccupied with individuals' shortcomings and deviance, such analysis emphasised the importance of focusing on the relationship between individual and society in order to show how social process would be manifest in various psychological states (Findlay 1978; McIntyre 1982).

It is not just social scientists who have expressed themselves through theories of conflict or consensus. Many people carry around cherished theories to explain normality and deviance, and the issue of poor people's behaviour has probably been the most popular subject for moral scrutiny as well as social science investigation. Those who hold consensus views of society explain poverty with reference to the lazy, disorganised or immoral behaviour of the poor. They ask few questions about the behaviour of the rich or about the policies and institutions which maintain social inequality. This view is popular with right of centre politicians, fundamentalist religious leaders, journalists who write moral judgments about the undeserving poor or personalities who compere radio phone-in programs which encourage intolerance among a certain constituency of listeners.

These commonsense consensus theories have been given a more sophisticated elaboration in accounts of the culture of poverty which moved away from stigmatising the poor and explained their condition as a way of life which was self-perpetuating because it was based on strong group values (Lewis 1965; Leacock 1971). A variant of this culture of poverty theory was the development of a theory of learned helplessness which emphasised the forces which socialised women into dependency roles. Although this theory of learned helplessness was first developed from laboratory experiments with dogs, it was transferred to explain the predicament of poor people in households headed by women who were black and who could be blamed for their children's deviant behaviour: the inability to delay gratification, juvenile delinquency and poor school performance.

The high incidence of depression among women and the predicament of women who were battered was also explained in behaviourist terms, in reference to lack of stimulation and the absence of rewards in these women's lives. Observations of these factors contributed to the theory that such women could only effect control over their circumstances by internalising feelings of powerlessness and learning roles to adapt to such experiences (Seligman 1975; Hendricks-Mathews 1982). However, feminist writers pointed out that the interplay of forces to do with social class, gender and context, including the monotony of household work, the low value placed upon it and the barriers to women having other choices, had been ignored. Deglau argued that the conceptualisation of learned helplessness had probably damaged women's progress in achieving equality and had certainly affected what happened to them when they sought treatment (Deglau 1985).

To avoid a preoccupation with individual behaviour to explain deviance and to avoid the tendency to blame the victim, various adaptations of systems theory became popular among social work educators. These adaptations included a general systems approach which used metaphors from engineering to explain the need for energy to contribute to equilibrium; an ecological approach which emphasised 'individuals' ability to negotiate and compromise with their social environment as they seek to adjust and survive' (De Hoyos and Jensen 1985 p.199); and 'the Parsonian Model' which documented the influence of values in socialisation and the function of society in providing rewarding roles which were also means of social control (De Hoyos and Jensen 1985, p.201).

Such development of systems theory also emphasised rules from the natural sciences, hence the importance of the neutral role of observers such as social workers. They provided a model to explain clients' behaviour not just by reference to psychological processes but also in terms of group membership and societal influences. Yet they also implied the value of orderly behaviour even if they did not explicitly acknowledge the disproportionate influence of the dominant values of American society. Such systems theorists relied on consensus perspectives, ignored the function of ideology and depicted social work as concerned with recovering individual and social systems to healthy and harmonious functioning (Howe 1987 ch.7) and described social workers as 'maintenance mechanics oiling the interpersonal wheels of the community' (Davies 1985 p.28).

With regard to a problem such as poverty, the power of theory, from either a conflict or consensus perspective, lies not only in the explanation of causes but in the corresponding prescriptions for intervention and reform. Depending on the explanation of causes, almost any form of treatment could be justified. If poverty was seen as caused by the values and behaviour of poor people, they could be deterred by being disqualified from social security benefits or they could be subject to programs of behaviour modification. Even policies to promote the alleged incentive value of regressive taxation and greater social inequality have the effect of rewarding the affluent and punishing those who have little to bargain with anyway.

At the other end of the ideological and theoretical spectrum, proposals for structural reform and the elimination of huge social class differences in access to resources and opportunities, emphasised the unjustness of society and the political powerlessness of the poor. Influenced by the works of Karl Marx and other social theorists who had documented evidence of social inequalities and social contradictions and who stressed the inevitability of struggle to resolve them, some social work theorists developed a radical or critical perspective (Bailey and Brake 1975; Findlay 1978; Corrigan and Leonard 1978). In Australia, the initiators of a project to give power to the poor, including the author of the subsequent insightful book on the subject, acknowledged their reliance on this theoretical perspective. It was a view, said Liffman '[which] possibly more readily than any other, accords with the intuitive experience of those whose concern with the problem of poverty is direct and passionate, and leads to a political approach for its alleviation, often directed at total transformation of the social structure' (Liffman 1979 p.21)

Even in this introductory section of the book, but with the wisdom of hindsight, Liffman was reflecting on aims which he had come to see as noble but somewhat unrealistic. He was confronting the difficulty of applying a theoretical analysis and of implementing any decision. The same issue is also addressed in the theory–practice relationship inherent in achieving the objectives of empowerment. The characteristics of that approach can now be described by using the three-level typology discussed above.

The nature of empowerment theory

The three levels of theory in empowerment will refer to the influence of theories of social conflict, the characteristics of empowerment as a theory of intervention and significant working concepts such as the constraints of working in an organisation and the primacy to be given to the views of powerless people.

At the level of overarching social theory, empowerment grows from the insights and ideology of those social conflict theories which have also influenced the need for an explicitly political approach to practice. For example, the influence of economic rationalism has been criticised for generating prescriptions for social order based on powerful interests which were also selfish. In these prescriptions there were few opportunities for economically powerless groups to be heard or to have their points of view taken seriously, even though the defenders of economic rationalism might argue that it has a human face and has not ignored social justice. Acknowledging a debt to the decades of campaigns to achieve social justice through social action and social policy has been another way of expressing the influence and value of a social conflict perspective. The goals of the peace and environment movements have also been judged relevant to empowerment in terms of those movements' concerns with justice and with equity, particularly in their challenging the dominance of corporate interests and in their promoting the principle of wider consultation in matters of national interest.

When applied as a 'strategic practice theory', empowerment would draw from ideas and techniques influenced by consensus and conflict traditions. This claim may appear tantamount to having fifty cents each way but it is also a recognition of the difficulties of doing social work and of working skilfully in spite of constraints. The empowerment approach recognises the need for practitioners to manage the personal tensions and conflicting demands in their jobs and to concede that theory developed in textbooks may be applied in different ways in practice. When discussing the different varieties of systems theory, De Hoyos and Jensen observed that 'most social workers appeared to be more interested in discovering new ways of expanding the medical model to include the clients' environment than in quibbling over specific theories' (De Hoyos and Jensen 1985). Leonard showed how apparently consensus-oriented versions of systems theory could be developed with radical goals in mind. 'It would seem more profitable,' he wrote, 'to rescue systems theory from the grasp of apologists for existing institutions and to use it for the purpose of understanding and changing those institutions' (Leonard 1975 p.48).

The difficulty of sustaining a conflict approach both to under-standing society *and* conducting practice was apparent in the experiences of the social workers and community workers in the Australian Brotherhood of St Laurence poverty experiment. Although committed to a conflict-oriented explanation of poverty, those staff improvised in their practice and used ideas which could be classified as conservative or radical. Did that really matter? They were faced with the dilemma of subscribing to the view that societal conditions imposed poverty on vulnerable people, such as the elderly, the unemployed, the chronically ill, the migrant and Aborigines, and recognising that providing material help was not the only way out of poverty. Although such help resulted in a clear improvement in some families' circumstances, in other cases it appeared to make little difference, 'hence the importance of processes within the Centre concerned with the development of self-confidence, social and practical skills, understanding of society and welfare rights and personal insight and purpose' (Liffman 1979 p.154).

In any efforts to enable people to achieve some element of power, it will be more important to give attention to skills than to judge activities unworthy because they did not appear to come exclusively from a social conflict perspective and did not immediately address radical social change. Throughout any discussion of empowerment as a strategic theory, the process of effecting change will be discussed in terms of the significance of small victories and achieving some progress, but always keeping the ultimate goal of social justice in mind.

This may not be as difficult as it sounds. Two examples of empowerment as a middle range strategy illustrate the importance of combining theory with interactive and political skills. The first concerns the placement of mildly intellectually disabled young people in job support programs. The second refers to the development of a support group for nurses responsible for caring for terminally ill cancer patients. In both examples, a humane and timely innovation was facilitated, at least implicitly, by the theory that vulnerable groups need support to move into new roles or to sustain the ones they are already playing. In neither case was there a preoccupation with individual problems but rather a focus on policy innovation and attention to group needs.

The structural problem of unemployment among the young disabled was addressed by linking prospective employers to the unemployed young people and those young people to the employers. Subsequently those who obtained employment were supported in the workplace by one person from the job support program. From the young people's point of view that support helped to convert the despair of being on the dole to a self-respect and happiness which the young people had not considered possible. In the second example, the social work practitioners on the cancer wards decided that their support for the work of the nurses was an effective use of time. Creating the support group for the nurses represented an expression of solidarity and an assessment of the importance of mutual support in conducting a stressful and at first sight unrewarding job. Even to encourage the nursing staff to value open discussion of their ideas about techniques for relating to patients and their families and to value the experience of sharing their feelings of dismay about their work, required political judgment and skill. So too did the task of finding the time to run such groups because the hospital hierarchy at first argued that time spent in discussion would have little to do with 'real nursing'.

Reference in this example to the hospital hierarchy and to the previously strained relationships between social workers and nurses underlines the significance, in any strategic theory, of including information about conditions of practice. A theory of empowerment should address the predicament of workers in organisations as well as point out ways to work effectively with the public. A theory which ignored organisational issues but made claims about solutions in working with vulnerable people, only to discover that the workers had left because they were burned out, could hardly be called empowering.

Organisational constraints and the perspectives of the powerless people who seek help will be addressed by considering these issues as day-to-day matters, which crop up at the working concept level of theorising. In this regard empowerment theory can be developed through awareness of conflicts and ways to resolve them. Conflicts may be apparent in individuals' ambivalence about their work and in feelings of disenchantment towards people they are supposed to care for. Tensions will be inherent in the task of reconciling statements of agency interest in people's welfare with official reluctance to provide the resources to achieve such goals. The conflict inherent in trying to do social work in a climate in which political paymasters only want practitioners to exercise control over people or in which they are expected, in the name of efficiency, to do more and more with less and less, depicts some disempowering aspects of working conditions. A specific example of potentially disempowering conflict in the workplace concerns agencies, such as probation and parole, where the practitioners are accountable to the courts and to the involuntary clients (Curnock and Hardiker 1979; Walker and Beaumont 1981; Cingolani 1984).

In the context of social work in the courts, if the contradictions inherent in the practitioners' jobs are not to become overwhelming, an adeptness in mediating and negotiating will be crucial. The conflicting interests of a juvenile court, families, the police, the probation agency and the values and interests of the probationer require attention to a political process to manage the tasks of care and control. That political process recognises that it is not the practitioner's task to ask for mere compliance from the probationer, even if that is what society appears to demand. To do so is to exercise power in that unimaginative, one-dimensional way which has nothing in common with empowerment.

If practitioners are to navigate a way between the probationers' points of view and the demands of officialdom, they will have to be effective in negotiating relationships in several contexts, not just with the young persons being supervised. Each practitioner's attention to the values and priorities of the juvenile court and the probation office and their ability to be seen as credible in these contexts will enable them to depart from official roles. Such a departure would involve searching for a workable compromise or, if need be, coming out openly as an advocate of all the young probationers' interests, even if that stance incurred the wrath of the agency.

The management of conflicting interests and contradictory instructions is not necessarily the major constraint which affects practice. Studies of front-line practitioners (Prottas 1979; Satyamurti 1981; Thorpe 1983) indicated that time was the resource in shortest supply and that 'all things being equal, the time saving alternative is preferable' (Prottas 1979 p.4). Whether the time-saving alternative is equitable will require careful attention to the negative and positive uses of discretion, an issue discussed in chapter 16 on the relationship between policy and practice.

The 'working concept' level of theorising is likely to show why and how students as practitioners use their discretion. A useful way of exploring working concepts is to think of them as something akin to the culture of the people concerned, as expressed by the assumptions which they have had socialised into them as to what 'appropriate' family relations should look like, or by their attitudes to the work ethic. The continued operation of those assumptions and attitudes might undermine whatever theoretical and practical commitments an individual might have, never more so than in working with those people who have not only been powerless but whom even welfare agencies have regarded as undeserving.

Following principles for conducting qualitative research (Glaser and Strauss 1967), empowerment theory should be grounded in evidence about the perceptions of all those who are the subjects of intervention. The theory has to be able to address the needs of those whom, at first sight, it is difficult and unrewarding to work with, as well as those who have traditionally been seen to be worthy clients because they were motivated, cooperative, spoke a similar language to the professionals and acknowledged the value of what was being done with them. For empowerment to make a difference it has to discourage the usual creaming off process which has seen some people rewarded with special attention and the problems of the undeserving compounded by being given scant attention, except on occasions of sensational and undeniable crisis. If the promise of biography is to be realised, constant questions about powerlessness and ways to change such a state will see attention being given to the predicament of people traditionally labelled undeserving, as well as those regarded as deserving. To do otherwise would be inequitable and disempowering.

Adapting concepts and theories

In spite of encouraging the development of theory by grounding it in examples from practice, students and practitioners may still see the exercise as abstract and of little value. How can this resistance be overcome?

Students, educators, practitioners and even client groups could elaborate the nature of their own and others' powerlessness and do so by linking their stories to surrounding social context and to the political and economic constraints of their times. Examples from individual biography will usually hint at the theories being used and indicate whether the storytellers were deriving their views from a consensus or conflict perspective. To acknowledge such ways of thinking is crucial for practitioners, so it would be valuable to ask them where they fall on the consensus to conflict continuum and the consequences of pursuing one perspective rather than another. Students and practitioners can do this by identifying their assumptions about normality with reference to the family, social order and appropriate behaviour (Figure 7.1). This figure is inserted in order to develop interest in consensus and conflict theory by encouraging discussion of common issues, and by asking students or practitioners to say which point of the pendulum would mark their position.

The pendulum analogy is also used to provide for the possibility that as awareness of the meaning of power, politics and policy increases, someone's theories may fluctuate, from week to week or over a longer period of time. For example, at some point in the thinking about empowerment, the cautious person who has accepted one interpretation of family or society and the values which characterise the good family and the orderly society, begins to realise that these consensus views are disempowering because they reproduce others' handed down versions of norms and values and the cultural and class origins of such assumptions. Acceptance of the characteristics of the normal family and the role of men and women and children within it can give way to an analysis which questions the influence of culture and examines how race, class and gender differences have affected people's economic standing and social influence. From growing confidence with that analysis comes a willingness to participate in debating the links between social order, social policy and social work, between the functions of agencies and the development of discretion to raise questions about social justice and the means of working for such an objective. That movement, from a consensus to conflict perspective, from one-dimensional to three-dimensional uses of power, would represent an interesting swing of the pendulum.

Reference to familiar concepts should develop students' confidence in taking risks and changing attitudes and be a bridge to ideology and theory, but what happens when there is a disparity between the claims made in the classroom and the values used in practice? Some educators and students may be convinced that a focus on power-lessness and oppression provides the motif for social work practice in the 1990s but that conviction is not shared by other students or by the bulk of the practitioners whom they encounter in agencies, some of whom may be their supervisors. The 'other' students appear to be fixed in their views. They expect social work to give them the opportunity to practice family therapy in the security of a semi-respectable job. Questions about powerlessness with reference to race, or class or gender, let alone about disability or sexual orientation only seem to get in the way of a smooth progress towards such professional respectability.

Figure 7.1   Identifying assumptions about issues such as the family, social order, and appropriate behaviour

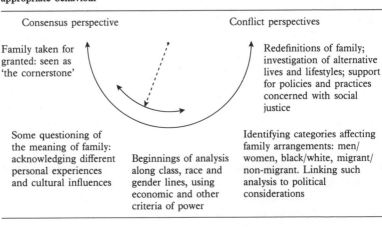

Consensus perspective

Conflict perspectives

Family taken for granted: seen as 'the cornerstone'

Redefinitions of family; investigation of alternative lives and lifestyles; support for policies and practices concerned with social justice

Some questioning of the meaning of family: acknowledging different personal experiences and cultural influences

Beginnings of analysis along class, race and gender lines, using economic and other criteria of power

Identifying categories affecting family arrangements: men/women, black/white, migrant/non-migrant. Linking such analysis to political considerations

The politically disinterested attitudes of practitioners, not the conservatism of students, may prove an even greater obstacle to any serious consideration of the merits of empowerment. Faced with advocacy of a political literacy in social work, some of these practitioners respond by complaining that students are no longer taught the holy trinity of casework, groupwork and community work. Or they respond to the word 'empowerment' by assuming that it merely means enabling. 'What's new?' they ask. They have always been 'enabling' and in that sense empowering. Besides, reference to oppression is just radical rhetoric and the use of the word 'political' in professional agencies would guarantee the loss of a job.

The combination of the conservative student and the politically indifferent supervisor looks like a recipe for intellectual and ideological constipation. Nothing seems likely to shift. Even the idea of equity through empowerment would appear as a threatening, inappropriate objective. What do we do with such an impasse?

The nature of empowerment theory affects the answers to the question. To suggest that only those students and practitioners who are familiar with theories at the conflict end of the continuum will understand and debate the claims being made here, is to preach to the converted. If relatively powerless people coming to welfare agencies can be encouraged to take one step at a time, so too can students and practitioners. The view that empowerment can only be weighed by a group of one ideological persuasion is also intolerant. Achieving power requires an aptitude for communication and cooperation, with students and practitioners with different values and different degrees of political understanding.

As a result of reading or from experiences in field placements or during conversations with their peers, students often question cherished beliefs, but they are not sure how to replace them. They accept the consensus—conflict distinction but remain cautious in their actions and some may have difficulty seeing the political connotation of individual powerlessness. On the other hand, those who display conservative attitudes today may throw caution to the winds tomorrow. The beginning-of-the-week self-proclaimed radical socialist may turn out to be Friday's conservative reactionary.

The question of how people change their views and adopt new ideas is addressed by the premise that in education as in politics, it is wise to anticipate the beliefs which an audience already possesses. When discussing empowerment with any group, it is a mark of respect to enable them to declare the contents of their own ideological and theoretical baggage. They should be able to do so without fear or favour, encouraged by the belief that it is not where you are coming from but where you are going to that matters. The process by which students and practitioners change and the possibility that their beliefs and actions may vary according to problems and context, is described in another pendulum figure (Figure 7.2). On this occasion, the respondents are asked how they would go about effecting change in various contexts of interpersonal relationships. One response would be to do nothing. For example, in relation to conservative parents, a potentially radical young woman decides to put up with her sense of subordination, at least for the time being. A wife who suffers physical violence from her husband tolerates such abuse because there seems no escape and no obvious alternative way of conducting relationships.

Figure 7.2   Effecting change: attitudes and actions
How do we effect change?   1   in the conduct of personal relationships
                            2   in relationship to the representatives of authority

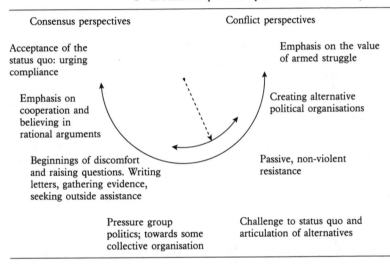

Consensus perspectives	Conflict perspectives
Acceptance of the status quo: urging compliance	Emphasis on the value of armed struggle
Emphasis on cooperation and believing in rational arguments	Creating alternative political organisations
Beginnings of discomfort and raising questions. Writing letters, gathering evidence, seeking outside assistance	Passive, non-violent resistance
Pressure group politics; towards some collective organisation	Challenge to status quo and articulation of alternatives

As students are invited to move around the pendulum, they begin to politicise their view of power in the conduct of personal relationships. They not only raise questions, they begin to develop the confidence that comes from the experience of solidarity with others and do so by learning the language used in analyses of social conflict. A second question in Figure 7.2 concerns the relationship of individuals to the state, or to the representatives of state authority. By virtue of their age, sex, race, class, health or sexual orientation, large numbers of people have experienced their lives as an essay in various forms of subordination. They may have resented their experiences but not have known how to change them. Their relationships to the representatives of authority have been perceived as oppressive, but like so many clients of social welfare agencies, they have been passive in their orientation to officials. Even if they had known intuitively what advice to pass on to others they had seemed unable to take action on their own behalf, like the mothers advising daughters in the Alice Walker poem 'Women'

> ...they knew what we
> Must know
> Without knowing a page
> Of it
> Themselves
> (Walker 1988 p.5)

Students' experience of practice placements provides the occasion to ponder their relationship to the state. As they risk new views and join organisations concerned with social issues, political identity begins and so does the knowing of the principle that personal issues become political when individuals ponder why they exercise power in a particular way in different contexts and why and how they have responded to the exercise of power by others. When individuals self-consciously think over this relationship, they are doing more than mouthing a familiar platitude that the personal is the political. If that link between personal and political is left at the level of slogan or platitude, it would be unlikely to lead to much insight by individuals, or discussion with others.

Invited to identify where they fall in the swing of the pendulum, the members of any group face the dilemma of choosing where they think they ought to be, as opposed to where they actually are. They can respond to that question privately but be encouraged to ground their answer with an example of their own experience. As long as they regard the descriptions 'passive resistance', 'creating political alternatives' (used in Figure 7.2) as apt, they can use such concepts and make the next step to being explicit about strategic theories.

Such intellectual exercises will always be supplemented by the experience of working, even with one person, to address a need for change and the steps to take to achieve that end. Although the search for equity and the attainment of justice are the touchstones for practice, a semblance of power can be achieved even in moving from one simple step to another. In so doing, working concepts will be translated into strategic theory.

8 Steps in empowerment

The processes of empowerment may cover the story of a lifetime. They may be apparent in a project which last for two years or be present in an educational and political experience which is completed within a few months. Whatever time it takes to achieve objectives, the process of change goes through stages. Several authors have described these and produced their own schemes to predict what is likely to occur. Each has depicted workers and their partners, practitioners and their clients struggling to comprehend political processes and to develop confidence in their abilities.

That process was not straightforward. Two steps forward might be followed by one step back. One step forward by two steps back. Each author has indicated that the responsibility to evaluate progress was a task to be shared in different ways at different times. It was not an activity which came only at the end of a project, neither did it represent work to be carried out by reliance on outsiders' expertise. These processes have been described by Freire (1972), Rose and Black (1985) and Rosenfeld (1989). The people they worked with lived in different parts of the world. Freire referred to peasants in South America, Rose and Black to ex-psychiatric patients in New York City and Rosenfeld in France to the poorest of the poor, whom he described as members of a Fourth World. For Freire the workers who might engage in the empowerment process were educators. Rose and Black were addressing case-managers or social workers responsible for implementing a policy of de-institutionalisation. Rosenfeld's manual for action recreated the work of volunteers in a Fourth World movement. Common stages in the process of dialogue and liberation (Freire 1972), of advocacy, empowerment and action (Rose and Black 1985) and of emergence and coproduction (Rosenfeld 1989) are apparent. Once those related schemes have been described (Figure 8.1), we can cull from them the ideas to be adapted for our own purposes.

Although each stage was recorded as a distinct step, to be completed before the workers proceeded to the next, each of the authors emphasised mutuality of interaction, the merging of one stage with another. The experiences engendered in each stage interacted with the ideas and tasks generated in another. The following figure is therefore an educational device, not some mechanical scheme to be rigidly followed. To avoid an impression of mechanics the stages have not been numbered, though in their original versions, two of the authors did so.

In addition to emphasis on the interrelatedness of initiatives occurring at different stages, responsibilities are repeated, which show continuity from one stage to another. The maintenance of trust, an awareness of exercising power in different contexts and a sensitivity to the use of language are features of all exchanges concerned with empowerment.

Even if credibility and trust have been achieved at one point in time, that is unlikely to be a permanent feature of working relationships. Successful completion of each step (Figure 8.1) requires constant attention to the gaining of credibility and the maintenance of trust. Enabling people to make connections between their lives and the political and economic trends in other contexts contributes to political literacy. This externalising, making connections between one context and another, is not only a means of focusing on the distribution of power and its consequences, it is also a guard against that easy tendency to privatise or localise problems—as though no one else shares them, as though they are only the product of individual shortcomings.

A scheme for practice, which applies to the development of policy initiatives with community groups, as well as to work with individuals, can be adapted from the stages described in Figure 8.1 and from the principles around which they were organised. In developing this scheme some of the ideas already spelt out will be acknowledged. The important additions and amendments derive from an emphasis on the responsibilities of practitioners to be explicit about skills, to address the constraints of working in agencies and to develop their responsibilities to interpret and implement social policies. Enough has been said already to indicate that the scheme which follows addresses practitioners' frequent sense of their own powerlessness as well as the fatalism and passivity expressed by others. The tasks of becoming policy literate, confident in comprehending the creative use of power and feeling at home with the political nuances of practice, applies as much to workers as to clients, as much to students of any helping profession as it does to specific practitioners in social work.

The following scheme illustrates phases in personal development and procedures for practice which were foreshadowed in the previous chapter's discussion of theory. For example, it will be assumed that the general problem being addressed is an expression of powerlessness, possibly poverty, illness or the membership of a group which is the subject of sexual or racial discrimination. Questions about inequality and inequity should flow from a familiarity with a social conflict analysis and that is the dominant theoretical perspective. The overriding practice requirements include interactive and political skills (outlined at greater length in chapter 10) and a sensitivity to the significance of the

Figure 8.1 Accounts of empowerment

Authors	Freire (1972 pp.81–95)	Rose and Black (1985 pp.60–69)	Rosenfled (1989 pp.51–54)
Key concepts	Liberation through dialogue: action/reflection.	Advocacy/ empowerment/ action	Emergence, partnership, coproduction
Stages in the process	Investigation of words which generate ideas	*Verstehen*: learning from each other and grasping the essence of oppression	Establishing credibility through alliances
	Evaluation of words and themes	Thematisation: pictures of objective conditions and subjective reflections	Acting as partners or coproducers
	Codifying the themes in ways familiar to the people who experience them	Problematisation: identifying problem to be solved	Discovering the families' suffering
	Presenting the codes by reflecting felt needs	Anomie: overcoming confusion and fear	Searching for expressions of hope
	Analysing and decoding: further listening and challenging	Analysing the consequences of action	Unveiling and constructing history
	Externalising: making links to wider contexts	Choice: ex-patients making decisions	Avoiding abstractions: maintaining the focus on living families
	Further decoding through inter-disciplinary studies	Action: self-conscious informed participation	Developing consent with coworkers
	Preparation of didactic materials	Evaluation: includes observations about personal development and changes in personal circumstances	Transferring goods and talents to other locations

potential creativity of all the parties involved. The stages by which the scheme proceeds can also be presented diagrammatically.

Figure 8.2   Stages in achieving power

Understanding themes
Evaluating self-image and knowledge
Specifying problems
Developing awareness of policies
Developing the notion of choice
Experiencing solidarity with others
Acquiring and using language
Resisting a return to powerlessness
Developing interactive and political skills
Evaluation

Discussion of the processes occurring at different stages will refer to work with individuals or groups concerned with various forms of problem solving. The same process could be applied to the implementation of a social policy or to the unfolding of a community development project.

A not dissimilar process of empowerment might also apply to practitioners rather than clients and in the following chapter on the politics of change in organisations, the powerlessness of practitioners and their need to work together to overcome agency constraints and to observe certain procedures in doing so, will be highlighted.

A balance of attention to the powerlessness of workers and clients is one way to guard against the patronising 'workers know best' attitude which has been identified in a brief earlier criticism of Freire's notion of consciousness raising. That criticism merits repeating. In discussing the stages shown in Figure 8.2, it would be easy to fall into the trap of thinking that because practitioners have a work plan and control certain information, they also have moral superiority or greater wisdom as to what ought to be done. To fall for that temptation would run counter to the ends and means of empowerment. One could hardly emphasise the value of rights, dignity and freedom and then treat people paternalistically. Striving to achieve equity in process and outcome could hardly be pursued by behaving as though a hierarchy of people and ideas should be maintained, as though the practitioner always has greater wisdom and better knowledge than the client. In this respect even the word client is a problem, but I will retain it as a means of identification and because it is unrealistic to pretend that power differentials of some kind do not exist.

Caution about professionals defining reality for those who appear to have less power than they do, is not the equivalent of saying that practitioners do not have a lot to share with clients and cannot influence them. They pass on information, provide support, generate ideas and participate in making plans. But in so doing they recognise that the other party possesses different information and has had different experiences. In his critique of what he saw as the patronising features of Freire's account of consciousness raising, Berger commented that educators could not be assumed to have superior information to the peasant. On topics such as plant and animal life, soil conditions, the weather and a multitude of manual skills and material artifacts, to say nothing of the intricacies of kinship and the true significance of dreams, the peasants very clearly had superior information (Berger 1974 ch.4)

A concern for equity, married to a recognition that client groups possess valuable energy, information and experiences, should highlight the wisdom of struggling for partnership not superiority. Consciousness is likely to be changed through the stages of empowerment but it is not a one-way process. For Berger the moral implication of his critique of consciousness raising was exceedingly simple. It was a lesson in humility (Berger 1974) and Rosenfeld had the same point in mind when he quoted from the Talmud to describe the premise of volunteers working with the poorest of the poor, 'Watch the children of the poor for wisdom shall come from them' (Rosenfeld 1989 p.33).

Another implicit assumption needs to be contested. Inadvertently it has almost certainly been implied that all practitioners always want to empower all clients. That is unlikely. Some people are more rewarding to work with than others. Practitioners may enjoy maintaining agency interests even though they may have little in common with client needs. Some practitioners, as a result of their professional education and socialisation, will have adopted a brand of professionalism which eschews any notion of partnership. In all those circumstances, fascination, let alone excitement, in what might be learned from clients is unlikely. Neither will such reactions occur if a scheme is presented as a set of marching orders.

Benefits of partnership and fascination for different ideas could be generated if the different steps are seen as having mutual benefits. Coherence should result from the successful pursuit of those stages and even if only one stage has been characterised by a degree of empowerment, the beginnings of coherence could be under way. Problems will begin to be understood if not solved. The promise of biography will begin to be realised.

Understanding themes

Themes refer to those aspects of biography which depict experiences of power and powerlessness, explained perhaps with reference to relationships of relative equality or those characterised by feelings of being dependent or being controlled. Expressions of powerlessness have been portrayed in examples of passivity and fatalism. Other manifestations may appear, paradoxically, in abuses of power, for example in violence towards women or children, or be apparent in undue deference to people in positions of authority.

Ignorance of the terms of reference of services and of the roles of professionals may also be evidence of powerlessness. Such lack of information may be coupled to assumptions that individuals have no particular rights or entitlements. Such assumptions say as much about general social issues as about specific problems and would reflect the sort of themes which a practitioner identifies in first meetings.

The concern with themes provides the opportunity for the practitioner to encourage people to tell a story and begin to gain confidence from knowing that one is being listened to and will be taken seriously. Concentrating on themes from biography creates the chance for an exchange about the possible link between personal and social issues. At least in this way, practitioners do not come to premature assessments of specific problems, without knowing who the people are and what resources they bring to the exchange.

Evaluating self-image and knowledge

If people are to become partners in an enterprise, they usually have to possess the confidence that comes from some element of self-respect. Without some evaluation of people's image of their ability to act in their own interests, goals may be generated which are unrealistic because they have overlooked people's aptitude for solving problems. In this respect a major task is to revive people's confidence by addressing that disparaging view of themselves which Lerner has said amounts to surplus powerlessness: a self-imposed burden which is additional to the objective conditions of their difficulties (Lerner 1983).

To evaluate self-image involves some exchange of information not only about past biography but also regarding current knowledge of services and ways to address problems. Even this shared evaluation can lead to a small sense of victory if it generates ideas and creates hope. Any interaction which assesses people's image of themselves and in so doing begins to channel it in a positive direction promises an unexpected achievement, however small.

Specifying problems

Those whose lives have been characterised by powerlessness may include people who have lived in institutions, who have experienced long-term poverty, or individuals with disabling physical and mental conditions and illnesses. This list is not exhaustive, neither is it meant to imply that everyone who has ever suffered such conditions is powerless. The point being made is that people with long experiences of powerlessness are likely to have had their problems defined for them. They have been on the receiving end of advice from a string of professionals. They have been the targets of an endless stream of envelopes containing demand notices, summonses to courts, hospital appointments or reminders of bills unpaid, appointments not kept or appeals for more financial and other help being denied.

Specifying problems involves encouraging people to have their say, but not in the tradition of anticipating what they think the professional wants to hear. The themes which the worker has picked up in an earlier meeting, or at an earlier stage of the same meeting, will give clues to specific problems, but the responsibility to say what the major problems are and to specify them, may not always reflect these earlier themes. The art of conceptualising problems and sorting one from another carries with it the seeds of self-learning, and some skills in analysing the relationship between themselves and the representatives of authority.

Sharing interpretations of problems even by the simple observation, 'This is what I understand you to be saying', facilitates the task of specifying problems and contributes to trust.

Developing awareness of policies

The predicament of powerless people is likely to be affected by social and economic policies and the professional services which are delegated the responsibility of implementing those policies. One effect of policies, such as those which influence prohibitive costs of rental housing or an absence of affordable public housing, is to contribute to powerlessness. Other policy outcomes with similar consequences have included social security payments which kept their dependents on or below a poverty line or the combining of official reluctance to address deep-seated problems of poverty with edicts about taking into care any child suspected of being abused.

The influence of economic policies on culture and social problems indicates that such policies are an important feature of the environment in which people struggle to effect some control over their lives. Yet this part of their environment is often a closed book. A young man who had had polio since childhood explained, 'I was intimidated at first about "policy". I didn't like people who called themselves policy makers yet I was deferential to them. After seeing the games they play, my views have changed. I am a policy analyst as good as them. I can be better because I know how poor bastards suffer from their misguided policies' (Rees 1988 p.8).

Discussing how policies and services affect people has two effects. There is the obvious outcome of enabling them to know that services and other resources exist to which they are entitled. Secondly, the act of demystifying what policy is about becomes part of an overall educational and political process. A well-informed public is seldom a powerless or helpless one. The motives to reform social policies and practices can spring from the intended beneficiaries, even if, historically, the professionals have not seen fit to consult and some people have been compliant in their acceptance of not knowing.

Developing the notion of choice

To be able to choose from among a range of people, services and ideas usually reflects a self-image which incorporates the feeling of knowing and the assumption that it is appropriate to have some control over one's circumstances. Years of not having the experience of making choices are not suddenly changed by the arrival of a social worker brimful of beliefs that even the most powerless people should be able to exercise their rights to choose. To develop ability in choosing involves assertiveness and a familiarity with the importance of choice. It requires moving from the assumption that there is no alternative to accepting one's lot, to deliberation over what might be possible.

Some people with a disability who have lived in institutions have spent years being encouraged to accept decisions being made for them, but their changed lifestyle in group homes, in the community, provides incentives to act as citizens with a variety of rights and entitlements. A young woman, a wheelchair user, said of her new life in a group home, 'I have to think for myself. I am no longer prepared to be beholden to others. I'm no longer prepared to be discussed by others just with a view to them putting me in a category' (Rees 1988 p.6)

Difficulties in encouraging a belief in the importance of choice and the confidence-boosting experience of choosing, are not the result only of people's passivity, poverty, disability, lack of confidence or limited knowledge. Despite protests to the contrary, powerful professions and institutions have vested interests in maintaining their own power and so hindering others' experience of choosing. Members of the medical profession place great emphasis on the public's freedom to choose their own doctor, but from the point of view of many patients, that freedom turns out to be a convenient myth. Without knowledge, contacts, money, private health insurance and some element of scepticism about being deferential to the medical profession, choice of health care may be difficult, perhaps impossible. Even the possession of money and private health insurance may prove insufficient. 'Choice is nothing if all they do is put pressure on you. They tried every trick to get me into a private hospital. The only ones who are doing the choosing are the doctors and they are deciding who they are going to treat,' said a man who had had two planned operations cancelled during a prolonged doctors' dispute in Australia (Rees and Gibbons 1987 p.96)

Thinking about choosing and making choices is an indication of some element of power being exercised and achieved. In deliberating over the factors which facilitate or hinder choice, a distinction can be made between two phenomena: the objective conditions which preclude choice; and the attitude which says that no choice has ever been possible and never will be. Those conditions and traits may have intertwined to become indistinguishable, yet it is important to know whether one or both issues exist.

Experiencing solidarity with others

The support group which brings together people experiencing the same predicament can be a means of education because it reveals a common grievance and encourages a sharing of ways to respond to such problems. From the sharing comes a confidence, trust and solidarity. 'It was good to know we were not the only ones,' said a young father following a meeting of parents whose teenage children had died from overdoses of heroin. 'In the discussions you began to see where you might go to from here, what to tell other kids and parents, whether methadone might be a good idea.'

This father said that through association with others in a similar predicament he acquired the language to explain problems in other than individual terms. The same lesson emerged from accounts of the value of women's activity groups which provided mutual education, strength to challenge positions of subordination and to develop new roles (Birmingham '81 1985).

Although the use of networks to provide support for people who share common problems—psychiatric patients, homeless children, adolescents from broken families and people in newly blended families —has been well documented (Whitaker and Garbarino 1983), it is apparent that the mere act of putting people in touch with others with whom they have something in common does not necessarily lead to empowerment. Support groups which discuss common problems but do not address the political processes which affect status and resources may only confirm the class-related myths about the psychological reasons behind individual powerlessness or individual achievement (Usher 1988).

In a critical analysis of the use of social networks, d'Apps argued that if groups were to contribute to solidarity and provide a sense of liberation, they would have to go beyond merely buffering people from stress by linking them to resources or just providing social bonds as a means of attachment (d'Apps 1982). Such groups would also have to encourage critical appraisals of the world and give support for analysis of the relationship between a new world view and new concepts of self. This process could be achieved not merely in association with kin, but with heterogeneous groups which would provide access to different relationships.

This stage of achieving solidarity as a means of empowering was foreshadowed in earlier description of the constricting one-dimensional exercise of power in contrast to the development of new agendas and the creation of possibilities where none had seemed to exist. The process of creating possibilities has also been described as involving an appreciation of belonging, through expression of solidarity with and responsibility for others, 'the sign of having emerged, of having won the freedom to act!' (Rosenfeld 1989 p.39).

Acquiring and using language

The language which expresses power, 'I want to make my own choices', 'The government has something to answer for', 'I don't accept what I've always been told by doctors and lawyers', 'We now know that there are alternative ways of thinking about this matter, we've got a shrewd idea of what's been going on', is likely to occur following those phases which have given information about policies, encouraged the idea of choice and developed solidarity among people who had thought they were alone.

An analogy can be made to the students and practitioners who followed a curriculum which aimed to spell out the objectives and skills of empowerment. They began by resisting the language of power and politics and the redefinition of social work that was implied by such language. Later, once connections were made between personal biography and the stories of others, understanding was signalled by new words.

Language is not merely a tool for communication but also a means of creating social relationships and realising the self involved in those relationships. The concepts 'promise of biography', 'interdependence of policy and practice' and 'achieving power' have been advocated, not to enlarge the vocabulary of students, educators, clients or practitioners but as a means of developing a political literacy in welfare. Such a literacy would question the language of conventional assumptions about helping professions, would make the word 'helping' problematic, and could thus move on to make manifest the political relationships involved in the work of such professions (Edelman 1974).

A test of the value of acquiring and using new language lies in the evidence that the users are making connections between one context of power and another. The language of power and politics enables people to understand some consequences of economic rationalism and the values which characterise that philosophy; it raises questions about policies which promote social divisions and thus avoids any preoccupation with private issues.

Resisting a return to powerlessness

At some point in a process of growing stronger, some people may experience doubts about the action they have been taking. These doubts may prompt a reconsideration of the benefits of returning to familiar lives and lifestyles: for example, toleration of incest, domestic violence or return to an institution.

To confront obstacles which appear insuperable, to live with the tensions of wanting to develop hopes without knowing for sure about means of achieving them, produces anxiety, fear or anger. Such feelings are associated with the unusual experience of being taken seriously, when a person 'comes to see and believe that one's life situation is different from what one had previously been coerced into believing it was, and that things do not have to be the way they have been' (Rose and Black 1985 p.65).

An ex-prisoner who was describing his experiences on release after serving a long sentence said, 'I only started to learn when I had almost given up.' He was refusing to collude with the idea that all was well or that progress was inevitable and his response was easier to manage than if he had just mouthed optimism. Better to have the expression of doubt and the glum look that poses questions than the permanent smile of a client, a student or practitioner who finds it difficult to express the tensions, contradictions and dismay that goes with any struggle to change.

However, a desire to return to the familiar is highly likely if people have been encouraged to assert themselves but have not been given appropriate support to do so. Assertiveness might have brought rewards to practitioners but for clients it may have provoked punishment, such as a further belting, continued sexual abuse, or eviction from home. Giving permission to develop new roles is not always accompanied by the protection to do so.

Expression of doubts about empowerment will usually show the difference between the concerns of the layperson and the professional. At that point the practitioner has an opportunity to validate the other person's position by saying that they recognise that they are not the one who is taking risks, but they should consider together the issue of protection and ways to provide it. Unless that happens, aspirations about empowerment will persist only as a scheme cherished by the practitioner. This stage of 'resisting a return to powerlessness' might appear to have its most obvious application to people in apparently subordinate positions, but it could be equally relevant to practitioners who have embarked on new ways of working but are discouraged by a lack of quick results. Faced with such discouragement they capitulate, resign, play the role of martyr or return to a comfortable agency niche (Wenocur 1983). But more on this in chapter 9.

Developing interactive and political skills

Students enjoy task-oriented ways of learning. Groups benefit from taking action on their own behalf. Provided the action has a tangible end product, such as obtaining a benefit, completing a letter or speaking out at a meeting, there is usually some pleasure and value in reflecting on what has been learned from such an experience.

Learning and practising interactive and political skills is a task for students and practitioners (which is discussed at length in chapter 10) but it can also be regarded as a criterion of progress for others. That progress can be assessed through the encouragement of action and reflection on action. For example, those who have seldom worked in association with others, such as university students who have been brainwashed into thinking that only their individual merits should be assessed, are usually cautious and fearful of embarking on cooperative endeavours. Once they have engaged with others in some shared task, they begin to revise opinions and make alliances with those to whom they had previously been hostile.

As with the conditions which facilitated learning a new language, so the unexpected experience of solidarity with group members contributes to the development of interactive and political skills. Communication begins to be open and appropriate. The idea of planning is inherent in the shared endeavour and makes inevitable the discussions of timing, tactics and strategies. 'We discovered "B" was a lazy bastard but we grew to like him. We discovered what he was good at, and I think he realised that we liked his humour and found him useful,' said a participant in a welfare rights campaign about a colleague whom she and others had previously avoided. The 'colleague' observed, 'It wasn't a bad experience. They discovered what I knew about people's rights. We all learned there were far bigger battles than the silly hostilities between us.'

Evaluation

One test of evaluation concerns whether the themes with which this process began have been redefined. Has alienation and isolation been replaced by involvement and participation? Has self-defeat given way to some element of pride and self-confidence? Has an apolitical approach to solving problems been replaced by political understanding and skills? Has compliance towards professionals and social institutions changed into timely and effective assertiveness? Has the tendency to see problems only as the product of individual shortcoming been overcome by an understanding of structural issues, and by the beginnings of pertinent social analysis? Has new knowledge and the confidence that comes from possessing and testing it, taken over from the powerlessness that had been maintained by ignorance?

Evidence of success, as reported by the people who say they have benefited from changes, may be apparent in a more confident self-image and in indications of tangible material improvement in the quality of lives. A combination of individual or family accomplishments and other distinct changes over time, could include a pride in being noticed in the present and a feeling of being able to evoke positive memories of the past. Or it could be evident in the formulation of opinions, however tentative, or in achievements of better health, improved housing and the opportunity for children to take advantage of education (Rosenfeld 1989 pp.33–40).

To evaluate is to examine the objectives of empowerment and to pay attention to the means of achieving small victories rather than making harsh judgments about failure to change the course of history. It involves some appraisal of the aspirations of all the people being worked with and this admonition draws attention to the creative use of power, to think, to criticise, to understand, to use any relevant event of biography which contributes to the freedom to act.

9 Politics of change in organisations

People go to work. They expect a demanding job and they hope for some rewards. Some meet their expectations and hopes. For others the work experience turns sour. These disappointed staff spend time telling stories about abuses of power by other staff, shortages of resources and the dominating culture of managerialism. Once their stories have been told, the analysis can begin with a view to encouraging staff to think and act politically and to contribute to mutual education and support.

Excessive control

Problems of low staff morale are apparent in feelings of being stuck in a bureaucratic cul-de-sac. A practitioner in a large public welfare bureaucracy commented, 'You can't respect the middle management but there's no way around them. Deadening is how I'd describe their influence.'

Disappointment and low morale also develop when expectations of autonomy have been replaced by the experience of excessive forms of control by superiors. After six years in a local authority department in Britain, a social worker commented, 'I came here valuing myself and this job. I still feel I want to do social work but I say to myself, "there's too much control here, too few rewards", there must be better things to do with my life.'

This 'better-things-to-do-with-my-life' feeling is a reaction to an atmosphere in which social work is neither understood nor valued. Superiors may be resented because they are seen as personally narrow, inflexible, intolerant or vindictive, but it is also important to ask whether such traits are fostered by the constraints of the organisation as much as by the idiosyncracies of personality. For example, a young social worker in a disability team felt dismayed and powerless because the team leader, a psychologist, encouraged nurses to conduct social assessments of new cases and insisted that proper teamwork depended on adequate psychological testing of the needs of the disabled child. The team leader behaved as though anyone could do social work. Creative service to the public was replaced by demarcation disputes between staff and one-upmanship games to gain professional territory. The young social worker explained:

> I'm isolated. I'm the only social worker. The nurses seem content to carry out someone else's orders. What do I do apart from write a better social work job description, that might impress her . . . I'd get out if I could. I've been trying to do so for ages. But she'd be pleased then, she could abolish the social work position. Social work with the developmentally disabled would no longer exist in that team.

It is small consolation to realise that the concern with control and even with punishment is a predictable feature of management in some bureaucracies. The cosmopolitan practitioner and leader who responds to uncertainty by encouraging creativity and some degree of autonomy is usually outnumbered by the bureaucratic personality preoccupied with order. That conformist fears the unknown, defends territory, hierarchies and status. The prospect of challenge and innovation reawakens their 'innate-tendency to smother the unfamiliar at birth' (Vickers 1965 ch. 6).

The psychologist in the disability team and the senior bureaucrats in the public welfare agency were exercising power in that consensus-oriented, one-dimensional way characteristic of line management practices, their decisions justified by reference to statutes and rules. Reverence for vertical lines of communication was matched by a taste for official job descriptions, practice manuals and rewards for conformity. The manuals and job descriptions were no substitute for the adrenalin and imagination that runs through creative working relationships. These examples match novelists' insights into some excesses of bureaucratic behaviour. In *The Caseworker*, Konrad described the personal becoming impersonal, and how administrative procedures affected social workers and the unsuspecting subjects of each file,

> which starts out with a petition, a complaint or denunciation, continues with a summons and a police report and ends with a judgement.
> Following a trajectory traced by the legal and administrative code, it rises high above the original lowly offence into a rarefied atmosphere that sparkles with procedural subtleties . . . I must admit to a certain malicious pleasure when, after the sharp acrobatics of official procedure, they crash land in my filing cabinet (Konrad 1969 p.12).

Whether the management of people and information is overt, such procedures may start out as reasonable, but can easily be abused. Before computers were being used to store information about staff, students or other clientele, Solzhenitsyn described the task of Rusanov, the master of personnel records' administration. 'It was a job that went by different names in different institutions but the substance of it was always the same' (Solzhenitsyn 1971 p. 217). The substance was a fondness for filling forms and secrecy in keeping records.

The disparaging remarks of team leaders or the cultivated indifference of the senior official may also have a stultifying, immobilising
effect. For Solzhenitsyn, authoritarianism was not obvious at first sight
but the storage of records of answers to questions on forms became an
administrative thread. 'If these threads were suddenly to become
visible, the whole sky would look like a spider's web and if they
materialized as elastic bands, buses, trams and even people would all
lose the ability to move, and the wind would carry torn-up newspapers
or autumn leaves along the streets of the city' (Solzhenitsyn 1971,
p.208).

The observations of Solzhenitsyn have echoes elsewhere, less dra-
matically expressed but still showing widespread experiences of dismay
and resentment. Authoritarianism and conformity to such dominating
exercise of power remain major issues in all sorts of bureaucracies in
different countries, in the private or public sectors (Rees 1984). In
response to resented controls, staff may comply or resist. Their protests
may be met with the disarming reaction of the persons whose behaviour
is the subject of complaint, that they were surprised that anything was
wrong, that they only had the best interests of the staff and the public
in mind. Nevertheless, the notion 'best interests' depends on compliance. Solzhenitsyn reminds us that the Rusanovs said they loved the
people, 'But as the years went by they found themselves less and less
able to tolerate actual human beings, those obstinate creatures who were
always resistant, refusing to do what they were told and, besides,
demanding something for themselves' (Solzhenitsyn 1971 p.208).

However, the visible disabling exercise of power in personal relationships often has structural sources which constrain the supervisors as
much as the supervised. These 'structural sources' are usually evident in
the familiar expressions 'too many demands and too few resources' and
'too much to do and too little time to do it in'.

Resource constraints

Constraints may include large caseloads and supervision which is not
supportive. A prescription for staff dismay and disenchantment includes a combination of infinite agency demands, but too few resources
of time, money or staff. Yet management may respond to these
shortages by thinking that they can be remedied by more efficient
controls.

The community worker's equivalent of the excessive caseload is the
ambitious project which the sponsors want to have completed in an
unrealistically short time. Linked to these demands is an apparent fear
by the officials of local government who employ the community
workers, that such staff may cause controversy and so tarnish the good
name of the authority. Shortage of resources hinders community

development but protects the establishment's good name. Deliberate underfunding also amounts to control.

Resource constraints can also eventuate due to the complexity rather than to the size of a job. The probation officer who combines probation supervision with parole responsibilities, voluntary prison after-care with a range of different court duties and participates in staff development programs is likely to finish up as tired and disillusioned as the child protection worker who is accountable for responding to every notification for child abuse and for the development of schemes to protect vulnerable families. The energy required to shift attention from one different task to another is greater than the energy required to pursue similar tasks over the same period. Without appropriate support, role complexity and conflict disempowers.

Other tangible shortages which impede practitioners include the absence of support from supervisors and the lack of appropriate back-up resources. Styles of supervision vary. Modelled on adult education, the supervisor-supervisee relationships focus on learning through a shared educational experience. By contrast the supervisor who is absent or indifferent or is preoccupied with counting visits, sick leave, mileage and expenses or with checking reports and compliance with agency rules is likely to be perceived as disempowering.

The physical resources of office space, appropriate technical equipment, secretarial and administrative services facilitate effective practice and also contribute to morale. The powerlessness of staff may be symbolised by offices which are badly equipped and located, and by the presence of one hard-pressed, poorly paid secretary who doubles as a receptionist–gatekeeper and treasurer for coffee and tea. Yet this gatekeeper can control access to people, information and other services. She (seldom he) is a tool in a policy aimed at controlling resources (Hall 1974).

Staff may have a well-documented list of grievances over this shortage of tangible resources. Yet the culture of the times allows management to argue the difficulty of addressing such problems and staff may be deemed professionally irresponsible if they complain. Offices may be closed, staff numbers cut, positions abolished but the surviving practitioners are expected to do more and more with less and less.

In the *Yes Minister* tradition that everything is possible if you can master doublespeak, statistical wizardry and plausible presentation, the impression persists that even if every public welfare office was closed and every staff member fired, the Minister for Social Welfare would still boast that every welfare requirement could still be met. Even a conscientious assessment of the tangible resources required to perform effective social work will be conducted in the shadow of the official ideology that all is well, as well as could be expected, or could be better if only the staff would improve their performance. Government and management only ask for improved performance. This latest piece of rhetoric derives from the language and values of the new managerialism, which has sought to reinstitute so many old forms of control.

The illustrations of excessive control are not confined to social work agencies. They occur whenever a superior is fearful and has little idea how to foster the abilities of peers and subordinates, when the assertion of control in an organisation is one-dimensional and almost military in outlook and intentions.

The staff in a criminology research unit had high hopes of their new director. At interview he appeared to share their philosophy regarding the importance of trust and the significance of taking themselves seriously but not too seriously. Over the next three months they stood by helplessly as they witnessed events which they had not expected but which have been imitated a thousand times in other bureaucracies. The new boss arrived and had great need to demonstrate who was in charge. He might have described himself as composed. His staff said that he seemed desperate to present an image of strength. He saw such strength as evidence of effective management, but his speaking and writing belittled the people he was supposed to support. Although his mistakes became obvious, the hypnotising effect of his own image of strong management ensured that he would never admit to being wrong, at least not openly.

This boss was quickly isolated from other staff and antagonism towards him increased. The staff continued to personalise their relationships and emphasised the value of horizontal communication. The boss sent memoranda explaining his concern to achieve 'efficiency and cost effectiveness'. The staff were angry but did not develop a common position in response to behaviour which privately they said was disempowering. Some staff resigned. Others waited passively for the situation to improve or deteriorate. The politics of empowerment were either unknown or not understood. The objective of providing high standard work was displaced by the misery of memoranda and staff fatalism.

A political economic perspective

Those examples have hinted at the power plays affecting relationships within organisations and the importance of a political–economic perspective on such politicking. Without such a perspective, the mere repetition of examples which caused frustration or distaste for the rhetoric of the new managerialism will only remind staff of their powerlessness. That predicament persists because the task of thinking politically about resources and relationships has not been regarded as an educational or professional priority.

Students' and practitioners' observations about behaviour within organisations can be part of a perspective which they can be encouraged to make explicit. It is a perspective based on assumptions that organisations survive not only through controls but also by bargaining, conflict and compromise over who has information, who distributes resources and who makes decisions. That perspective, which can be developed by students from the examples of first placements or from the gripes of experienced practitioners, should make sense because it derives from the commonsense way in which these people construct their accounts of reality (Schutz 1982).

However, 'commonsense' uninformed by political and economic knowledge may merely result in the reproduction of simple, one-dimensional pictures which lead nowhere. Viewing an organisation as the interplay between political and economic processes within and without, should put together the pieces in the jigsaw: the personal stories, the shortage of tangible resources and the reasons for the trend towards controls. 'Political' is the process by which the power of personnel is legitimated and distributed within the organisation. 'Economic' refers to the process by which 'resources needed for the service technologies of the organisation are acquired, distributed and used' (Hashenfeld 1980 p.508).

That definition may be easy to comprehend because it follows from the earlier discussions about the meanings of power and the centrality of politics in practice, but it is far too easy to spell out terms in the abstract and overlook other significant issues. We still need to demystify the meaning and practice of politics in organisations by paying attention to ideas found in most organisational literature: questions about the primary and secondary status of social work, the meaning of 'rational', the links between empowerment and the conditions of secrecy and uncertainty.

The distinction between social work as a primary or secondary activity within bureaucracies tells something of the lines of communication and the locus of power. Primary functions occur in deliberations over the means and ends of social work because such practice is the only or the priority function of an agency. Secondary refers to social work as one of several competing occupations within an organisation in which it is seldom the most important, or in which its major responsibility is to contribute to an atmosphere of teamwork and to directly facilitate the work of others. These distinctions between primary and secondary activity point to some characteristics of agency politics, to the number of people involved, their different lines of accountability and their diverse roles.

To question assumptions about the meaning of 'rational' will also be part of the stock-in-trade of thinking about the distribution of power within the organisation. For example, official versions of the way an agency works usually incorporate pictures of hierarchies and a pyramid of responsibilities. Calls for efficiency, effectiveness and cost-effective controls on money, personnel, clientele and policies are presented as inherently reasonable and rational. So too is the demand for deference to respected professionals and conformity to agency rules and procedures, even if such a response looks unlikely to enhance the lot of vulnerable people. These rational pictures of the way an agency should work rely on an uncluttered one-dimensional view of power, promoted to foster the interests of those politicians and managers and even front-line practitioners who have an investment in the all-is-well, provided-we-have-conformity-approach to administration and government. It is a perspective which looks irrational to people who are powerless. A political–economic perspective, on the other hand, emphasises the tension between the rational and the irrational, conformity and non-conformity, the concern with order and the creativity which should come from realising the potential power which exists if you can deal with uncertainty.

When agency staff are locked into the conflict provoked by damaging government policies, rigid ideologies about professional conduct, and even the feeling that other front-line colleagues are not to be trusted, there is little sense in wringing hands in familiar circles of despair. Almost everyone knows and may be disillusioned by the routine. Few are willing to trespass into unfamiliar territory, yet it is the recognition of areas of uncertainty and the ability to move into them which facilitates empowerment; a process which requires careful evaluation, planning and mutual support.

Creating certainty out of uncertainty depends on identifying those informal networks of influence which are probably stronger than formal relationships. Informal relationships can build trust and take for granted secrecy based on trust. With regard to such informal alliances, political scientists have argued that secrecy is 'a major aspect of informal organisation . . . a political act par excellence. It is a response of power' (Feldman 1988 p. 87).

Secrecy may not always facilitate empowerment. Some of the worst authoritarianism depends on secrecy: the keeping of records, the refusal of leaders to say what they really think and believe, control by favoured cliques and other forms of exclusion. Nevertheless, in adopting a conflict-oriented, political–economic perspective on the way power is exercised within and between organisations, secrecy is an appropriate topic of analysis, and is usually associated with that uncertainty which is anathema to those who are preoccupied with control.

Making rules and distributing resources are meant to reduce uncertainty. Yet social work is often about developing resources where they do not exist, interpreting policies which match local conditions rather than the letter of regulations. The inventiveness which can be the outcome of an energetic political perspective on the operation of organisations depends on a willingness and aptitude for moving into areas of high uncertainty and handling them. For example, when an agency has a high turnover of staff because the demands to investigate new child protection referrals far exceed the number of available front-line practitioners, it appears impossible to work out different ways of responding to such demands. The 'different way' requires just one small team to question the resource problems and policy issues behind the assumptions about child protection, poverty and agency priorities. Those priorities would include the building of networks of volunteers whose visits to the families of children at risk have been shown to reduce abusive behaviour and are an important form of support for parents (Zimrim 1984).

The criticism that practitioners are not cost-effective can create a sense of powerlessness because the question of financial costs has seldom been part of their agenda. Yet those staff who can address both financial problems and new ways of working are likely to consolidate their positions. They have responded to the criticism of management, not defensively, but by creating an opportunity for change. If staff recognise the relationship between the phenomenon of uncertainty and the practice of organisational politics, they are likely to be able to innovate and achieve solidarity.

Some typical staff responses

Common problems facing staff in social welfare bureaucracies will be the product of conflict between opposing forces: the emphasis on rules and conformity versus a need for autonomy and creativity; the infinite demands of difficult tasks versus limited time and few other resources; the demands for compliance by the new managerialism versus the retention of some high professional expectations.

Awareness of these conflicts and the manner of their resolution will vary according to the experience of staff. Kramer for example, identified four stages in nurses' socialisation into hospital bureaucracies, beginning with a honeymoon period followed by social integration when protection from difficult demands was slowly removed. This period gave way to a sense of moral outrage when the staff became aware of double binds inherent in clients' anger and frustration, and the refusal of agency management to provide resources to enable difficult problems to be solved. Resolution of these conflicts was the final stage (Kramer 1974).

The manner in which staff resolve conflict is likely to reflect their ability to assess the problem and their capacity for successful organisational politics. The language of powerlessness identifies those who resolve conflict on their own terms but leave the problems untouched (Sherman and Wenocur 1983). The capitulator is the ten-year survivor, who says, 'you're usually beaten before you start, you just have to put your head down and get on with the job.' Others distance themselves from the organisation by finding a niche in the practice of their own specialty. Some staff withdraw, resign and months later you hear them reassuring themselves, 'I don't know how anyone could continue to work in that organisation.' Others play the role of victims or martyrs and end up in a cycle of powerlessness with a fatalism embodied in the attitude 'nothing has ever changed, nothing ever will'. There may be those who protest but unless they do so in solidarity with colleagues and with a plan, they will change little and threaten no one. They are likely to be dismissed as merely the mavericks or the house radicals (Sherman and Wenocur 1983).

None of these responses shows much political understanding or action. They are defensive postures which are the result of a work force which has not seen fit to organise with one another and which, in political terms, has been deskilled. Even trade unions, said Lerner with regard to an industrial work force, have been characterised by a similar fatalism, more interested in collecting dues than what was happening in the personal lives of members. The unions may have sided with management or found other means of reminding workers of their importance, as in the case of meetings being 'dominated by a format that is at once boring and virtually impossible to understand by anyone except those who have attended them for years' (Lerner 1986 p. 68).

Developing a capacity for negotiation

Others may experience union membership as characterised by equity in relationships and by effective political strategies, but the issue remains, how do staff provide mutual support on a day-to-day basis? How do they move from disenchantment to victories and consequent empowerment (Figure 9.1)? In the final sections of this chapter, informal negotiation between staff will be described as the process which precedes the formal stage of negotiation when certain aspects of power relationships are redefined. The skills required in the formal stage of negotiations will be discussed in Part IV.

Stages in the process preceding a formal negotiation can enable staff to collect information and make plans concerning the following issues: whether to call in outside assistance, how to locate and assess the major staff problem, assessing the attitudes or compliance of members, defining the audience, i.e. the people who have to be influenced, and finally, being explicit about the best way to keep records to contribute to a political literacy.

'Yes' or 'No' to outside assistance

The process of change depicted in Figure 9.1 respresents a strategy based on the assumption that staff will not necessarily need the help of outsiders. The development of a political orientation to practice often begins with the question, can we go it alone, or will we need outside assistance?

Figure 9.1   Empowerment among front-line staff: the process

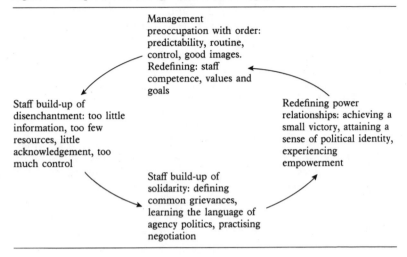

An immediate rush for outside help may mask the resources which exist within the disaffected group. In an age which has seen a burgeoning of subcontracting in counselling and management, this caution about outside help needs to be emphasised. However, it staff are locked into a conflict with management, they may perceive little alternative to seeking ideas from a third party. If so, that person should be chosen because he or she shares the staff aspirations to locate power and to decide how it may be redistributed.

There are two kinds of outside advisers who should be avoided: the expert counsellor who diagnoses problems and prescribes remedies in terms of individual models of explanation of behaviour; and the management expert who is preoccupied with malfunctioning systems, ignores inequities within the organisation and who pays little attention to the politics of personal relationships. The political understanding of the staff groups is not enhanced by such outsiders' intervention.

Locating and assessing the problem

'Locating the problem' includes an appraisal of the wider world of power relations of which this agency is only a part (Figure 9.2). Such contextualising, i.e. locating the exercise of power in relationships at a particular point in time and showing how decisions in one context have a ripple effect in another, can be carried out in each of three contexts (Figure 9.2).

In the relationships between the agency and the wider political issues emanating from federal, state or local government policies, key words depict the exercise of power: cutback, support, disinterest, indifference, ambivalence. What words and concepts do the members use, what colourful and easily remembered examples illustrate their ideas?

Identifying the locus of power in the second context, i.e. with regard to agency and inter-agency policies and practices, would begin with questions about the historical tradition of management practice. Is it hierarchical, democratic, or authoritarian? In what style is power actually exercised? The answers to that question might include 'condescending', 'by informed consent', 'sensitive but indecisive', 'open but not supportive'.

The relationship between members who are meeting on the assumption that they have something in common is the familiar context for front-line personnel, yet its immediacy may make it difficult to comprehend. Are those relationships characterised by suspicion or by trust, by anxiety or confidence, by feelings of competition and resentment or cooperation and mutual support?

Assessing compliance

Investigating problems of low morale in organisations requires not only a focus on the conduct of people in positions of power but also a focus on questions about the compliance of their subordinates. The bully bullies but the bullied put up with the bullying. The inflexible manager dictates but his staff comply with his wishes. They have seldom discussed their common grievances.

In assessing compliance, people produce reasons why they should not act and have resorted to capitulation, niche-finding, withdrawal or martyr roles (Sherman and Wenocur 1983). Those responses can be transformed into a capacity to negotiate the conditions of work, the opposite of passive compliance.

Figure 9.2 Context of agency politics

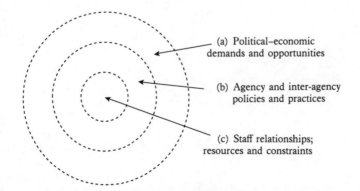

(a) Political–economic demands and opportunities

(b) Agency and inter-agency policies and practices

(c) Staff relationships; resources and constraints

Defining the audience

An essential political skill is to know whom you wish to address and influence. If the task is to effect change with regard to a wide-ranging policy issue, the potential audience is diverse. Adopt the language of political theatre and ask, who will we need to talk to, who will we need to influence? What sort of people are they: humorous, serious, flexible or inflexible? What models of explanation of behaviour do they carry around in their heads, or, in the language of some organisational theorists, what is their 'mode of rationality'?

Communicating about the problem: talking and writing

In coming together, the staff group are implicitly making a statement about wanting to know and change the exercise of power within their organisation. They are venturing into politics even if they have previously considered themselves apolitical.

Keeping records as a resource to achieve a goal does not have to be cumbersome. In their fascination with questions of power and powerlessness and the changing attitude to compliance, and with it the group's changing biography, those records differ from the conventional keeping of notes and minutes. The recording of some verbatim quotes will give colour and easy recall to what might otherwise read like a dull document.

Members of the group take turns in keeping these records. Writing is almost always illuminating and thereby empowering. To make points, the records might also be peppered with cartoons, poetry or other illustrations. These processes of collecting and recording information about conditions of employment and some causes of low staff morale are an indispensable preparation for formal negotiations. The plans and rehearsals for such negotiations will be addressed in Part IV in relation to the specific skills required to be successful in negotiating a change of attitude and practice by management.

IV Identifying and developing skills

10 Interactive and political skills

Skills refer to a facility in doing something, an ability that comes from knowledge and to a practice or aptitude to do something well. Several points emerge from these definitions. Skills are indispensable to perform even unambitious tasks but do not exist in limbo. They are linked to the values inherent in ideology, to the knowledge contained in theory and can be practised to achieve excellence. In discussions about educational priorities in social work and social policy, there is a case to be made for teaching skills not only in field work placements but also in tandem with other parts of a curriculum.

Apart from contributing to the false knowing—acting distinction, which is to be discussed with reference to the interdependence of policy and practice, separate teaching of theory and skills brings dismay to students. They want the confidence that comes from developing skills and knowing that they possess them. They become impatient with what appears to be abstract discussion if skills development is not addressed. They deserve to be able to identify significant skills, say what they are good at and in what areas they intend to improve.

The skills discussed in the following six brief chapters may come as something of a surprise, even though they have been foreshadowed in the elaboration of the steps of empowerment and in the description of the means of overcoming disempowering conditions in an organisation. The surprise is in the absence of the attention usually given in social work and social welfare to skills associated with nurturing, sustaining and facilitating. Instead, the following discussion will emphasise the value of workers seeing themselves as assertive, powerful and able to take risks.

This shift may prove difficult if these latter qualities are not the ones which young women, young men, or any student or practitioner for that matter, have expected to develop. However, acquiring skills is part of a process of personal development. In the shift referred to, which is as much cultural as educational, professional as well as personal, students and practitioners will be in process of 'becoming' not 'being'. No one is expected suddenly to see themselves differently or to become overnight a highly competent administrator or advocate.

It should also be reassuring to say that the business of practising new skills does not mean that familiar qualities, such as being empathetic or being concrete as a communicator, are devalued or discarded. They remain indispensable and contribute to other skills associated with the objectives of empowerment.

There is a danger that this acknowledgment of the significance of skills will play into the hands of those who emphasise social work only as a technology, whether in counselling or therapy, or to achieve cost-effectiveness and demonstrate efficiency as priorities for practice. Skills will contribute to cost-effectiveness and efficiency but may divert attention from the questions of whether efficiency promotes powerless people's welfare, or whether saving money contributes to empowerment? The importance of these questions gives reason to ponder the relationship between skills and the ideology and objectives of empowerment.

Students, practitioners and an even wider public can easily become fascinated with skills as though developing them is an end in itself. If that happens it may soon be accompanied by sterility of thought and boredom with practice. It would represent some vacuous idea of efficiency without equity, of management without the wit or patience to consider management to what end. The skills given prominence in empowerment will include interpersonal skills but will also be associated with questions about the purpose of a policy, the objectives of an agency, or for that matter the meaning of welfare in society. For example, in chapter 14, skills in formal negotiation will be identified through an exercise aimed to enable students to practise (as members of an agency's staff) to obtain concessions from management. That exercise in negotiation is spelled out as a process of mutual education. Even if management concedes and the staff negotiators feel successful, such skills in bargaining should be seen only as part of a process. The aim of that process would be to establish the organisation as an encouraging place to work, characterised by equity in relationships as well as by efficiency in the performance of tasks. From such an atmosphere would come a feeling of community, which would also be conducive to fostering a range of views to provide the potential for the organisation to reform itself.

This distinction between different skills and the link between skills and the empowerment approach to practice will be made by reference to the tasks of working in an organisation, but that is only being done by way of illustration. The use of skills to foster a community capacity for problem-solving can be applied in any context.

To contribute to the capacity of an organisation to question its purpose and reset its direction would be more demanding than to develop skills in negotiation merely for the purpose of obtaining concessions and not changing the fundamental values which support familiar forms of control. This more demanding activity would include the resolution of conflicts and has been described as 'double-loop learning' (Argyris and Schon 1978). It is a philosophy and a process 'in which conflicts of value and purpose are resolved instead of being suppressed, and in which solutions emerge out of frank discussion instead of being imposed by the victors in a struggle for power' (Marquand 1988 p.230).

Related to the skills of empowerment, such double-loop learning would enable the participants to develop confidence in the subtle and liberating three-dimensional exercise of power. When tempers are cooled over personality differences or over resented agency practices, such an approach seems eminently sensible. It involves informal negotiation skills which will be in almost constant use. Informal negotiation will be described in terms of a combination of interactive and political skills to facilitate the choice and exercise of other specific skills. These latter include skills in evaluation, assessment, administration and planning, formal negotiation and advocacy. They refer to the performance of tasks at specific points in time.

For the purpose of distinguishing one set of skills from another and to demonstrate the contexts in which they are used, the skills in constant use can be plotted vertically and those used to perform specific tasks horizontally (Figure 10.1).

Figure 10.1 Skills of empowerment

Specific task-oriented skills	Constant-use skills in informal negotiation
Evaluation and preparation →	
Assessment →	Interactive–political skills
Planning and administration →	
Formal negotiation →	
Advocacy →	

The order of specific task-oriented skills is not set in concrete, though a case will be made to argue the importance of beginning by practising skills in evaluation and preparation. The emphasis on each practitioner's interactive and political skills implies something about their creative use of self in an atmosphere which would be stimulating because of the struggle to address the objectives of empowerment.

Even in statutory settings, social work does not depend on strict adherence to rules and would be highly unlikely to contribute to empowerment if it did. That principle notwithstanding, there is still the job of obtaining agreement with all sorts of people on what is desirable and possible. This task requires the interactive and political skills used in those informal negotiations which occur virtually every day in any setting. Such negotiations have infinite and unpredictable possibilities. They involve practitioners in a web of relationships in the community, with representatives of numerous agencies and with their colleagues.

By confronting the incessant and unpredictable demands of informal negotiation, practitioners can comprehend important features of their agency, the customs and the constraints, the leaders and the cliques, plus information about whom to rely on and trust. Through the same informal practice they also derive a picture of the world of their local public, including people with resources who may be leaders and the members of vulnerable groups who may be clients.

This attention to informal negotiation marks the difference between the roles of social work practitioners and the roles of members of other occupations. 'Social workers,' said Jordan, 'are different precisely because they characteristically prefer informal negotiation to formal rule-bound decision-making, and discussion and agreement to solutions imposed through professional authority' (Jordan 1987 p. 141). Emphasis on the central importance of informal negotiations does not indicate the skills which are crucial to the successful conduct of such practice. Even a reference to the creative use of self, a quality of self-evident importance, is too general to produce common agreement about the actual skills being used.

By identifying a combination of personal attributes which indicate an ability to communicate and to exercise influence, the quality of interactive and political skills should become apparent, though at first sight the link between the two may not be obvious. The ability to communicate through listening, talking and writing represents skills in action which have political implications in the sense that they include efforts to influence the distribution of power. The political element in the creative use of self also emerges in the attention paid to informal negotiation which gives practitioners leverage within agencies and credibility with clients.

Avoiding definitions of skills is disempowering because it leaves things vague, but to yield to the temptation to say 'here's the definition, these are the skills' may also have counterproductive results. Faced with the task of identifying the qualities used in informal negotiations, it may be too hasty and too threatening to stress interactive and political skills unless the students or practitioners have had the chance to say what skills they think are important. With this principle in mind the following exercise can be repeated in almost any context with any group. It starts with general questions, 'what are the characteristics of the practitioner who is successful in informal negotiations?' 'what attributes hinder the conduct of such negotiations?' From general descriptions of the positive and negative qualities of the hypothetical practitioner common denominators emerge and specific skills can be identified.

The following ideas were generated by twenty social work students in five groups of four. They were asked the general question about skills in informal negotiations and it was explained that their answers would produce a picture of an ideal practitioner. A second step in the exercise was to bring the small groups together and ask each to report its answers to see what they had in common. The results of this exercise produced descriptions of a practitioner who was flexible, creative and critical, was seen as decisive, self-confident and attentive, and who would be open-minded, responsible and approachable. This list of positives also included references to practitioners being articulate, assertive and able to demonstrate skills in being an advocate, a negotiator and an effective communicator.

At this point the blackboard containing the ideas was becoming crammed with pictures of perfection, as though tomorrow's practitioners would be bionic women and supermen gifted with political skills of timing and empathy. Such fantasy was brought back to earth by reference to negative characteristics.

There were as many ideas about negative characteristics as about positive ones. Judgmental, authoritarian, unimaginative and vague practitioners, who might also be confused, jargonistic, rigid, compliant and lacking humour as well as being inaccessible were seen as likely to be harmful and incompetent. They were regarded by the students as being poor practitioners even if they possessed sufficient humility and self-awareness to admit to some of these traits.

From the almost infinite lists of ideas, several were common and produced a portrait of the practitioner who was open-minded, creative, sensitive and a good listener and whose opposite was seen as vague, fearful and inarticulate. The exercise to identify these personal attributes was also intended to begin the process of developing skills. Frankness about personal qualities was encouraged by identifying the correspondence between students' views of skills and the conclusions of writers and researchers. From such correspondence the virtually synonymous nature of valuable personal attributes and interactive–political skills became apparent. It was implied in the students' emphasis on qualities required to contribute to dialogue. It was made explicit in their reference to traits which were disempowering because they contributed to dependency not to dialogue.

In weighing his evidence about clarity in communication as a political skill, Bardach pointed out that an argument which was hard to follow would be hard to believe and he also observed the political significance of timing in making contacts with people, and in accumulating and releasing information to selected audiences. These were political skills, he said, and they required 'traits like high ego strength, tolerance of ambiguity and a readiness for prudent risk taking that I call poise' (Bardach 1972 p. 261).

A study of the political influence of social workers from the point of view of state and federal legislators in the United States emphasised attributes such as visibility and expertise (Mathews 1982). Visibility made it likely that the practitioner would be well known and could develop a reputation for being accessible. Expertise was the ability to offer timely and important information in personal relationships, in letters and more formal presentations. There is a tautology in the idea that the politically skilful practitioner is someone who is influential. Nevertheless, the practitioners who were visible and credible would not have earned high marks politically if they had not also possessed a record for obtaining resources, making decisions or having them made. These last attributes describe what was meant by influence.

The association of skills in interaction with political judgment has been shown to be a valuable feature of practice in contexts such as schools (Lee 1983) and hospitals (Murdach 1982) where social work was not the primary function of the agency and where practitioners had to establish credibility to gain influence. But in any informal negotiations about the meaning of welfare or the means of empowerment, interactive and political skills are indispensable.

In a multicultural society, the idea of welfare may vary from one ethnic group to another and between the members of one family. The interpretations of men and women may not match, their teenage children may not want to comply with the parent's interpretations of fairness or welfare and the idea of equity may be unusual, even alien to the groups in question. Their stories may display values and be expressed in words whose connotation is unfamiliar to practitioners, yet all these issues have to be weighed in informal negotiation: through perception and sensitivity in discovering something of the biographies of the interviewees. Key aspects of their private world would include expressions of need, evidence of attitudes and interests, biases and preferences, ways of communicating and habits of cooperating (Jordan 1987).

Interactive and political skills might be exercised in informal negotiation about the general good, from an agency or policy point of view, or concerning fairness in interpersonal relations, but they will also be required in order to achieve trust and cooperation in almost any endeavour. Stages in empowerment, from the first task of understanding themes to the midway phase of facilitating choice, to the step of encouraging people to conduct their own evaluations, depended on relationships which gave support and created trust. Work with ex-psychiatric patients highlighted the constant attention to creating trust, achieving validation, providing support, obtaining legitimation and so consolidating the initial achievement of trust (Rose and Black 1985). William Carlos Williams, famous poet and doctor, recalled that the two-way process in achieving trust showed a crucial but fragile quality in relationships. 'Even when the patients knew me well, and trusted me a lot, I could sense their fear, their skepticism. And why not? I could sense my own worries, my own doubts' (Coles 1984 p. xii)

Being creative

Reference in the discussion of interactive and political skills to the creative use of self recalls the promise of biography. If ideas from poetry, music, pictures, dancing and politics motivate people to develop ideas and to arrive at goals and solutions where none previously existed, use them. If the business of writing a report feels boring, break away from it, talk to friends and colleagues, make connections with other ideas and events, perhaps films or books. Out of frustration conjure opportunity, from the boredom with routine look for the alternative suggested by Frost's lines:

> Two roads diverged in a wood, and I
> — I took the one less travelled by
> And that has made all the difference.
> (Frost 1973 p.77)

Students can be encouraged to think creatively when they share in discussion of experiences they have valued, when they recall events which they found inspiring and which perhaps made them feel powerful. Over the years they may have listened to Bob Dylan, Joan Baez, Peter, Paul and Mary, Bruce Springsteen, Tracy Chapman and Peter Garrett singing the songs of protest, or derived inspiration from classical composers, or may have been intrigued by the impressionists' multidimensional pictures. They may have admired the courage of activists who risked lives and careers in challenging authoritarian regimes in countries and regions as wide apart as South Africa, Singapore, China, Eastern Europe and Central America.

We learn and communicate in different forms, from concrete thinking to abstract ideas, from examples offered by others, from words spoken by one person to diagrams, pictures and stories. Creativity can be encouraged by saying 'no' to the one-dimensional routines of work, or the top-down solutions imposed without consultation; and criticism of stories about practice can have a particular educational value. An Indian social work educator observed, 'The students should be encouraged to express their personal emotions and attitudes towards the characters, social interrelationships and environments as depicted in the story, and helped to relate them to their own personality moulding and value judgments' (Desai 1985, p. 30).

Desai's recommendation to her students mirrors the prescription of a theorist and educator such as Gramsci who paid attention to folklore in his letters to his family. He gave a very positive evaluation of storytelling as an aid to the development of imagination and as a means of practising skills in communication.

Creativity in informal negotiations is usually evident in being proactive not reactive, in creating choices where none had seemed to exist. Practitioners can and do develop choices, as in the creation of alternative forms of care for children at risk, or in probation officers' proposals for alternatives to imprisonment, or in the consideration of projects in community development, or in the alternative accommodation and support for the frail elderly, or in the different ways of ordering priorities in the crowded office and congested caseload.

Although this discussion of interactive and political skills has focused on the education and training of practitioners, its emphasis on creativity is just as applicable to laypeople as to professionals. They meet to define objectives, examine choices and unearth resources. Each is capable of resisting the imposition of top-down solutions, though the alternative means of problem-solving — the politics of mutual education — will not be easy even for those who may regard themselves as already possessing interpersonal skills.

In an echo of the student exercise which produced a picture of practitioners who demonstrated interactive and political skills, Marquand also concluded that a new politics would be open to people from all walks of life struggling to achieve collectively agreed goals. Such a politics would not rely on quick fixes or on the illusory solutions achieved by the introduction of a new technology. Rather,

> Its style is humdrum not heroic: collegial not charismatic, consensual not ideological: conversational not declaratory.It depends on the slow process of argument and negotiation. It requires patience, open-mindedness and above all, humility before the astonishing and sometimes exasperating diversity of others. At its core lies the belief that men and women may learn if they are stretched; that they can discover how to govern themselves if they win self goverment (Marquand 1988 p. 246).

11 Evaluation and preparation

Stretching exercises prepare the athlete and dancer. Quiet contemplation is necessary for the poet and composer. For those engaged in helping services, rehearsing skills of evaluation is also a valuable means of limbering-up, mentally.

Practitioners, students and educators may perceive evaluation as highly scientific and in consequence so difficult that it can be accomplished only by outside experts. Wedded to assumptions that science means objectivity, they may believe that evaluation will have little in common with the alleged subjective world of social welfare, and will therefore not concern them. Yet practitioners, students and educators do conduct their own evaluations, albeit using knowledge derived from others, including perhaps those researchers who show what practitioners do well and under what circumstances (Rees and Wallace 1982; Sheldon 1987).

Although regarded as important, evaluation has also been perceived as a procedure which comes at the end of a project, an interview or a group meeting. Homage is paid to evaluation with the retrospective comment, 'Now let's think about what we did.' It is just as appropriate, however, to think of evaluation as a preparation type skill, used at the beginning as well as at the middle and end of social work and social research. Evaluation of one's mental and physical state is unlikely if the space so essential to the unhurried frame of mind is absent, so we need to ponder the value of creating space and contemplate the disposition generated by being in a hurry, 'that poisonous 20th century attitude' (Pirsig 1974). The story of the famous scientist who was late for a meeting and coped with the stress of his lateness by slowing down as he approached the building in which the meeting was being held, may be apocryphal but it highlights the importance of control over self-space. Within that space, the ordering of priorities and the sorting of complex information begins.

Consciousness of the different interpretations of power (see chapter 4) and of the value of checking features of biography to recall experiences of powerlessness and the ways to overcome such feelings or predicaments, should have highlighted the significance of skills in evaluation through preparation. More specifically, such skills can be developed from answers to several questions: how am I thinking about the concept of power? what will be the consequences of my thinking about power in different ways? and what are some common characteristics of the powerlessness of client groups?

Perspectives on the exercise of power

Given that skills are usually perceived as the technical paraphernalia of doing a job (although we have argued above that they reflect attitudes, ideologies and theories), there is value in pictures to facilitate preparation through evaluation. For example, in answer to the question of how am I thinking about the concept of power, it would be valuable to use Figure 11.1 to address three issues. First, in asking about the personal exercise of power, a feature of biography is to be unmasked. Professionals of any description can hardly make claims about the value of developing self and social awareness in other people if they have not addressed that issue in their own lives (Alfrero 1972).

Second, we are recalling the vocabulary in which this approach to practice is embedded. One, two and three-dimensional power, located on a continuum from consensus to conflict perspectives represents ways to think critically about practice and the consequences of acting in one way rather than another.

A third point is that in using this pendulum to ask, 'where do I finish up at this point in time?', no absolute moral imperative is being implied. Acquiring skills takes practice. It is therefore satisfactory to say, 'I am currently thinking one-dimensionally but I am struggling to suspend some assumptions, to question some familiar habits. I am trying to think and act more imaginatively and am prepared to take risks to do so.'

With regard to a prospective interview or group discussion, students and practitioners can be asked to judge where they think their exercise of power locates them in the accompanying figure.

Figure 11.1 Checking our understanding of 'power'

Consensus	to	conflict perspectives

one-dimensional
(the status quo)

three-dimensional
(searching for and
creating alternatives)

two-dimensional
(a pluralist conception of interests)

Different consequences from different perspectives

Evaluating the consequences of exercising power in different ways, even with reference to the conduct of one interview, does not have to be abstract. Three characteristics of interviews: auditions, some sharing of information and alliances reflect practitioners' exercise of power in different ways (Figure 11.2). In the audition, control is maintained by the professional person: the doctor, teacher or social worker displays a take-it-or-leave-it attitude to the respective patient, student or client. In such an exchange, a considerable gap marks the difference between the power of the professional and layperson. By contrast, the sharing of information, depicting the second type of exchange, sees a diminishing gap between professional and layperson. Achievement of the third position, the alliance, is characterised by the ideal of equality. In the achievement of alliance and trust, the differences between lay and professional person are quickly transcended by the nature of exchange, as in the introduction, 'I am pleased to work with you. Let's try to have a look at this problems together.'

Figure 11.2 Differences in the exercise of power in meetings

Types of meetings	Auditions	Some sharing of information	Alliance
Types of power as exercised by a social worker	Official, conservative, maintains status quo One-dimensional	Pluralist: acknowledges several points of view but focuses on individual behaviour Two-dimensional	Questions official agendas, examines class and institutional issues Three-dimensional
The changing exercise of power:	Control retained by professionals and social distance maintained	Begins to share information and identify different tasks	Sharing information contributes to trust and a sense of alliance
Individuals' and groups' perceptions of the conduct of practitioners	This person differs little from others in authority	This person might be different from others in authority	This experience enhances knowledge and self-respect: 'I do not have to accept others' versions of events, I feel able to exert control'

In evaluating the exercise of power, the perceptions of the individuals and groups who are participants in the exchange provide important criteria (Figure 11.2). In auditions the experience is impersonal, the client might feel anonymous and would have little reason to perceive the social worker as any different from others in positions of authority. Compliance has been expected and is usually given. At the other end of the continuum, in the meeting characterised by a sense of 'alliance', the spontaneity of the exchange gives every chance that the status of client can be forgotten. In that type of meeting, even a poor self-image

begins to be replaced by a sense of dignity. Such a changed consciousness might not last much beyond this first meeting, but that is a
beginning and it takes practice.

In anticipating the different ways of conducting meetings (Figure
11.2), the management of information is a common issue. There are few
skills involved in being deceptive, in keeping information to oneself. By
contrast, openness and sharing in such a way that a sense of partnership
is effected may not come easily. On the contrary, professions have
sustained their power and privilege by maintaining the public in a state
of ignorance and the status of personnel in organisational hierarchies is
marked by the information they control. The creation of alliances to
share information stands in contrast to professional conventions about
the value of hierarchies, even though the disempowering consequences
of such ways of organising have been documented.

Recalling characteristics of powerlessness

Whatever may have been said in some educational circles about the
structural causes of problems, an ideology of individualism and consensus is likely to survive and even flourish in agencies.That ideology
would be apparent in the argument, often heard in practice, that every
person is unique, hence the impossibility of identifying common
features in backgrounds, common attitudes, expectations or resources.
Such a tendency represents a poor use of time, as in the reluctance to
evaluate what is already known. For example, in preparing for the tasks
of assessment, we do not have to reinvent the wheel. Powerlessness
among practitioners and clients has common causes and characteristics
which can easily be recalled.

For the purpose of rehearsal, we will concentrate on recalling the
confusion about social work experienced by people who have been
clients. Other issues, such as identifying the consequences of the stigma
associated with welfare, thinking through the differences in people's
orientation to solving problems (an issue addressed in chapter 3) could
also be used to sharpen skills. For current purposes, the issue of people's
confusion about social work and the consequences of that confusion will
be addressed.

In the model of an ideal exchange between the so-called helper and
the helped, the layperson knows about the terms of reference of the
professional person or enough about their job to seek help in the
manner which confirms the professional person's role. Such game
playing may not get to the heart of a problem but it leaves the
interaction undisturbed. The professionals play their role because the
other parties are playing theirs. What happens when the person referred
for help barely knows where they are, let alone the nature of the social
worker's job? For example, a young man who had just learned that he
had a chronic disabling disease and who had been referred by a

physician to a social worker in a hospital expected help for a problem which he defined as 'practical'. He explained, 'I didn't really know what was going on. I just wanted these forms filled in. She kept on talking about the disease, what I felt about it, what the wife felt about it. Coming to terms with it. All I want to come to terms with is these forms' (Blaxter 1976 p.123). A man, in his thirties, who had been referred to a voluntary welfare organisation explained, 'I associated them [the social workers in the voluntary organisation] with the sort of thrift shop type. You know, the bachelor ladies doing their best to keep up the moral support of the community. But what they do has surprised me' (Rees 1978 p.12). A 14 year old youngster, who had pleaded guilty to stealing property worth $50.00, described his expectations of a Children's Court. 'Scary , I mean, and sort of trying to scare me [the court would have] the judge, solicitor and twelve jurors ... [it would operate] like a computer and type each of the things that I did — like I was sat down and they took pictures of me while I was sitting down, writing down what I was saying' (O'Connor and Sweetapple 1988 pp. 39-40).

In these examples, the social worker's tasks included clarifying their role and the nature of their agency. The greeting 'Good morning, my name is, can I ask whether you have been here before?', and then, 'Do you feel that you know exactly what this organisation does?' begins to demystify a process which is likely to be confusing. At least those questions would not bypass the problem of people's fear of authority and confusion over what might be going to happen to them.

Explaining a role does not necessarily mean that it is understood, appreciated or accepted. Such understanding, appreciation or acceptance may only be achieved over time and not within minutes of a first meeting.

In role plays, students in classroom and practitioners in workshops can practise the skills of giving information in such a way that it enhances the respondent's feeling of control over what is happening. In probation services it has never been assumed that the magistrate's or judge's explanation of the purpose of probation would be sufficient. A first meeting with the new probationer usually requires a probation officer to explain the nature of probation and the 'advise, assist and befriend' responsibilities listed in this legal contract. Such goals may be clearly printed but they still require careful face to face explanation.

Clarification of agency function and social worker role depends only partially on what is said in first meetings. The character of the relationship and the style of the worker will connote the meaning of social work in the layperson's mind and attention to that connotation requires not only skills in evaluation but also skills of assessment. Evaluation of what is already known will facilitate assessment, a task which is often the priority in a week of work.

12 Assessment

Much social work begins with assessment and practitioners' competence is often judged by other professionals in terms of whether they are considered to make appropriate assessments of people and situations. Of course, 'appropriate' in the eyes of other professionals may mean a judgment which matches what they already think, but may not be an assessment which is apt, or fair.

Assessments are influenced by the theoretical perspective of the person doing the assessing: psychoanalysts pursue a line of questioning which matches their preconceived picture of key stages in an individual's development; defence lawyers engaged in plea bargaining steer their client towards admissions which that defendant originally had no intention of making (Scheff 1969). The empowerment approach to practice recognises the potential power of the assessor to steer people in one direction rather than another but the safety valve against this happening is the principle that assessment is, as far as possible, a process in which the individuals or groups being assessed are partners. Assessing people and their circumstances should not be conducted like some mystery, to maintain the professional person's image of expertise and to keep the subjects in ignorance and at a distance. On the contrary it provides the opportunity to engage people in a way which they have not hitherto experienced.

Assessment which reflects the ideology of empowerment implies an understanding of individuals' or groups' powerlessness and their means of moving away from that predicament. Expressions of powerlessness and the resources to combat it are almost always a focus of interviews concerned to make assessments. Skills in assessment will be influenced by the three-dimensional approach to raising questions about the exercise of power. Such an approach should unmask the predicament of clients and so lessen the chances of uncritically adopting official agency views, or any other predictable account. Skills in assessment should also be influenced by the principles of triangulation recommended in social science research (Denzin 1978). Maximising the number of sources from which information is derived and checking the degree of correspondence between those sources is at the heart of these principles.

An explicit point also needs to be made about the link between interactive and political attributes and skills in assessment. The ability to engage with people to try to develop trust in what might otherwise be an unfamiliar and threatening exercise is an inseparable part of the assessment process. But the worker will also need to recognise that as a consequence of their accountability to the agency as well as to the public, they will not always be able to play the role of the good guy. Establishing trust should stay as an ideal. But in statutory and non-statutory settings, constraints such as time and workers' responsibility to represent certain values in the conduct of relationships will mean striving to establish understanding and a working agreement. That agreement may or may not be accompanied by trust but the work still has to be done.

Assessment begins with themes from biographies in which assessor and respondents exchange information for the purpose of achieving understanding. Whether trust follows will depend in part on past experiences: the respondent's view of people in positions of authority or the worker's recall of the reliability of client groups. It will also depend on each party's perceptions of the attitude and skills of the other person or persons.

The emphasis on comprehending the exercise of power and recognising that it can be used creatively is a first step towards unmasking people's powerlessness, but the reliance on this approach does not exist in some kind of vacuum separate from all the other approaches which may have been crammed into the worker's theoretical wardrobe. Students and practitioners will already be carrying assumptions which may need to be discarded, by acknowledging which theoretical approaches they are familiar with, and by identifying how these approaches affect their analysis of power and powerlessness.

The relationship between other theoretical approaches and the political literacy which is being emphasised here has been discussed in chapter 7, but the following points can be re-emphasised. Students and practitioners make their own choice of theory but it is important for them to ponder their choice and its consequences, otherwise the basis for assessments is blurred. In general terms they could ask whether theirs is a consensus perspective, which reflects a point of view that there is nothing much wrong with the institutions and professionals who represent society's dominant interests. Or do they pursue a conflict analysis which assumes that competition, struggle and controversy are more likely to explain social problems than any concern with the smooth operating of systems and individuals' lack of fit with such systems, or their failure to adjust to them?

The commonplace view that society's problems are caused by people who allegedly refuse to work, 'bludgers' in Australian parlance, is a familiar example of the consensus-oriented point of view. To bludgers can be added blacks, migrants, homosexuals, single parents, AIDS sufferers, adult criminals and juvenile delinquents, in fact any relatively powerless group which does not appear to contribute to the maintenance of a society according to dominant social mores. This list of social deviants does not include senior white-collar employees, managers, leaders of national and multinational companies, owners and representatives of the media or politicians of any persuasion. The empowerment approach to assessment requires an appraisal of the resources and constraints of the powerless in relation to the behaviour of the powerful. You cannot have one without the other, though consensus approaches convey the impression that the behaviour of alleged deviant and non-deviant groups is somehow not connected.

With a view to showing the limitations of a consensus-oriented perspective in assessment, the following case study will focus on the exercise of power in different contexts and should therefore show the nature and consequences of conflict in daily lives. A couple in their twenties have two children, a 3 year-old boy and a 9-year-old girl. The father and mother have been unemployed for over a year and a general practitioner had once referred the mother for help with depression to a social worker in a community health centre. In this referral, approximately a year ago, the doctor had mentioned his suspicions of domestic violence but had not suggested that the children were being abused. The visit by a social worker from the local welfare office had been prompted by neighbours complaining about physical abuse of the girl. In a political climate of increasing concern about child abuse, and in a part of the world where reporting of suspected child abuse was mandatory, the social worker had little alternative but to follow up the anonymous dobbing in by neighbours. What did the social worker assume, what would she see and what should she have looked for?

Before making the visit to the couple's home, a visit which has been pre-arranged by a telephone call, the worker mulls over what she already knows. This sifting of prior knowledge amounts to a pre-assessment phase. Here are some of the assumptions which the social worker takes with her to the interview.

1   There has already been a referral for alleged domestic violence.
2   The family live in a city neighbourhood where private rents are high, incomes are low and there is a disproportionate amount of unemployment.
3   There is a relationship between poverty and domestic violence.
4   Although this is a relatively routine visit for me, it is likely to be perceived as a crisis by the family.
5   It is not clear who the 'client' is: maybe the 9-year-old girl, or all the family members, or one or both of the parents.

The social worker's ability to make an assessment during the visit depends partially on her skills in engaging the family but at this point we merely want to spell out the questions which the social worker poses in her own mind. The interview is conducted with both parents present, the two children running in and out. The worker wants to investigate the suspected child abuse but is not preoccupied with it. She mulls over the contexts in which the family experience different forms of power and powerlessness: within the family, the daughter's school, and the agency, the latter being represented by subsequent meetings between this practitioner and the family members (Figure 12.1).

In each of these contexts, there is a major issue which needs to be clarified and there are a series of key questions which reflect the social worker's interests.

1   She wants to know about family relationships, not in isolation but in terms of what power dynamics reflect socially, what they suggest about class-rooted values and constraints.
2   She wants to know about the child's experience in the school. The child's teachers are a potential source of information and support.
3   She wants to reflect on the exercises of power in the current meetings with the family. She correctly assumes that such meetings are the latest in a succession of exchanges with people in positions of authority and that in the eyes of the adults, both of whom feel threatened by the arrival of this person from 'the welfare', there is no reason to believe that these current meetings will benefit them.

The relationship between contexts, major working concepts and key questions is set out in Figure 12.1. Given the objectives of empowerment, the social worker's task is to protect the vulnerable, but this does not only mean pondering whether to remove a child to care. The vulnerable people may include all or only some of those involved, the child or both children, perhaps the woman only or the total family.

For the purpose of concentrating on the questions which contribute to skills in assessment, details of the outcome in this case study are omitted. Suffice to say, agency constraints influence social workers' attitudes to cases and so affect assessment. The skilled assessors do not pretend that these issues do not exist, but perceive the context of their own work as having a bearing on their attitudes and decisions. Political understanding presupposes both a familiarity with the demands of an agency and a striving to ensure that these demands do not unduly affect the conduct of tasks such as assessment.

In cases of suspected child abuse, most practitioners will be aware of the need to avoid making mistakes, to avoid being too cautious in removing a child. Influenced by the clichés 'better to be safe than sorry' or 'prevention is better than cure' and unduly influenced by what Rose and Black (1985) called the 'thought structure' of the agency, practitioners may find that their initial concern to assess the degree of care being shown to the child has been displaced by a current need to be

Figure 12.1 A focus on contexts: practitioners' thoughts and questions in assessments

Contexts of power and powerlessness	Major working concepts	Key questions
Family	Social class	What are the family's resources? How has power been exercised? Can it be less oppressive than hitherto?
School	Nature of education	What is the parents' interest in the school? What is the child's performance in the school? How do the parents perceive the school's interests in the child?
Agency: as manifest in social worker/ parent/child meetings	Stereotypes of professionals and authority	Have I clarified who I am and what I do? Have I explained the process and the major actors? Have I explained my tentative assessment of what I observe and what I think might happen?

seen to exert control over allegedly abusive parents. The social worker treads a tightrope in managing the conflicts of care and control, never more so than in such an assessment.

In another case, the same social worker inherited responsibility for a 10-year-old boy who had been removed from home. In this case the social worker's tasks included the support for the child through the court system and, subsequently, in dilemmas over the choice of temporary foster parents. Using the same framework of contexts of power and powerlessness, major working concepts and key questions (Figure 12.2), the social worker continues the tasks of assessment, aware that she may be the only person able to make sense of a confusing and threatening set of procedures.

In humanising the process, the social worker is not complying with people in power, she is enabling the different participants—child, parents, and foster parents—to perceive the power plays and ploys of which they are a part. This does not mean to say that the social worker is only pragmatic when it comes to articulating standards for the care of children for which she has some responsibility. It does mean that the whole notion of standards of care and the identification of the people accountable for such standards is a topic for negotiation. The attitudes and actions of court officials, lawyers, social workers, foster parents, senior agency personnel and the representatives of the media who love to make moral judgments about such matters, are all part of the process of assessing this one vulnerable 10-year-old and his parents.

A perspective which labels the behaviour of all these participants as political throws up different tasks in assessment than if the idiosyncrasies in the story of the child's life were regarded as the only fit subject for appraisal. Key questions in this perspective on assessment also address those agency constraints likely to affect the practitioner's actions. The major working concepts in trying to weigh a case such as this are hierarchy, language and conflict of loyalties (Figure 12.2).

Figure 12.2 Some consequences of agency constraints

Contexts of power and powerlessness	Major working concepts	Key questions
Social worker in the agency	Hierarchy, convention, pressure of time	Am I using my *discretion* creatively? Am I resisting compliance to superiors and traditions? Am I addressing the care versus control dilemma?
Courts: arenas for contesting justice	Symbolism and power: language and procedures	Have I conducted the assessment of the child's needs exhaustively and creatively? Have I communicated effectively to the other players? Have I demystified the process for the child?
Substitute care	Conflicts of loyalties, different line of accountability	Have I clarified 'right' to the child, natural and foster parents? Have I clarified the time scale of substitute care to the child, natural parents, foster parents, myself, and my supervisor? And always, am I carefully evaluating the merits of the different solutions?

At this point, we will leave the students and others to ponder the questions, and return them to the tasks of administration and planning.

13 Administration and planning

Talk of empowerment without the ability to contribute to decisions and implement them would be rhetoric. Credibility would be lost. Colleagues and the public would be reduced to comments of the flavour 'Those managers . . . or those practitioners . . . cannot be relied on to do anything.'

Effective administration draws on political skills in timing and releasing information to selected audiences but the concept also implies attention to the organisation of thoughts and time. Such organisation depends on an ability of staff at different levels to plan. Although such planning implies an element of control over events, it will also involve the management of uncertainty: it is not possible to anticipate every change in public demand or other crises which may occur within an organisation.

The hope of exerting control, through careful administration and planning, may often prove illusory but the vision required to plan should increase staff chances of influencing events, not merely reacting to them. Demands on these skills would vary according to practitioners' levels in a hierarchy but the administrative tasks which are being discussed here will apply to management as well as to front-line personnel. The latter could include the probation officer in a crowded city office or in a single office in a remote rural area, the community project officer in a multiethnic urban estate, the community development worker located in a suburb with an apparently homogeneous population and common problems, the social worker in a small or large hospital, or the lone social worker in a school.

The administrative skills which reflect the empowerment approach to practice presuppose a view of the organisation as a political–economic environment. In this environment, processing people and information depends on knowing about the location and distribution of financial and other material resources and being familiar with the attributes of the personnel who control information. This perspective exposes the never ending political eddies in which administration is conducted. It does not emphasise adherence to rules as the way to administer. On the contrary, the competence of manager or front-line administrator will be enhanced if they view their office and agency as an ever changing political arena, which reflects the dominant values and language of economic policies, as well as management priorities and senior bureaucrats' aptitude for exercising authority.

A common and conventional perspective on organisation and administration might emphasise the value of keeping one's desk clear, moving correspondence up and down a hierarchy according to rules and according to the equally predictable arrival of memoranda from superiors. The formal rules and mores of an agency should be known and used creatively. Without knowledge of such rules and how they are applied, practitioners teeter on the edge of organisational powerlessness, but to be preoccupied with good order by compliance with rules is a reactive way of organising and administering and we are not talking about that here.

Predictable skills in planning and administration include the storage and retrieval of information, which is often dependent on a highly competent secretarial colleague, a filing system or an appropriate use of word processors and computers. Then there is the task of keeping written records which facilitate planning.

In subsequent discussion, in chapter 17, of the economic literacy of practitioners, the management of budgets and the interpretation of different costs and benefits are addressed as a feature of empowerment. Demystifying the meaning of economics and enlightening practitioners on the breakdown of budgets should benefit those who previously felt ignorant or confused and it is worth recognising the importance of such demystification, even though the existence of some special skills in financial management should also be acknowledged.

To empower others through administration presupposes precision in contributing to decisions rather than building a reputation for getting things done. Efficiency in contributing to and implementing decisions will also require careful attention to consultation, a task of two extremes, neither of which may have much in common with competent administration. The first extreme is the familiar temptation to hasten decisions by consulting no one or as few people as possible. Such a practice is usually counterproductive because it provokes resentment, often leads to decisions being reversed and is thus a time waster not a time saver. The second extreme refers to the practice of wanting to democratise every decision however trivial. While laudable in principle, such a practice demonstrates a degree of political naivety, and perhaps worse than that, shows little evidence of trust in immediate colleagues of whatever status.

Three issues will illustrate the process of implementation as a central feature of good administration. The first concerns the creation of time for and giving time to administration; the second refers to an ordering of priorities; the third asks for identification of the stage which an item of work has reached, and the characteristics of that stage.

Creating and giving time

This skill presupposes an attitude to the significance of administration. The overheard conversation between staff in a community health centre persuading themselves why they would not apply for a senior position displays familiar attitudes. 'Why aren't you going to apply for that senior position?' asks one. 'All that paper work,' replies the other, 'I'm too busy with the real business of practice to want to be bothered with administration.'

Related to these exchanges is the belief that competence in practice is rewarded by promotion to a position with responsibility for tasks in administration. Yet front-line practice also demands competence in conceptualising tasks, ordering priorities and keeping records which analyse rather than describe. That takes time.

Administrative skills are inherent in the ability to create time to think and plan and require that attitude and aptitude already referred to in the limbering up process of 'evaluation and preparation'. Identifying the time to think through a day or week's work and to anticipate the unpredictable events that might throw this planning off course, should facilitate competent practice. At least it will increase the chances of the practitioner being in the right frame of mind to weigh the disaster situations or crisis telephone calls that seem to be the stock-in-trade pressure in many agencies.

The skill in creating space to think can be done with a colleague or colleagues informally, or formally as in a meeting designed to plan work, though it is the constructive informal use of time which is so easily overlooked. Even the observation to a colleague, 'let's close the door, take the phone off the hook and think through the likely priorities for the week before we look at today's correspondence', would be indispensable practice for creating time. This capacity to create the space to think about administration is not the equivalent of time spent in meetings, though the effective timing and efficient conduct of meetings will be one feature of good administration. After all, a purpose of such administration is to increase the accessibility of practitioners to colleagues, other professionals and the public. Such effective administration is the opposite of time spent in marathon meetings protected by a secretary who has to tell an increasingly impatient public, 'They're in a meeting,' or 'I'm sorry, they're still in a meeting.'

Ordering priorities

A great deal of administration has to address the question of priorities; and skills in making such choices can be learned. For example, the following tasks in a busy, urban welfare office would take approximately eight hours to complete but only four hours are available. Students or workshop participants are asked to rank order the priorities and explain, in two brief sentences, why two tasks were selected at the top of the list and two at the bottom (Figure 13.1).

Figure 13.1 Towards skills in planning and administration

Tasks	Scores out of 10 in importance	Rank order
(a) Completion of report on a union meeting about in-service staff training		
(b) Undertaking a second home interview of a family suspected of abusing their child		
(c) Group meeting with six single parents about the common problems of managing alone		
(d) Telephone calls to the Public Housing Department and to a private landlord regarding a family threatened with eviction by the landlord in two weeks' time		
(e) Proposed assessment interview with the parents of a runaway teenager who is to appear in a children's court at the end of the week		
(f) Reading and summarising chapters from a recent national report on youth homelessness in relation to welfare policies		
(g) Arranging a meeting with colleagues to plan the coverage of the work of a colleague who has just resigned and is not to be replaced		
(h) Planning for tomorrow's meeting with a supervisor whose habit is to check on the progress of alleged difficult cases		
Reasons for choice of two most important tasks		
Reasons for the choice of the two least important tasks		

Evaluation skills are also involved in this exercise, but this ordering of priorities in relation to available time is intended to show a capacity for administration and planning. The scores out of ten should precede the rank ordering and make that latter task easier to complete. The exercise can be completed individually and the results shared with a group. Alternatively, the exercise can be completed in several group discussions and the results compared between one group and another. The important tasks concern the explanations of the choice of priorities rather than the rank ordering. Those 'explanations' will also have to include thoughts about how they are going to deal with the repercussions of 'failing' to do the other tasks.

This exercise should be completed within twenty minutes. Such a task could keep students and others occupied for two hours or more but there is an irony in discussing priorities if they become blurred in importance on account of the time taken to dicuss them. Competence can be indicated by the efficiency with which complex tasks are completed, within a sensible time frame: not in a rush but not by endless meandering.

Characteristic of the stage of work

Knowing the stage of intervention or the stage which a project has reached can facilitate the organisation of managers' and practitioners' own work and their support and supervision of others. It is also a skill which enables practitioners to anticipate the nature of the demands likely to be placed on them by other professionals and by volunteers.

In the organisation of work, judgments are made about the progress which can be expected and the degree of frustration which should be tolerated if no progress is obvious. The characteristic of each stage of a piece of work would provide a baseline against which to make judgments. Examples from familiar problems should illustrate the point.

The beginning stage of a community development project or of a research enquiry conducted through participant observation is characterised by the 'liabilities of newness'. All that can be said with any certainty at that beginning stage is that all sorts of leads have to be followed, many different contacts made and varieties of information collected without anyone being certain that the leads will go anywhere, that the contacts can be trusted, or that the collected information will be used or useful. Lack of certainty about direction, trust and usefulness are liabilities which have to be tolerated and used. They cannot be ignored. Such liabilities are normal: they characterise the beginning stages. They become somewhat abnormal, almost pathological, if the lack of certainty about key people, destinations and information continues beyond about a three-month period. It may take longer but it is not endless. In planning work, the liabilities of newness stage will be replaced by a period of consolidation or by further planning and predictions about specific goals to be achieved within a specific period.

The administrative skills evident in the ability to anticipate future events and organise workloads involve a thinking ahead which can be shared with colleagues and other groups. For example, in that phase of work when practitioners are encouraging others to resist a return to the familiar experience of powerlessness, it should be encouraging for people to know that the experience of wanting to return to what seems safe because it is known, is not unusual. The prospect of change may be unfamiliar and even threatening, because old habits are being discouraged and predictable relationships challenged. A feature of the effective management which characterises good administration is the ability to forecast the onset of any stage in the process of change and to plan to provide the necessary support.

Good administration aims to enable people to take responsibility for their lives in such a way that they confront the temptation to revert to the familiar. Examples of the wish to return to the familiar might include the desire to return to an institution in the case of ex-psychiatric patients; to the safe way of working alone as a social worker rather than to experiment as a member of a team; to retreat to one's own privacy in the case of people who have joined a community project but are impatient because their aspirations are not being fulfilled.

The specific events discussed above, the characteristics of the beginning stage of a community project and that stage in the steps toward achieving power when the participants are almost overcome by doubt about the wisdom of what they are doing, can be forecast. The performance of such work requires skills in predicting the onset of change and such forecasting will be referred to as administration through anticipation (Figure 13.2).

Figure 13.2   **Administration through anticipation: skills in predicting the characteristics and onset of change**

Examples of practice	Participants' reactions: obstacles to change	Predicting onset of change
Beginning stage of community development projects	'Liability of newness': key people and key sources of information unknown	'Liabilities' can last for several months, but not much longer
Support for ex-residents of institutions	Period of 'anomie': fear of unknown, wanting to return to the familiar	Occurs through participation in making choices, an experience which may require six months work, or more

The political dimensions of practice which have been stressed already with regard to evaluation and the conduct of assessments are also significant in administration and planning. The performance of those tasks displays an attitude. It marshals or dissipates energy for being creative. Competent administration empowers. It frees the practitioner, immediate colleagues and other personnel to spend time on other demanding issues, including perhaps the conduct of formal negotiations with senior management, within their own or in other organisations.

14 Formal negotiations

The distinction between informal and formal negotiations matches Cohen's description of the process stage of a negotiation and the formal event (Cohen 1988). The practice of skills in informal negotiation can enhance practitioners' chances of being successful in formal negotiations if these practitioners have developed trust and achieved credibility in the eyes of those whom they want to be their allies or others whom they wish to influence. For example, in the earlier discussion of a political–economic analysis of low staff morale in an organisation and the suggestions about ways to solve that problem, the discovery of common ground between disaffected staff members sowed the seeds of trust. The process of thinking and acting politically began at that stage.

The aim to build alliances and trust was kept in mind by staff members throughout informal negotiations. In addition to identifying a common cause of low staff morale, other steps in informal negotiation included the decision to say 'no' to calling in outside experts, assessing other staff members' compliance with management, being sure which audience they wished to influence and recording information about objectives, alliances, strategies and tactics. These activities usually build confidence between people and generate information to formulate a case to present to the opposition. Of such preparations in the 'process stage' Cohen said '. . . fortune will favour the person who uses his lead time to seed an environment of trust that will grow and ripen during the event. This ability, to use the present in anticipation of the future, will make the difference' (Cohen 1988 p. 165).

Skills in formal negotiation are linked to other aspects of empowerment. For example, efforts to achieve equity can be a purpose of specific negotiations, as in the case of achieving fair employment conditions for staff and overcoming oppression experienced by client groups. In both instances the negotiation plan is facilitated by establishing its ideological and moral base. Negotiation in the empowerment tradition does not mean every man and woman for themselves. If it did, the powerful would always win and the values surrounding the free hand of market forces would have invaded every sphere of human relationships.

The empowerment approach should build confidence and optimism and those feelings should influence the negotiators' attitude to bargaining with people in positions of power. Students and inexperienced practitioners usually underestimate their ability to challenge either people in authority or the rules which those people uphold, and when a successful challenge is mounted, the importance of success to these previously inexperienced negotiators is also underestimated. For example, a young university student who had participated in negotiations to change the requirements by which degrees were awarded to part-time students expressed her surprise at the successful outcome of several meetings. 'I never thought it could happen. I was pessimistic. I had no idea that change could be achieved like this. I thought we would either fail or it would take ages and involve lots of unpleasantness and conflict.' Her new optimism and the valuable political experience which she gained also generated confidence which could be drawn on in subsequent encounters.

Although we are now in a position to spell out principles for the conduct of formal negotiations, the excitement of participating in almost any kind of negotiation and the importance of the skills being acquired in the process should not be overlooked. However, no one is suggesting that because some form of negotiating is an everyday occurrence, it can be carried out by hunches and intuition, with little practice and no guide lines. In other fields of endeavour, in commerce, law and foreign affairs, comprehensive descriptions and projects have been completed on the best ways to negotiate (Cohen 1988; Fisher and Ury 1987).

The following guidelines for the conduct of formal negotiations are directed at staff who are intent on bargaining with their superiors but they could be applied in other contexts, as in the resolution of disputes between community groups, or in inter-agency controversies. The specific exercise to practise skills in formal negotiation arises from the discussion in chapter 9 on the problems of low staff morale in a large welfare bureaucracy. The students who participate in this exercise will have to operate as though they are members of staff intent on obtaining concessions from management. In preparation for this exercise, six guidelines will be used. They refer to timing, planning, trust, clarity, observation and the pursuit of principle.

These guidelines are not rules set in concrete. They represent a general framework which can be amended in the light of discussion and practice.

Timing The time and occasion for formal negotiations needs to be chosen carefully. Not only should the date of the formal meeting occur following sufficient preparation by the staff representatives, it should also fall at a time convenient for representatives of management. They should not feel they are being ambushed into a hasty meeting. In the run-up to formal negotiations, therefore, avoid impromptu discussion in corridors or elevators because these exchanges usually involve off the cuff comments, may give the wrong impression and become a hiccup in deliberations about the timing of a meeting.

Planning If the objectives of the formal negotiation have been discussed with all the interested participants, that discussion should help to compose the minds of the staff representatives. Agreement about objectives is a first step in planning and a second step is to have contingency plans, to anticipate reactions if management appears inflexible or proposes a compromise. Even the most experienced negotiators will flounder if they have not thought about contingency plans. Knowing of alternative solutions if the management will not accept the original submission usually provides negotiators with a sense of security, calmness and even power within meetings. Without those contingency plans they are unlikely to feel calm or secure.

Trust Although trust in relationships has been discussed with reference to the stages of empowerment and the development of interactive and political skills, it is just as germane to the business of formal negotiations. Even the pleasant greeting at the beginning of a meeting may be a start if it expresses the hope that a mutual solution can be achieved in the best possible atmosphere. Such an opening statement may be, in Cohen's terms, 'the equivalent of asking for approval of apple pie, the flag and a hot lunch for orphans' (Cohen 1988 p.167). But at least it displays an attitude of cooperation and a regard for reciprocity.

This effort to achieve trust can continue throughout the formal exchanges but it does not imply even for a minute any tendency to be ingratiating. Showing interest in the other side's point of view is not being ingratiating. The observation, 'I think I understand but would you please clarify your point to make sure there is no misunderstanding', is a valuable technique because it shows you taking seriously the other side's point of view and thus contributing to an atmosphere of trust.

Clarity When the formal negotiation begins, but not necessarily in the first few minutes, state clearly the interests which you represent. At an opportune moment this general statement can be followed by clarification of the specific points which you wish to pursue.

A reputation for clarity can be achieved by written communication and by articulating in a brief and concise manner. Such clarity contributes to understanding and affects whether that practitioner will be taken seriously. For example, politicians who spend a lot of time dealing with lobbyists appreciate intelligible, informative and accurate presentations. They do not like arguments which they perceive as 'cryptic, deceptive or obscure' (Mathews 1982).

Observation The role of the negotiator has something in common with the participant observer in research. The consequences of your own presentation of self as well as the attitudes of others can be noted. To recognise feelings generated by attitudes and to make mental notes of what was said, enables negotiators to play an energetic and pertinent role and prepares them to respond to almost any occurrence.

Perceptive observations will help to compile information, which is one purpose of negotiations. Without that attention to collecting information, the negotiators will find it difficult to make sense of the content and outcome of any one exchange, let alone be better equipped to conduct the next round of meetings.

During the formal negotiation it may be appropriate and a real ice-breaker to make observations explicit. For example, if the representatives of management appear tense, a non-threatening even humorous observation about the meeting's atmosphere could reveal their attitude and position. They may dislike the personality of one of the staff representatives or they may feel that the communication by another staff representative is woolly, inflexible and has been going on for too long.

Pursuing principles The objectives underpinning empowerment should rule out the possibility that you intend to get your way by whatever means and at whatever price. An objective in formal negotiations would include focus on an outcome of mutual advantage, each party coming away feeling they have gained something from the experience and that the outcome could be regarded as an innovation for both sides.

This focus on mutuality of interests and outcomes is what Fisher and Ury had in mind when they argued the merits of principled negotiation as compared to the concern to win positions, and in doing so not being too bothered about offending people, if such offence contributed to a feeling of defeating the opposition. Principled negotiation in their terms required a focus on interests not on positions, the invention of options for mutual gain and an insistence on objective criteria for judging the conduct and outcome of negotiations (Fisher and Ury 1987).

Even the practice of ending negotiations on a positive note, by expressing the hope that a solution can be reached, or by recording your appreciation if some agreement has been attained, follows a tenet of principled negotiation. That positive note also contributes to trust which is a valuable investment to use in subsequent work. The positive note, 'We appreciate your time and consideration, we feel sure we can solve this problem in future discussions', is not a concession. It does not mean you have agreed to disagree. You have kept your options open, though you have not ruled out open partisanship through advocacy at some later date. But the skills required in advocacy will differ from those we have just discussed with reference to formal negotiations.

Rehearsing for formal negotiations

The above guidelines for conducting formal negotiations can be tested in the following piece of theatre which aims to give students an experience of being on both sides of an issue and involves all the participants, including the audience, in evaluating the performance. Solidarity can be built through rehearsals which give people confidence to play new roles and share ideas. When confidence is built through rehearsals, the actual meeting with management is likely to be conducted skilfully.

Consider two possible scenarios. In the first the negotiators ignore all the guidelines which have just been discussed. The negotiation is unsuccessful. In the second the negotiators follow the guidelines and their experience is very different. The scene is a room in which three representatives of management face three representatives of staff. The issue is the need for staff to have space and time during working hours to discuss improvements to working conditions. The exchange lasts fifteen minutes and is played out twice. On the first occasion the staff play into the hands of management. They say different things. They are uncoordinated, almost incoherent. They come away feeling dismayed and disillusioned. Their worst fears about bargaining with the establishment are confirmed. Given the way in which this exchange is conducted, the management side has also learned almost nothing. The experience could have been as disempowering for them as it was for the staff.

In the next presentation the staff group are deliberate, firm, coordinated and coherent. Even if management does not agree with them they cannot fail to be impressed. In this exchange, a sense of dialogue between the parties is empowering for both, even if they continue to disagree. In this second and competent piece of negotiation it is best to have the same staff who had played out the incompetent performance. In that way they experience the contrast between feelings of dismay and powerlessness and between feelings of competence and power.

In the first performance the staff are all over the place. Convinced that they could react and speak on their feet, they are ill prepared. This is politically naive and almost always ends in failure. Management comes away with the impression that these people were speaking off the cuff, did not know what they were talking about and should not be taken seriously. In the second performance the staff clarify their position and indicate their solidarity. They know but keep secret their fall back position, which includes their resolve to enlarge their contact with staff in other parts of the agency and distribute their record of this meeting.

Clarifying their interests will usually provoke questions and some other response from management. The quality of active listening is played out with management: asking for matters of interpretation, summarising what they think have heard and not being bothered by silence. Even the request, 'can we just think this through for a minute' conveys that they are reacting to events, not just asserting preconceived positions. Such a request is unlikely to be turned down and will create space for the actual 'thinking through'.

A restatement of the staff's interests can be introduced by the observation, 'We realise we have said this already but in order to avoid any misunderstanding can we just repeat our concerns?' Following that statement comes the effort to clarify the management's views, their feelings of like or dislike and some discovery of the room for compromise, even if, at this stage, the staff have little intention of compromising.

It is unwise to enter into argument with management about their negative views on the staff position. An empowering stance is inherent in the refusal to be drawn into argument, even if the content and style of management's views are provocative and unpalatable. Besides, the negotiation group has to report back to their colleagues and, as in any poker of politics, they should not be showing their hand, at least not prematurely.

The staff finish, as far as possible, on an optimistic note and with a summary of what they think has been achieved and agreed in that meeting. This summary is a statement of coherence which can also identify areas of disagreement which remain and so foreshadow the topics for a future meeting.

Evaluation

The participants in the negotiation finish with an evaluation. If they do not evaluate, they leave with a sense of unfinished business. Of four specific tasks in the evaluation, two are undertaken by those who represented management, two by the staff representatives' group. In each evaluation, the different participants are identifying feelings, techniques and outcomes. Those four tasks are as follows:

1   Management evaluates their feelings about exercising power, including their reactions to the incompetent performance by staff.
2   Management evaluates their reactions to the competent staff performance. They compare the different experiences.
3   Staff identify their feelings during and following the incompetent performance.
4   Staff go through the same process regarding the competent performance.

Completion of evaluations by all the participants, including the audience, enables the staff players to judge their actions and their feelings. By contrast, in the language and ideology of some management practice, evaluation is a task carried out be experts: the quality control person, production personnel in a policy unit or the team of management consultants.

The value placed on evaluation, and the language in which it is expressed, confront the familiar claims of management and some researchers that this is a specialist, scientific activity. A political–economic perspective on behaviour in organisations does not deny the merits of scientific method in evaluation but it also emphasises the interdependence of evaluation and political action. Immersion in such organisational politics produces a literacy for workers which should enable them to redirect their own and their agency's biography from disenchantment towards an empowering redefinition of roles. These staff have participated in negotiating conditions of employment, have paid attention to developing skills and have done far more than merely survive the organisation.

15 Advocacy

Advocacy refers to the act of pleading in favour of something or someone or urging a cause by argument. Some dictionary definitions also refer to an advocate as someone who is qualified to conduct such pleading or urging. Qualifications in advocacy do not necessarily derive from legal training or practice. Advocacy to achieve a particular outcome can be facilitated by familiarity with the exercise of power in different contexts and with an attitude which says that in matters of social injustice, the realm of public affairs should become a political domain where people can be enabled to represent their own interests.

Previous discussion of economic policies and their consequences, and about the disappointing conservatism of professions and professionals who settle for their own interests, has been aimed at preparing practitioners for advocacy. A picture of power being exercised with a view to creating alternative ways of thinking about issues and solving them has provided the theoretical approach which should serve the advocate well. More specifically, the practice of skills in formal and informal negotiations should have given practitioners a feeling for the politics of practice, as in the careful specification of a problem, the identification of coalitions of common interests, and the choice of the target or audience to whom the advocacy might be addressed, if and when negotiation has failed.

The distinction between negotiation and advocacy is blurred but presupposes activities of different style, intent and time frame. The interactive and political skills in almost constant use in informal and formal negotiations are used in advocacy to focus on a particular end in which partisanship and conflict will be very apparent. For example, in advocacy, an awareness of injustice should be coupled to a determination to pursue the interests of the parties who are the subject of injustice, and to do so with a conviction uncluttered by considerations of tactics and compromise.

Although advocates are partisans pursuing goals single-mindedly, in doing so they are not trying to imitate the charge of the Light Brigade, determined on glory but guaranteeing a premature and usually fatal end to their efforts. Advocacy requires contemplation rather than an immediate outburst of feelings. It begins with an appraisal of an injustice and a decision about the best way to address the issue.

Case or cause

Two types of advocacy can usually be distinguished: that which relates to an individual's interests or to an issue affecting many individuals; the one referring to the pursuit of justice in a case, the other to class advocacy in the interests of a common cause (Rose and Black 1985 p.130; Hepworth and Larsen 1982 p.504).

For several reasons the experience of advocating for justice in a particular case prepares a practitioner to extend the number of people being represented. A piece of single case advocacy can be converted to collective social action. The one often leads to the other. In pursuing advocacy of a single case, a practitioner becomes aware that this one person or one family's grievance is shared by numerous others. For example, the advocacy of the interests of patients who were being refused medical treatment because they did not have private health insurance began with the uncovering of a few cases of injustice (Rees and Gibbons 1986). The decision to pursue a widespread campaign on behalf of uninsured patients came with the accumulation of information showing that discrimination was widespread. This trend would also be familiar to those who have participated in advocacy to obtain civil rights whether in poverty programs or in campaigns to dismantle apartheid and other forms of racial discrimination.

The experience of advocacy in a specific case also provides the means of rehearsing the skills which will contribute to a wider and perhaps longer campaign. Success in single-mindedly pursuing arguments in one case will mentally prepare for the testing demands of collective action, though the latter may be more complicated simply because more people are involved, the storage of information has to be more systematic and the maintenance of alliances will require greater reserves of energy.

The decision to pursue the advocacy of a case or a cause, or a combination of both will usually have been preceded by the identification of an injustice which it is felt cannot be rectified simply by efficient administration or negotiation. The identification of an injustice and the sense of conviction that the removal of this injustice should become a priority, even in a congested workload, goes hand in hand with the advocacy process. It is not sufficient merely to recognise an injustice. You have to believe that this issue should be fought for, and if necessary over a long period of time.

On what specific issues would practitioners play the role of advocate? The answer to this question will be affected by a reappraisal of the objectives of empowerment. In this regard the advocate will be mindful of that principle of justice which is concerned with better treatment for those who are most disadvantaged. That task is not the same as trying to secure equal treatment for everyone. The list of injustices could be almost infinite. It has included discrimination against people because of race, religion or creed, the delivery of services in a dehumanising manner (as in the case of rape victims being humiliated) or evidence of hardship being caused because no benefits or services exist (Hepworth and Larsen 1982 p.505).

These examples cover two issues. Each addresses the relationship between policy and practice and each highlights the potential for practitioners to use their discretionary power as advocates. The first issue concerns policies which are non-existent, or situations where policies may exist but the resources to implement them are too few. The second issue concerns adverse ways in which policies are being implemented. The intended beneficiaries are denied access or the process of providing a service becomes so complicated that the outcome is the same as if access had been openly denied in the first place.

Of course, to say that individuals either obtain a service or they do not is too simple. Such a picture obscures the possibility that people may not be able to pursue their own interest effectively because they are relatively ignorant of their rights, or because their orientation to authority, perceived perhaps as too passive or overassertive, adversely affects their contacts with others.

All the issues of knowledge, orientation and attitude are present in the experiences of people who suffer injustice because they do not speak fluently the language of a host country. In the experience of ethnic minority groups, the problems of language barriers, isolation and reluctance to take action on their own behalf may be compounded by other aspects of disadvantage. For example, an advocacy program on behalf of Spanish-speaking people in the United States established self-help groups to overcome problems affecting the delivery of social services. These problems included arbitrary denial of services, the inflexibility of institutions, red tape with long delays and silences, undignified or callous treatment, long waiting lists, inaccessibility by telephone or in person, a run-around from agency to agency and even a 'lack of clear, simple directions and explanations' (Cameron and Talavera 1976 p.427).

These issues of bureaucratic inflexibility and professional misconduct would have to be linked to subsequent or parallel advocacy concerning fundamental problems of unemployment, housing, inadequate medical care, poor systems of transportation and a lack of suitable child-care facilities. The manner in which these shortcomings or injustices are addressed can be as varied as the issues which merit advocacy. At least twelve different techniques were listed in one study (Panitch 1974) and several texts, usually dealing with ways to plan and organise for social change, have been cited as important sources on the means of advocacy

(Hepworth and Larsen 1982). The techniques included planned arguments with agency personnel, the preparation and presentation of expert evidence before legal or parliamentary tribunals, the use of letters or petitions, the formation of coalitions, the creation of consumer groups and the conduct of survey research to be used in educational campaigns.

From this myriad of means the prospective advocate may choose. Some of the techniques require close association with others, colleagues or clients. Some may depend on the skills of one individual. All will probably require careful consultation with the people to be represented.

Preparation for the skills of advocacy begins in the atmosphere of debate, criticism and creativity which characterises the politics of mutual education, from which the optimism about empowerment grows. In spite of that claim, people who have never been advocates, not even on behalf of their own interests, will need opportunities to practice. Students can join with others in writing a letter to a newspaper, to describe an injustice and to advocate the means of dealing with it. They can conduct small-scale surveys about the conditions of vulnerable groups and work together to decide the best audience at which to aim their data. They will also need to decide the most effective way to present their information and determine at what times its release would achieve maximum impact.

Some specific issues

For the purpose of enabling students to gain confidence in themselves and identify with key principles of advocacy, two small exercises will be referred to. The first concerns the need for practice to be openly partisan, irrespective of criticism, veiled threats from more powerful officials or other means of making someone feel that it would be easier to stop the challenge and to cease being controversial. The second example concerns the need to include citizen groups in plans for advocacy, not least because the extent of an injustice and the relevance of solutions are best known to them.

In the first exercise, parts can be played in an exchange between three people. They are discussing rules concerning access to a service, in this instance the provision of a place in a tertiary education institution. In the view of the person arguing the case on behalf of students who had been denied a place, the discretion to interpret the rules had not been used. In the view of the officials the rules had been administered as they had been written.

There is an imbalance of power in the exchange because the two officials are able to control the agenda and they have the power to make decisions. The person playing the role of advocate is using the meeting to change the balance of power, get the agenda reinterpreted and the decision changed.

The exercise aims to provide practice in sticking to a point of view even if the weight of an institution's authority and its rules seem likely to prevail. In the following brief dialogue the officials are represented by 'O_1' and 'O_2'. The person arguing the case of the students denied a place is denoted by an 'A'.

O_1: It is impossible to admit these people under the resolutions. There is no way it can be done.

A: It may be your job to interpret the resolutions, my task is to also interpret them and to look for exceptions to the rule.

O_2: We know you would like to but there is no way we, or you, can ignore the rules. They provide for fairness, for everyone.

A: Those rules were only written years ago by another set of human beings. We have to interpret those rules and if need be remake them. Equity is the issue, not the rules.

O_1: In spite of what you say, a letter will have to go out to the unsuccessful students explaining that it is unlikely that anything can be done.

A: I do not accept that. I am against sending totally pessimistic letters to anyone.

O_2: There is little alternative whichever way you look at it.

A: Of course there is an alternative. We are only just starting the debate. It is not going to be so simple as to just tell them 'no'.

O_2: You are entitled to your point of view but it has probably been tried before and it does seem a waste of time. It is almost certainly out of order.

A: It is never a waste of time to try to create opportunities for people. You should know I am now a party in this process. It is not just between you and these applicants. We have to search for the alternatives, we have to try to effect change. There is a lot more to this than rules, which in any case are open to interpretation.

In the second example the purpose of the exercise is to ensure careful consultation with the group whose needs are to be represented through advocacy. This careful consultation is part of the advocacy process not only to enable people through self–help to represent their own interests but also with a view to the practitioners becoming informed about an injustice to which they may hitherto have given little consideration.

The issue concerns legal representation of people who are deaf. It is an exercise which challenges cosy consensus views of society, points to the injustice inherent in conservative one-dimensional exercise of power and poses explicit questions about the language of power and powerlessness.

With a group of people who are deaf and through an interpreter, issues concerning consensus views of institutions, the use of language and the search for an alternative way to represent a very disempowered group are to be discussed. The discussion produces evidence of considerable inequalities of power and the previous failure of reasonable negotiation with authorities to produce understanding let alone a solution. From discussion emerges the need for advocacy and the case to be put for a different attitude to people who are deaf and different means of representing them in courts of law.

The discussion challenges the official legal view which, put simply, says that criminal courts recognise the difficulties in obtaining access to proper legal representation for hearing-impaired people and the difficulties in ensuring that such defendants fully understand the charges against them. This point of view takes little account of the disempowering effects of legal mystification for anyone, let alone for people who cannot hear and whose low status is confirmed in a context in which lawyers say they are concerned with justice. The second issue requires an unmasking of assumptions about the language to be used to communicate. Issues about the importance of language can be recorded in point form.

Even before any hearing-impaired people may appear before courts, they will have been disempowered by contact with institutions which have obliged them to use an unfamiliar language. As members of a minority group with its own distinctive culture, their status has been denied by notions of normality and the consequent insistence that it is a hearing world that must be lived in, irrespective of difficulties in communication. Searching for alternative ways to ensure justice for hearing impaired people in courts, these previously disempowered citizens not only wish to make the point about language but also about the habit of professionals thinking that they can intervene to represent the interests of such a group. In the discussion in question it was obvious that the people concerned had experienced services being dominated by the medical model in which they were expected to depend on a small group of specialists who always liked to behave as though they knew what was best. Such specialists were happy to mediate between the hearing-impaired people and other representatives of the hearing world.

In discussing ways to represent hearing-impaired people in court, it was apparent that a repeat of experiences with medical practitioners was the last thing that was wanted. On the contrary, advocacy was to include a challenge to assumptions about the fairness of professional practice, and an exposure of the illiteracy of powerful people and institutions when communicating with this group. The powerful people had given no thought to the value of being bilingual. An acknowledgment of previously disempowering attitudes and the humility required to begin to shed an ideology and learn another language would produce a creative and empowering alternative. To achieve that goal would be a revealing, humbling but testing exercise. So is the pursuit of most forms of advocacy.

V Policy–practice controversies

16 The interdependence of policy and practice

There would probably be widespread acceptance of the premise that practitioners derive their jobs as a result of policies about welfare and that implementation of these policies depends on those practitioners' resourcefulness. Yet the professional worlds of policy and practice are inhabited by brands of experts who develop specialisations and polish a language to protect their separate interests.

The maintenance of these separate worlds is disempowering. The intellectual lifeline between the two is constantly being turned off whereas a coherant relationship between policy and practice should provide a vigorous and stimulating supply of fresh air and other nutrients. That growth-enhancing supply should benefit both practitioners and the public.

Even though there are numerous arenas in which the design of policies and ways to implement them are matters of daily discussion, the following examination of the policy–practice or practice–policy relationship will be conducted with reference mostly to front-line practitioners. They are well placed to implement policies in the spirit as well as the letter of the law, and if need be to remould those policies with a view to achieving equity in the treatment of people and the distribution of resources. This responsibility for implementation provides the lens through which the relationship can be discerned.

Implementation occurs through interpretation and improvisation, hence the somewhat unexceptional point that policy and practice are interdependent. Yet the nature of that interdependence is not always apparent, not only because of interests in maintaining the separation but also as a result of the ways in which practice and policy are defined.

Practice, in the empowerment tradition, is the implementation of the responsibility to effect access to services and participation in making decisions. Such practice will not always be conducted in association with the intended beneficiaries of services, but the focus on access and participation addresses some aspects of people's powerlessness. Such concepts are also familiar to the architects of social policies who couch their objectives in these terms.

Social policy is the articulation of values and rules which deal with relationships between government and governed, between agencies and their staff and between professionals and laypeople. For example, mental health policies which aim to empty psychiatric hospitals and support ex-patients in their return to the outside world are attempting to replace one set of relationships, in an institution, with another set of relationships, in a community.

An agency which provides services to people with a disability may never include disabled people on its board of management. They are kept in their place, at the bottom of a hierarchy. Alternatively, the agency might determine that at least half of the board of management should be people with a disability. Whatever else happens as a result of this change, the relationships between the people with a disability and the practitioners will never be entirely the same again. The change in structure will affect practitioners who in turn are accountable to a board of management and could thus affect deliberations about policy.

At this point defenders of the exclusiveness of policy and practice will be edgy but it is not being claimed that policy is always practice and that practice, via the opportunity to implement objectives, is always policy. Not only are there areas of public policy, such as economics and defence which have nothing directly to do with social workers, there are also areas of social policies which are not immediately concerned with the process of implementation. The design of a family policy to introduce a means test for family allowances and subsidised child-care for single parent mothers on low incomes, has to address the questions of political justification and the availability of financial and other resources before it is announced. Some professionals such as policy analysts and specific civil servants will undertake that task. The policy, for which they are calculating the resources and the probable consequences, does not involve social workers, in part because questions about implementation may have not been raised and when they are, may involve other kinds of workers.

Three issues in the policy–practice relationship

Reference to the disempowering features in which the policy–practice relationship has been construed also suggests an ideal state of affairs in which writers and practitioners, educators and activists acknowledge what they share and harness common ideas and objectives. The essence of this ideal would be a community of interests and scholarship, a fascination with debate and experiment in the tasks of acting equitably and efficiently to influence and implement polices. Such implementation would facilitate access to services and increase people's involvement in decision making. Attention to access and participation should ensure that equity is both a part of the process and a characteristic of the outcome.

Specific features of this ideal state include exchange and reciprocity between practitioners and other policy makers and between educators of various descriptions. However, the maintenance of those separate worlds indicates obstacles to achieving the ideal. In any conceptualisation of the policy–practice relationship, the factors which contribute to separation cannot be ignored, though it is the failure to make connections, not the physical separation, which is the essence of the problem. The failure to make connections solidifies the two world views.

The significance of the politics of relationships is a second feature in the policy–practice debate. Fiercely competitive relationships in different contexts show links between policy and practice, not least because these controversies may occur between different people with similar responsibilities who work under one roof.

A third feature depicts conditions under which policy and practice merge to become virtually indistinguishable. The use of discretion by front-line practitioners is germane to the discovery of when and how policy may become practice and vice versa.

This preamble sets the terms of discussion about the nature of the policy–practice relationship. Separation, interdependence and synonymity are three ways of describing that relationship and some characteristics of the contexts in which various personnel meet. In each of those contexts, the exercise of power provides a criterion to view the subject matter and to indicate how the subjects, such as prospective clients and practitioners are treated. That perspective begins with the disempowering conditions of the separation game.

The separation game

The subject matter of policy and practice has been separated by a division of labour in social welfare agencies and in academic institutions which has been described as the difference between knowing and acting (Rein and White 1981 p. 620). Staff responsible for developing policies, or others who teach about policy, possess knowledge derived from research findings but may have seldom trespassed into the acting sphere carrying with them answers to the question of how is this to be done. The values and knowledge used in practice are generated in the context of practice and not from the expectations of policy makers (Rein and White 1981 p. 621).

With regard to the planning and delivery of services for the elderly, Graycar has agreed with this distinction between knowing and acting and has bemoaned the consequences of its existence. He identified a hierarchical relationship between policy and practice and observed that 'many of those who plan don't know much about delivering and many of those who deliver do so without effective communication with those who plan' (Graycar 1989 p.3). In his experience the gap between policy makers, planners and front-line practitioners is often filled with anger and frustration. The policy makers are saying 'these practitioners don't know nothing' and the practitioners are saying 'these policy makers are living on another planet' (Graycar 1989 p.11).

Academics may do little to overcome this gulf. Teachers with similar responsibilities may be located in the same department but to all intents and purposes are miles apart. They play a separation game as though the rules of science and research govern the roles in one arena and improvisation through intuition prevails in the other. One activity, uncontaminated by the responsibility to examine implementation, can claim prestige. The other, which includes the evaluation of students in field work, is practical, characterised by the unpredictable, messy business of influencing what people do, and therefore less prestigious, at least, in the eyes of the tertiary institution which values the production of publications and research grants. It has seldom known how to put a value on other activities such as the development of an initiative to give greater access to educationally disadvantaged groups, or the project which sees previous consumers being employed to work alongside those experienced staff who hitherto have operated in some kind of professional isolation.

Such initiatives and experiments could change educational cultures and if so, what is prestigious would be redefined. In educational institutions, and within health, welfare and judicial contexts, that is a challenge for the last years of the twentieth century. Within those years lies an opportunity to create joint endeavours in which excellence can be married to equity, in which some classroom activity is replaced by the project which involves and rewards many parties.

To make the point about the fascination with prestige hindering the growth of a community of interests and the development of theoretical coherence, I shall describe some stereotypes. For example, a derisory description of practice teaching as soft, may confirm some policy specialists' conviction that their discipline is concerned with hard data and measurable outcomes which would impress scientists in other parts of the college or university. The so-called practice staff collude by engaging in meetings peppered with contemplation of individual cases, whether of student or clients, and so, by inference, confirm an image of having little to do with policy. It is possible too that a disproportionate number of the policy teachers are men and most of the practice staff are women. A division of labour between policy analysts and social work practitioners is maintained by gender differences, as well as by claims about the scientific merit of the allegedly different activities.

The idea of practice being low in an academic pecking order survives in some educators' feeling of fatalism. 'What else do you expect?', 'It's always been this way, they don't really understand', 'Our job is labour intensive, we have to work all year round, we seldom have the privilege of going away to do research', 'When the students are in trouble they come to us and we have to sort out the problems.'

These expressions of resentment also illustrate relationships of subordination and compliance. The energy consumed in such activity does not allow space to consider the disempowering consequences of the separation game.

Inviting different personnel to consider what they have in common, by conceptualising policy in practice terms and vice versa would be one way to end the separation. For example, Schorr has shown how policy can be redefined to challenge the orderly but separate views of teachers and practitioners (Schorr 1985). In his terms, even the choice of a model of explanation of behaviour amounted to a policy: controversies between diagnostic and functional schools, or the choice of an 'eco-systems model' influenced the questions which practitioners asked and the questions they did not ask.

Schorr contended that the structure of agency practice could also be construed as 'policy'. 'Structure' include the location of agency offices, cultural traditions, such as the way secretaries were treated and the way they treated others. Practitioners could be encouraged to listen with a policy-sensitive ear; an individual's reference to loneliness could be connected to a policy of deinstitutionalisation; an elderly person's expression of anxiety about the future might reflect an absence of coordinated plans for subsidied health care and sheltered accommodation.

A definition of policy which includes models of explanation of behaviour, the structure of agencies and the way staff listen, addresses questions about the politics of relationship and the exercise of power. In assessing client interests, the policy-sensitive practitioner will also be evaluating the appropriateness of agency culture and routines. Any redirection of agency practices based on that assessment may have immediate consequences for individual empowerment and well-being. Schorr argued that such agency changes could effect more immediate improvement in the quality of individuals' everyday lives than the large-scale government initiatives more commonly regarded as policy. This point will be pursued in subsequent discussion of front-line practitioners' use of discretion.

Interdependence through relationships

Definitions of policy and practice which include references to agency structure provide examples with which practitioners can identify because they see them as related to their experience. Such non-threatening examples facilitate learning. By contrast, if an area of knowledge is regarded as difficult because it is only within the reach of specialists, it remains mysterious and threatening.

The value attributed to an understanding of relationships is usually taken for granted as an indispensable feature of good practice, and in the empowerment tradition, the significance of examining the exercise of power in different contexts and the politics of relationships in most encounters, has been emphasised. Yet this emphasis on the politics of relationships as a hub of practice also suggests how policies are made and has been a focus for research questions into the priorities of bureaucrats at different levels of bureaucracies. It would be surprising to discover that front-line practitioners were concerned with 'acting' through relationships but their superiors had been programmed so that their values, biases, alliances and animosities had virtually been removed. Neutered and neutral they acted to ensure that policy making was not affected by the usual human foibles.

That may be a rational view but it is inaccurate. Senior public servants and politicians do acknowledge their adherence to hierarchies, roles and administrative rituals but only a consensus view of policy would construe the outcome of their deliberations in those terms. Accounts of policy making which highlight the conflict in relationships between key people dismiss the consensus perspective which nurtures a view of policy as emanating from an orderly system.

A British text which examined how social polices were introduced and modified, documented tensions between partisans who were trying to clarify choices and effect changes. Key partisans included private citizens, pressure groups, the mass media and the political parties (Hall et al 1975). Others to depict policy making as the product of conflicting relationships between partisans have described such a process as muddling through or incrementalist (Lindblom 1959), interactionist (Higgins 1978) and as subjectivist (Edwards 1981). The latter author described this approach to the study of policy process as giving primacy 'to the perceptions, social constructions, assumptions or "world views" of key actors in the policy making process and which have their foundation in phenomenological and ethno-methodological sociology and, more particularly, in the notion of grounded theory' (Edwards 1981 p.290).

Of course, uncovering the motives and weighing the actions of key people produces a predictable picture of jockeying for position and influence, but it also highlights the importance of relationships in context and therefore addresses matters of conflict as well as co-operation.

In his portrait of policy making as a study in the art of judgment, Vickers spoke of the constraints which affected the behaviour of key people (Vickers 1965). The rules and procedures of government bureaucracies were imposed limitations, but they were not inflexible. They were open to interpretation. The ability to interpret brought into play another set of constraints, the self-imposed rules, which include the refusal to take risks and the reluctance to exercise initiative, and the lack of skills inherent in the inability to make good judgments.

The policy-making process, in Vickers terms, emerged as a conflict between the officially imposed and the self-set limitations. The rules which were applied were the product of relationships characterised by struggles over values as to who ought to be contacted, what documents should be read, which information might be withheld and what decisions must be taken. In such bargaining over values, moral, social, legal and political relationships became grist to the mill of the civil servants and the other partisans. The goals they sought, said Vickers, were changes in their relations or in their opportunities for relating, 'but the bulk of our activity consists in the relating itself' (Vickers 1965 p.33).

Almost ten years later, in a study of how public expenditure decisions were made in the highest echelons of British government, Heclo and Wildavsky also highlighted the need to penetrate relationships in the 'work-a-day world of these political men'. Policies emerged not only from powerful men bargaining but also from 'puzzled men learning to adapt their minds and operations to emerging problems' (Heclo and Wildavsky 1974 p.xix).

That adaptation occurred in relationships which required the participants to work hard to create and maintain trust. To do so they made calculations about precedents and about individuals' reputations, and they weighed their deliberations in relation to the political and economic climate of the times. Decisions about shifts of money from one program to another and massive expenditure of public money in general, were explained in the context of a community of relationships, a product of forever moving customs, rules and incentives. Heclo and Wildavsky concluded,

> However quaint and faintly ridiculous the idea may seem at first, the
> distinguishing feature of the Treasury men who deal with public
> spending is not their intellect or their ideas but their emotions. Their
> supreme skill lies in personal relations. When they succeed where others
> fail, it is because they recognize the overriding importance of giving and
> getting a personal commitment (Heclo and Wildavsky 1974 p.xiv).

Uses of discretion

It may seem a quantum leap from Whitehall to the responsibilities of front-line practitioners, yet in the arrangements for implementing policies, the high-ranking officials depend on subordinates. An examination of this dependence has produced a distinction between policies and the arrangements for their implementation but under some circumstances, these 'arrangements' have a considerable influence on the character of policy (Hill 1983). When implementation depends on the improvisation skills of the front-line practitioner, policy and practice merge and could be seen as virtually synonymous. For example, the people who are the target of policies may only experience the behaviour of the one social worker whom they happen to meet. Although practitioners may deny that their work is a matter of policy, the public will not see it that way. The attitude and efficiency of that front-line practitioner may be the only visible sign of policy in operation.

The views of the intended beneficiaries are an indispensable source of information about the implementation of policies and a reminder that the principle of accountability to the interests of such people is an important measure of the front-line practitioners' use of discretion.

Conditions which contribute to the use of discretion can be traced by considering the strategic position of front-line personnel and the characteristics of social welfare policies which make inevitable some freedom to act. An account of some uses of discretion in pursuit of the objectives of empowerment will follow the discussion of these conditions.

In a seminal paper on the sources of power of lower participants in complex organisations, Mechanic (1962) demonstrated how senior executives were dependent on front-line personnel and powerless to check their actions. Those personnel, such as nurses or doctors, prison guards or social workers and community workers met daily with patients, inmates and members of the public and usually did so at some distance from senior staff in a central bureaucracy. In addition to their invisibility to the centre, such personnel also possessed expertise without which organisations could not provide a service.

The specific efforts and special interests of front-line personnel are also a source of influence. For example, nurses in a psychiatric hospital may make special efforts to facilitate a policy of deinstitutionalisation, but they could display complete indifference to that policy or take more specific action to hinder its implementation.

Mechanic also described how the attractiveness of 'lower participants' provided them with leverage within an agency and in a wider network. This is not a tactless reference to physical appearance but a repetition of emphasis on the personal attributes used in the exercise of interactive and political skills. The person perceived as credible in the eyes of peers, superiors and subordinates would be attractive to them and therefore stand a better chance of obtaining resources than a colleague who was not perceived as credible. The front-line practitioner's ability to build coalitions among colleagues with common interests has already been discussed with reference to skills in formal and informal negotiations. In that discussion, the point was also made that the successful pursuit of an objective usually required staff to know the rules of the organisation. This 'knowing the rules' is doubly important with regard to social welfare policies because they may give specific discretionary power to some practitioners, or are written in such an ambiguous way that the person who checks the small print and reads between the lines may thereby take full advantage of their already strategically convenient position.

Compared to services which are to be uniformly distributed, such as cash entitlement from social security, personal social services rely on discretion because their form of help is open to interpretation and will have to be 'individually applied' (Sainsbury 1977 p.xvi). Such application requires practitioners to walk the tightrope between exercising care and control, between taking responsibilities themselves and fostering those responsibilities in others. With reference to services such as child-care and probation, Sainsbury described this balancing in terms of 'liberating people from socially generated distress and with controlling some aspects of their social circumstances and behaviour' (Sainsbury 1977 p.3).

The ambiguity of some social welfare legislation provides opportunities for interpretation, a not surprising outcome given that the goals of such policies are the product of unexceptional compromise between partisans. For example, policies to consolidate the interests of the family or to promote the welfare of the community, leave unanswered the questions of what is meant by family and community and who is to achieve those goals and how.

Ambiguity in the small print provides one opportunity for discretion. An absence of resources creates another. If specific objectives are accompanied by few resources, improvisation is inevitable. For example, faced with a policy of mandatory notification of suspected cases of child abuse, social workers may be swamped with referrals and so develop their own rules to deal with excessive and unexpected demand.

Responsibility for housing all ex-psychiatric patients who have been currently registered as homeless, throws social workers in a community health centre back on their ability to improvise. Without that quality, which includes skills in informal negotiation, the policy goals would exist only as a statement of good intentions.

It is not merely that policies are written ambiguously or that their intentions are specific but the resources few, the suspicion also exists that governments are ambivalent about their legislation and the policies of which they boast. Perhaps no one really intended all the mandatory notifications of suspected child abuse to be investigated or all the ex-psychiatric patients to be properly rehoused. In cultures which worship the value of citizens being financially independent, some ambivalence over policies dealing with dependence is to be expected. Front-line personnel can use discretion to manage this ambivalence but how they do so will affect ordinary citizens' own freedom to act. Discretion to enhance this freedom, by pursuing the objectives of empowerment, will involve some appreciation of the relationship between the liberty of some people and the control of others.

Discretion and empowerment

In the face of the moralism and other controls so beloved of some promoters of economic rationalism, the freedom to exercise discretion is a privilege. Even when totalitarian governments have been replaced by reformist ones, the drift towards regulation and the stifling of initiative in organisations survives. Therefore the maintenance of the opportunity to exercise freedom, to interpret, choose and act should be greeted with enthusiasm and guarded carefully. Its exercise is a quality of intellectual energy showing people striving to make the most of their talents and engage with others in the process. This is the potential in discretionary power that Bertrand Russell had in mind when he spoke of a human being's 'freedom to examine, to criticize, to know and in his imagination to create' (Russell 1918 p.46). He later spoke of such creative energy and the wish to be effective as being 'beneficent if they can find the right outlet, and harmful if not — like steam, which can either drive the train or bust the boiler' (Russell 1977 p.95).

In describing the freedom to act to enhance other people's liberty Isaiah Berlin reported his own aspirations: 'I wish above all to be conscious of myself as a thinking, willing, active being, bearing responsibility for his own ideas and purposes' (Berlin 1958 p.16).

This statement emerged from a description of two concepts of liberty and the associated distinction between negative and positive freedom. Negative freedom included unnecessary interference in the lives of the others and would be equivalent to some aspects of social workers' negative use of discretion to implement policies. For example, there is an influential school of thought which argues that discretion can easily lead to a diminution of people's freedom and should therefore be curtailed. Proponents of the welfare rights movement have argued against discretionary powers on the grounds that they can be unfairly discriminatory, that they are almost always exercised arbitrarily and that the staff who exercise power in this way are not accountable for their actions. An alleged solution to such arbitrary, discriminatory and non-accountable use of discretion is to ensure that this room to manoeuvre is replaced by legal prescription. That argument presupposes a clear dividing line between the application of law and the exercise of discretion and that the law will always be implemented in the spirit which the statute writers had in mind.

This law-better-than-discretion argument is flawed for other reasons. The law has to use constraining words to fit the myriad circumstances of human life. It thereby obliges all to conform to the words which describe ideas which get transformed into legislation.

Even if there seems to be nothing wrong with the law, you might not want to trust the lawyers. Their interests in supporting clients or pursuing causes might have little in common with the principles of fair treatment which characterise the goals of empowerment. In the area of welfare rights, Titmuss warned that if this area of social welfare activity became the preserve of legal experts, the public as well as social workers would become further disempowered (Titmuss 1971). Once specific experts cornered an area of activity, the non-experts became dependent. Numerous areas of law are already inaccessible to ordinary citizens. Converting bargaining over welfare into another legal preserve would enhance the power of the legal profession but leave untouched the predicament of welfare claimants.

However, the negative use of discretion by practitioners occurs when practitioners do not intervene as well as when they do. Action which impedes access to information, a sin of omission rather than commission, hinders people's chances of acting in their own interests. For example, documentation of the experiences of families caring for a severely handicapped child showed that the existence of an allowance to which they were entitled was unknown to a majority of parents (Rees and Emerson 1985). This lack of information persisted, for years in some cases, even though the families had met with doctors, social workers and community health nurses, each of whom could have given information about the entitlement. Even though this had not been their deliberate intention, the professionals had kept the potential beneficiaries uninformed.

The professional who plays the role of expert by keeping people at arm's length, never sharing, always making decisions with little consultation, is also using discretion negatively. So too is the professional who interprets every policy according to agency interests, who colludes with a legacy of practice which ensures that clients come last (Stanton 1973).

In the implementation of policies with a view to achieving the goals of empowerment, the distinction between positive and negative freedom and positive and negative discretion may not be as simple as it sounds. The judgment required to implement some social welfare policies has characteristics of the balancing act or tightrope walk referred to earlier.

Intervention in the lives of families suspected of abusing a child appears at first sight to interfere with freedom of all the family members. The social worker seems to be exercising unnecessary control. On second consideration, a judgment about the way the practitioner uses discretion is not that simple. The freedom of several family members, of the parents and all the children is at stake. The use of discretion may be negative in the eyes of one party but positive from the perspective of another, and at this point we ought to immerse ourselves in the predicament of the hard-pressed practitioner who is trying to be fair and act responsibly.

Empowerment through good policy making

The manner in which accountability for the implementation of policies can bolster empowerment will be depicted with regard to each of the several steps in a particular area of work. This illustration could be regarded as merely showing what most observers would assume to be good practice. It is the supplementing of the idea of good practice with the responsibility for good policy making that should enable practitioners to perceive their role in more imaginative terms. They could contribute to long-term planning about policy goals by documenting information about current consequences of policies and they could use the practice–policy concept to assess their conduct of immediate cases.

Illustration of practice being empowering if it also addresses policy considerations will refer to the predicament of families with a severely handicapped child. They are entitled to various benefits but are unaware of their entitlement and of the criteria used in their administration.

Almost any other group of people whose quality of life may be affected by the terms of reference of social policies might also be discussed: ethnic minorities who are newly arrived migrants, single parents for whom new family assistance packages have just been introduced, young people who have just been severely disabled in car accidents, parolees newly released from prison or the residents of old people's homes. Where the objective of the practitioner is to increase access to information and services, and participation in making decisions, the list of examples is almost infinite. For the current purpose we will stick with families with a severely handicapped child and spell out the use of discretion in a process which has much in common with the phases of change described in chapter 7.

Discovering themes   Practitioners do not immediately rush in with a view to discovering whether families have taken up their entitlement to apply for a child disability allowance. It is more important to discover their accounts of the meaning of their child's disability and to consider the connotation of policy-oriented notions such as 'care and attention for the child'.

Providing information about entitlement   Information can be given so that the parents of these children appreciate the purpose of the policy and realise that no stigma is attached to acceptance of help. The mere provision of a pamphlet is unlikely to be empowering. Careful discussion of the terms, 'disabled child' and evidence of need for 'care and attention substantially more than the care and attention needed by a child of the same age who does not have such a disability', can involve the parents in the process of translating policy into practice.

Facilitating participation in decisions   The process by which a family's eligibility is determined should not be entirely in the hands of officials such as social security personnel and doctors of various descriptions. The parents have a right to know who is involved in the decision-making process, how these professionals view the family's application and what criteria they use to come to conclusions.

Although the family members are not sitting as judge and jury to reach a verdict about their own interests, they should know that what they say and write is part of the policy process. Their awareness of themselves as political actors as well as private citizens will enhance their chances of influencing the implementation of policies.

The management of conflict and controversy Assume that the parents of this child have been judged ineligible for the benefit. The policy process does not end there. They have a right of appeal, though that may sound daunting if the unwritten motto of their lives has been to keep themselves to themselves and never to disagree openly with authority. The social workers support the parents by enabling them to realise that the appeal process is as much a part of policy as the application for the benefit.

Policy is often redesigned on appeal. The accumulation of information about the merits of the policy in operation depends in part on the challenge, conflict and controversy that is part of appeal. The practitioner becomes better informed by participating in such controversy, in particular because it evaluates the use of discretion.

Towards political identity A last step in this process may also be a first. The family can be told that freedom of information legislation entitles them to the case records which contain evidence of the professionals' judgments. Families may not regard such information as important during first meetings, but when controversy over appeal for a benefit has become a central topic in their exchanges with the social worker, they are probably ready to exercise their rights under freedom of information and prepared to read adverse comments about themselves. They have become aware of the politics involved and the policy process in operation. They accept that this affects them. They can play an advocacy if not an adversarial role. They too can use discretion to enhance freedom. The policy–practice relationship is expressed in their words and illustrated by their actions.

17 Towards economic literacy

It has just been argued that students and practitioners can achieve coherence, and thereby power, through their understanding and handling of the policy—practice relationship. A similar coherence can be attained by an understanding of the links between social work tasks and economic policies.

How should the staff of human service organisations, mostly untutored in formal economic theory, respond to current economic programs and policies? For example, simple equations for complex problems, as in disdain for the value of investment in the public sector and respect for the ability of market forces to achieve efficiency are characteristics of a school of economics called rational. The ideology and language of such rationalism dominates current political and economic thought; in the face of that domination it is imperative that practitioners develop their responsibility towards vulnerable groups of people by becoming economically literate.

The need for the development of an economic literacy for social work is a response to two major forces which affect educators, practitioners, clients and the general public. The first is the dominant influence of this particular brand of economics. The second is the assumption that social, behavioural and political issues are to be formulated and remedied according to that dominant economic thinking.

In the United States, former President Ronald Reagan justified huge cuts in taxes on the rich on the grounds that this would have a trickle down effect on economic growth but he also ensured that some industries, such as weapons manufacture, would thrive and human services such as those to people of colour would decline (Centre for Popular Economics 1986).

In Britain, Mrs Thatcher defended her economic rationalist policies before the General Assembly of the Church of Scotland where she produced a Christian justification for individualist effort to obtain wealth, even if that meant an increase in social and economic inequality (*Guardian* May 1988).

In Australia, the Senior Executive Service of the federal bureaucracy contains a majority of staff with degrees in a particular school of economics, or in business administration and accounting. A majority of those staff show little belief in the value of social welfare provision but great faith in the achievements which can be attained by deregulating financial and capital markets (Pusey 1988; Pusey 1991).

The creed of the rationalists, especially their emphasis on the freedom of market forces to achieve a healthy economy contains little room for dissenters. To raise alternative views is to be dismissed as wet. To emphasise the value of services for dependent people who do not appear to be contributing to economic growth is to risk being regarded as soft and to invite more cutbacks on those allegedly unproductive services and people.

By insisting that the use of their language and values is the way to conduct analysis, the proponents of economic rationalism have set the terms for debate about psychological and cultural issues in contemporary life. Alternative values and views are strangled by aggressive managers, appointed to put their mentors' policies into effect. How do educators and practitioners respond?

Social work educators' and practitioners' fascination for the concept of empowerment and the theories which are derived from it may appear at first sight to be the expression of a latest fashion. Even if it is that, it is also, at least in part, a response to the sense of powerlessness generated by the undue influence of economic rationalism on contemporary life and thought. One implication of this premise is that any theory about empowerment should reflect an economic literacy which exposes the values of economic rationalism and provides a view of welfare that not only focuses on powerless people but does so in a language which describes the quality of their lives with reference to values, benefits and costs. Economic literacy involves the demystification of economists' claims, by refusing to be overawed by their forecasts, by insisting that projections about a country's welfare should include social and economic statements about the impact of policies on people's lives. That economic literacy will articulate the different meanings of costs and benefits and the different ways of judging efficiency and productivity.

There are alternatives to this approach. One is to remain ignorant yet continue to flail against the tentacles of an intolerant and all-embracing school of thought. That response guarantees powerlessness. Another alternative is to train in the dominant brand of economics or to pursue a training in the degree of Master of Business Administration (MBA). That route might provide a semblance of wisdom, the prospect of power and a guarantee of lucrative remuneration. But it is a form of cooptation which looks like a surrender to the cliché 'if you cannot beat them, join them'.

The task of demystifying some economists' projections and prescriptions will be facilitated by the opportunity and responsibility to examine the relationship of policy to practice and practice to policy. The opportunity comes with linking the claims of policy makers to the consequences for ordinary people. The responsibility lies in challenging economists' habits of dealing in aggregates and abstractions, and economic journalists' explanations via a maze of metaphors, such as taking hands off the throttle in order to enable the economy to take off, priming pumps and pulling levers, entering uncharted waters and flying blind. If the metaphors confuse, then reference can be made to apparently scientific symbols such as the J curve, with its attraction of proving that things will get worse before they get better, or presumably they will get better before they get worse.

In these metaphors, aggregates and abstractions, the idea that people matter in economics is lost. Yet the disparity between the daily concerns of poor people and the language of economists is difficult to ignore. Greater productivity in economic rationalist terms is effected by economising, as in contributing to unemployment by cutbacks in public sector welfare. Even such a liberal economist as Kenneth Boulding in (for him) an offguard moment has said 'there is no aspect of human life in which economising is not important. Beauty is a matter of right proportion . . . ' (Boulding 1984 p.13–14). For poor people, however, economising contains no elements of beauty. Jenny Trethewey's study of changes in income and expenditure among low income families in Melbourne (1986) shows that food was the discretionary cost area in which they could cut back in times of difficulty. A single parent with one dependent child, living on a widow's pension, was described as economising on food to pay fuel and power bills. 'She invariably cuts down on food when she has bills to pay. She likes her son to eat as well as possible. She gives him bread while she makes do with dry biscuits' (Trethewey 1986 p.29).

These families were making their own economic impact statements, addressing a topic which seldom interests economic commentators, namely the link between private lives and the trends affected by economic policies.

It is not only that economists seldom address the stark reality of poor people's lives, but also that social workers often ignore the evaluation of policies, even though the evidence may stare them in the face. They do not make sufficiently explicit the connections between examples of individual powerlessness and the economic constraints which distinguish one social class from another. Those 'constraints' are often described as being internalised so that people blame themselves, or as in *Living Poorly in America*, 'they do not learn that they can overcome obstacles, they learn that obstacles are insurmountable' (Beeghley 1983).

This focus on poor people's apparently self-defeating behaviour is not inappropriate if links are also made to the economic sources of their powerlessness. In spite of considerable odds, poor people often make the links which elude professionals. In the study of changes in income and expenditure among poor families, a 40-year-old mother said, 'I would get out of this house if I could. My kids would not get so many colds if they had a better diet and a damp free bedroom. I suppose if years ago I'd got qualifications, I wouldn't be doing this lousy job.'

Another respondent explained, 'I can see that I've got to get out of this hole: better job, better money, better house, lower rent. Jeesus, you must be joking' (Trethewey 1986 personal interviews).

In these insights some self-blaming occurs but not without reference to economic trends. They linked their low self-esteem to things they could not afford for their children. They talked about the huge financial and social costs of unemployment. People did say, 'it's my lack of education and training which is keeping me out of the labour market.' They also said, 'I'm spending too high a proportion of my income on rent.'

This language of survival provides cues for educators and practitioners. Poor mothers and fathers struggle to make sense of their lives, in part by demystifying the language of experts who claim to have their welfare in mind. The development of practitioners' own economic literacy also depends on demystification, with three specific objectives in mind: avoiding powerlessness through lack of information, constructing their own social and economic impact statements and becoming familiar with issues of power passed off as economics (Figure 17.1).

In perusing these objectives, I have identified four topics which are affected by economic policies and which overlap to provide the context of most current practice. Those four topics are household economies, claims about the merits of the public and private sectors of welfare and the relationship between agency budgets and case management.

Figure 17.1 Demystification and enlightenment

Areas affecting the activities of social workers	Some implications for economic literacy
Household economies	Distinctions between control and management: class differences
Public sector welfare expenditure	Merits and demerits of the welfare state; defining mixed economy
Private sector welfare expenditure	Questioning the idea of free markets; costing the voluntary sector; defining mixed economy
Agency budgeting and case management	Combining financial and other professional considerations; budget control affecting client and staff well being; differentiating costs

Each topic provides an opportunity to question and demystify, starting with the connection between the management of private lives and the meaning of the term economy.

Household economies

If the term economy is linked to its original association with household management, it is apparent that most people possess some understanding of economics. Pemberton identified the origin of the term economy from the Greek *oikos* meaning house or clan and *nomos* meaning law—hence *oikonomia* or 'oeconomy' meaning the art of household management or the wise government of the family, but she also showed that economics had come on a long journey, 'a continued extension away from the basic household meaning' (Pemberton 1988 p.191).

On the assumption that a dimension of household management and control is the availability and distribution of money, an understanding of household economics is germane to understanding politics and power. In a study of the distribution of income within households, Edwards referred to control as the decision-making functions of any enterprise and management as the implementation functions, the carrying out of decisions already made elsewhere (Edwards 1984).

The exercise of control over a household's finances is a significant indication of power even though the controller might not make many purchasing decisions. The management of a household budget could be evidence merely of powerlessness; showing the person who manages as seldom knowing how much money is available but always having to show ingenuity, perhaps managing to do more and more with less and less.

This differentiation of power according to the distinction between control and management varies along class lines. Edwards concluded that finances generally were more likely to be controlled by husbands than by wives, and that the lower the family income the greater the probability that the wife would have the management responsibilities. When a wife's income was high she was likely to exercise control and management, but in the lives of wives who had almost no financial role, that key form of powerlessness was compounded by other considerations. Such wives were less educated than their husbands, they had young children and felt guilty about spending on themselves (Edwards 1984).

Steps towards economic literacy among different practitioners could be facilitated by impact statements depicting the quality of families' lives and the effect of social and economic policies. That 'quality' and 'effect' will seldom be evenly distributed. Edwards explained, 'Because financial resources are neither shared nor pooled equitably within some households, policies should relate more to individuals and less to family units

... criteria of efficiency and to a lesser extent simplicity suggest the superiority of the system which treated tax payers as individuals' (Edwards 1984 p.135).

Although it is tempting to become absorbed in family economics, and more high quality work on family economics would help, critical discourse demands an examination of wider issues, such as the merits of the private and public sectors of welfare. These topics represent the contexts in which social work is practised and they expose the arguments that commitment of public money to welfare is unproductive and that support for private rather than public services would be in everyone's best interests.

Demystifying the public sector

In these tugs of war about the merits of different types of ownership and control of services, the public sector is usually treated as synonymous with the welfare state, 'in which citizens have rights or entitlements to goods and services independently of rights based on property or income' (Collard 1984 p.176).

The stereotype of the welfare state as 'wet' because it is committed to unproductive, incentive-lacking services cannot be answered merely along the moral plane of claims about altruism, redistribution and equity. These values may be indispensable as guidelines and statements of overall objectives but left as they are, they remain as abstract as the arguments about greater productivity, and the alleged incentives of the market place. An examination of the disparaging welfare state stereotype can include some acknowledgment of the complexities of welfare state activities, and an answer to the charges that services were wasteful, created dependency and were seldom innovative.

The point needs to be made by social workers that assessing the effects of the transfer of money through social security is a very different form of evaluation than any assessment of the effects of social work. In the latter there are many more actors, different forms of service and a variety of criteria for assessing effectiveness, including several ways of listing the meaning of costs.

An appraisal of the social and economic costs of unemployment shows the complexity of the relationship between investment in public sector services and the outcomes. The costs for the long-term unemployed include poor self-image, loss of skills, depression, increased prospect of marriage breakdown and negative effects on their children's welfare and education. Community costs include an increase in mental illness and delinquency and extra demands on public housing, health and welfare services. The costs to the government are substantial in terms of income foregone through revenue lost, estimated by Dixon in Australia as 'an amount equal to some 40% to 50% of the private income lost through unemployment' (Dixon 1988 p.14).

The argument that public sector services such as job creation programs are wasteful, merits challenge from a reverse thesis, namely that waste is explained by the economic costs of not having the public sector. Dixon concluded,

> Policies involving major reductions in government payments and services, especially those directed to assisting the unemployed, should be viewed with skepticism. Apart from the adverse social impact of such policies, there is a real possibility that they could add to unemployment. The resulting cost of such increased unemployment would frustrate the achievement of the very budgetary objectives given as the raison d'etre of the expenditure cuts (Dixon 1988 p.24).

The argument that the welfare state is wasteful has usually been mounted on evidence that universal services did not alleviate social inequality and on claims that they were unnecessary because the private sector services would have achieved better economic results (Saunders 1988). On the one hand economists have said that welfare state services amounted to a leaky bucket (Okun 1975) because the poor did not receive what was intended for them and on the other it has been argued that public sector services have made significant contributions to a country's economy by operating as an irrigation system (Korpi 1985).

Judgments about the merits of either argument will depend on the social and economic impact of services on government as well as on individuals, in particular with reference to questions about equity and efficiency (Barr 1987). The responsibility for defining those terms cannot be left merely to economists. For example, the point needs to be made that the welfare state has had a positive effect on economic morality because there is no self-interest in protecting the rights of weak minorities (Collard 1984).

A second charge against the public sector, concerns its undermining of individual initiative. In this charge what appears at first sight to be a debate about economics, turns out to be a controversy over values in which numbers are only one part of the language.

In the United States, critics such as Guilder (1978) and Murray (1984) claimed that welfare state services produced dependency and undermined character. The provision of aid to families with dependent children allegedly produced a climate in which men lost sense of personal responsibility and young women developed unrealistic expectations. In similar vein these critics argued that public housing contributed to a culture in which householders had few opportunities to acquire autonomy and independence, and in black ghetto areas welfare systems maintained a culture of disadvantage.

Social workers can address the culture-bound nature of these arguments (which make no reference to the value of services provided in developing countries) yet the economic rationalists' arguments about the demerits of the welfare state will persist, as in claims that the private sector is enterprising, while the public sector is stifled by bureaucracy. The evidence on this is inconclusive. Kramer, for example, compared the role of voluntary and state organisations for the physically and mentally handicapped in Britain, the USA, the Netherlands and Israel. He judged the state sector innovative and the voluntary sector conservative (Kramer 1981).

The demystification of stereotypes about the benefits of the public and private sectors in welfare will rest largely on showing that these claims are based on a false distinction. In several countries, state and private sectors are mutually dependent and integrated to a point where they are often indistinguishable. Private provision of health, education and welfare depends on heavy commitment of public subsidies and confounds any economic theory that there is a free market in services, let alone a free market in labour. It is more appropriate to talk about a mixed economy of welfare. The public services can and do impose charges and thus exhibit some of the characteristics of private organisations, raising revenue and revealing consumer preferences. 'Moreover,' says Glennester, 'the largest part of social spending takes the form of cash given to individuals in welfare benefits that they spend on privately produced goods and services. We already have a mixed economy of welfare' (Glennester 1985 p.6).

Demystifying the private sector

In spite of the evidence of this mixed economy, the argument persists that if individuals are left to pursue their interests under far less government regulation and direction, economic welfare for all members of society can be maximised. This commitment to the value of the invisible hand of the market is attributed to one of the founding fathers of classical economics, Adam Smith. Yet his commitment to the means of free trade does not match the values of today's rationalists who justify their activities in his name. Smith advocated a tax on wealth. He regarded the division of labour for the single-minded pursuit of profit as likely to produce mentally and politically crippled human beings and his nineteenth century followers supported various forms of government intervention including government schools, 'to even out the economic playing field' (Boulding 1984).

Claims that the private sector is efficient because it calls on voluntary initiative are simple and politically influential. The revival of charities and the claims about the ability of other private organisations to deliver a service free of bureaucracy and relatively free of costs represent a convenient stereotype. People in many countries do spend a large proportion of their time (as much as 40%) doing unpaid work (Szalai 1972) and an impressive percentage of people (14% identified by the Wolfenden Committee survey in Britain) undertake work with an identifiable voluntary organisation (Wolfenden 1978). Such work adds to the quality of life of a society as a whole and revives the emphasis on altruism, a significant feature of any society concerned with equity and reciprocity. But such voluntary work is not free.

Social and economic impact statements compiled by social workers and social researchers can put a price on the value of voluntary work, and should differentiate between one set of costs and another. In a study of the costs of the care of the handicapped elderly, care of the elderly person took on average 4½ hours per day and in a quarter of all cases 6 hours per day. The major proportion of that time was given by women who, if they had been in paid work could have earned an estimated £4000 per year (Nissell and Bonnerjea 1982).

To the opportunity costs associated with these women's lost employment could be added the social costs of caring, such as restrictions on leisure, the material costs of transport, food and accommodation and the emotional costs of strain, stress, guilt and fatigue (Knapp 1984 ch. 8). By documenting these quality-of-life-criteria, management and front-line staff can make decisions about the costs and likely impact of one form of service compared to another. To do so will probably depend on their being responsible for a form of case management which will include accountability for a budget.

Agency budgeting and case management

A comparison of experiences in household and agency management suggest that the absence of a responsibility for the expenditure of money amounts to powerlessness. In both contexts, social workers' understanding of the politics and economics of resource distribution can be enhanced if their job descriptions include budget responsibilities.

If front-line staff do not have some control over financial decisions, they may be held accountable for the way they spend their time but they will have no means of putting a realistic price on their different activities. If such practitioners can weigh the financial with other costs in their case management, not only will their morale be high but it also seems that they will make the most appropriate decisions on behalf of others.

This conclusion is demonstrated by a significant longitudinal study of comunity care of the elderly in Kent (Davies and Challis 1986). The power and responsibility of the social workers were enhanced by their knowing what financial resources they had and by becoming experienced in combining professional and financial judgments. They did so in relation to a group of elderly people, of whom one third would have died within a year, one third would have been admitted to hospital for long-term care and one third would have continued to live in their own homes. Special conditions facilitated the social workers' tasks in caring for this vulnerable group and in making the link between their financial decisions and the social consequences. These conditions included small caseloads, a clear responsibility for case management and a budget from which they could draw to mobilise community resources or pay for agency services.

The outcome of combining financial and management control produced lasting benefits for the elderly people, for their informal carers and for the practitioners. The social workers' case management decisions halved the probability of the elderly people entering an institution and doubled the probability of their continuing to live in their own home. The elderly persons' perceptions of their well-being were improved along with the quality of care as seen by them and an external assessor.

The verdict on cost savings and cost benefits is salutary for those who find it difficult to put a figure on the benefits of the personal social services. The social workers not only achieved high standard care for the elderly but also reduced the average cost to the social services without imposing additional costs on the health services. In addition, they relieved the informal carers of the psychic costs of caring and they appeared to reduce the social opportunity costs of care.

These relationships between budgets and verdicts, financial decisions and case outcomes show a greater sophistication than a simple cost benefit analysis. The researchers showed the social workers differentiating between social opportunity, capital and personal living costs. They were able to make statements about impact because they were accountable for costs.

The alternative is to delegate the responsibility for assessment of efficiency and cost-effectiveness to outside experts. Their value-for-money criteria will probably oversimplify the different costs and result in reports which are regarded with suspicion or are ignored.

The ability to combine economic with other judgments is not enhanced by the deployment of outside experts, a process which creates dependency for practitioners and that sense of powerlessness inherent in believing that money matters should remain a mystery beyond their ken. As with mothers trying to do their best in the management of households, practitioners' economic understanding is not likely to advance if they are asked to make decisions without participating in deliberations over budgets. When management and control functions are combined, the self-respect and well-being of practitioners are enhanced and beneficial services are available to the public.

Implications

In the tradition of empowerment, analysis is facilitated by action which practitioners and educators can refine in the light of experience. Some specific steps to develop economic literacy can be numbered as tasks for practitioners, students and teachers.

1 To consider the management of households as the equivalent of small economies, to be analysed in terms of: the impact of wider social and economic policies; the distribution of resources within households; and the class differences in the management and control of money.

2 To consider the mixed economy of welfare and to avoid being trapped into either/or debates in which the public sector is pitted against the private and vice versa.

3 To keep a record of the different costs to the practitioners of conducting social work: the social and psychological as well as the financial costs.

4 To work with vulnerable individuals and families to assess the impact of costs on items such as child-care, transport, rents, mortgages and food.

5 To develop some familiarity with arguments about the allegedly cheap or free costs and benefits of using volunteers. The assessment of such costs and benefits becomes an important dimension of the evaluation of social work and a task which can be developed in professional supervision.

6 To insist that all social workers' contract and job descriptions should include a reference to the budget which funds their work and a description of accountability for the specific moneys entailed in running a project or managing a case load. Team members' accountability for a small budget should be matched by agency accountants' accountability for overall operating costs, hence the next proposal.

7 To conduct regular meetings with the agency accountants or controllers of budgets. In those meetings, the financial managers are held accountable for their deliberations and decisions. Social workers' economic literacy goes hand in hand with administrators becoming familiar with the different costs and benefits of practice.

These specific points emerge from a general premise about economics and social work. Front-line staff can take advantage of their strategic positions. To do so they should not be overawed let alone intimidated by accountants' or economists' claims. Much of economics is about a struggle for power to control resources, a process which social workers witness and in which they participate.

The process of achieving power starts with those who feel uninformed refusing to remain mystified by those who control apparently technical information and who like to make moral prescriptions for the behaviour of others. That refusal has to be followed by more than a protest. It involves the development of a literacy in politics and economics, in policy and thereby in practice. As with any groups trying to comprehend their rights and redefine their opportunities, practitioners learn language in association with others who have also felt mystified by events which affected them, but about which they felt ill informed. As they respond to economists' claims, keep records about the costs and benefits of their own work and the human impact of economic policies, these practitioners will develop their own economic literacy.

18 Coherence

The past decade has seen leading politicians and their advisers absorbed by a brand of economic thinking which defined as rational the provision of huge financial rewards to those who were already extremely well paid. The same school of thought described financial commitments to health, welfare and justice as irrational, as though those areas of public life had little to contribute to national wealth or well-being.

The economic policies which have been influenced by this rationalist ideology have been offensive. The concern with deregulating markets and with treating health, education and welfare, including shelter, as though they were just economic commodities has produced enormous personal and social costs. Policies which deny unemployment benefit, which cut back on employment training programs, which prune investment in public education, abolish educational programs in prisons or limit the supply of affordable homes, have been unjust in two significant respects. They have been manifestly unfair. That unfairness has been compounded by other policies which gave cash in the hand to increase the standard of living of those who already appeared to have more than enough.

These 'rational' policies have been justified as likely to motivate individuals and increase economic productivity, yet they have been economically stupid as well as socially unjust. The organisation which is seen by all its staff as fair in its conduct of relationships and in its distribution of rewards is likely to be a productive place to work. By the same token, the society which struggles for justice in the treatment of all its citizens is investing in equity. It is therefore less likely to have to spend time or money to cover the costs of excessive ill-health, or to pay for security and penal systems to protect the gains of the successful from the increasing anger of those who feel they have been defined as second-class citizens.

In different countries, the homeless living in cardboard accommodation in and around the centres of cities bear witness to some consequences of economic rationalism. No society and no welfare organisation should be waiting for a violent backlash from people with little hope before it reasserts the values of justice. In this regard, the goals of empowerment include immediate individual aspirations and the wider goals of social justice.

Harnessing energy for common aspirations will involve using the ideas of all those who have addressed issues of injustice. Poets, novelists, social scientists, clients, volunteers as well as workers, social policy analysts, other social work educators, some lawyers and theologians can all contribute. The coherence that comes from joining people and ideas provides an experience of being creative, and without the confidence generated by such activity, the task of tackling issues of social injustice may seem overwhelming.

The achievements of the women's movement and the proposals for liberation spelled out by writers and practitioners following different feminist perspectives, provide one significant source of political literacy about justice. To that movement and their literacy, the values and the language of the peace and environmental movements can be joined. The task may not be easy, even though it looks as though their methods and goals—to protect the vulnerable, to conduct political analysis and to achieve solidarity—are the same.

Reasserting the values of justice and opposing the fascination with greed will not be helped by spending valuable time and energy protecting professional interests and identity. For example, community workers have been known to say they have nothing in common with social workers. Some of the latter have claimed that they are very different from, or even better than welfare workers. Policy makers keep themselves apart from front-line staff. Researchers have had few means of communication with practitioners. Many managers have achieved an aura of their own, as though control is the major objective and economy the only criterion of evaluation.

The means of simultaneously addressing individual problems and social issues has been depicted in 'the promise of biography'. The proposition is that in the telling of a story, people see themselves in a different light, and from having others listen to their account of their experiences they build a political analysis and identity. That analysis is facilitated by seeing politics as an activity concerned as much with relationships in the household as with competition over scarce resources in an organisation. Politics includes participation in decision making at local levels as well as politicians' deliberations over the choice of national priorities.

Achieving power is as much about humility as about political skills and appropriate assertiveness. It requires a willingness to listen and to learn from those who may have been ignored: men from women, practitioners from clients, managers from front-line personnel and educators from students.

Europeans and North Americans can respond generously and unselfishly to the ideas and values of people who do not live in their hemispheres and dominant white populations will gain from the time taken to hear what indigenous peoples have to say. For example, Australian Aborigines have a strong tradition of storytelling and they want the chance to speak the truth about the future of their children. They know that racist attitudes are an impediment to their children's development. They are not against competition between tribal and other groups but they show a disdain for efforts aimed only at individual material advantage. They value social networks as crucial features in their lives and they know about the pleasure in solidarity to preserve cultural and spiritual values. Yet their anxiety about the future of their children concerns the disapperance of their language, land, values and customs and a consequent cultural and spiritual deprivation.

In describing the promise of biography, key concepts have come in clusters of three. Researchers have identified three orientations to solving problems: passive; vulnerable but resource-seeking; and circumspect and problem-solving. Empowerment occurs in movement from a passive to a problem-solving orientation and in that change, at least three stages, education, solidarity and confidence in taking action are traversed. These stages apply as much to partnership between people in groups as to the negotiations which occur in individual, face to face encounters.

At risk of being accused of replacing one holy trinity of casework, groupwork and community work with another, it is important to repeat the distinction between very different ways of exercising power. One-dimensional power is the way of economic rationalism or of any other powerful interests which want others to comply with their views. The compliance of powerless people who have learned to be passive is as much an example of the one-dimensional exercise of power as are the assumptions of professionals that they know best and are therefore entitled to protect and enhance their interests. The constricting, one-dimensional exercise of power is apparent in familiar, everyday transactions as well as in examples of extreme authoritarianism.

Two-dimensional exercise of power appears to hold out a promise of reform. The client groups who were vulnerable but tried to be assertive, albeit without much success, were at least saying 'there must be a better way for us to be treated' and 'there must be some opportunity for us to make our own decisions'.

Within agencies there are always reformers keen to talk about a pluralist conception of interests, who want to address questions of hidden conflict as well as those observable controversies which make it to official agendas. The questions they raise are within the parameters of officially sanctioned rules and policies. The wisdom of these policies is challenged and their fairness questioned, but changes are made in style not substance. To the powerless outsiders, this two-dimensional exercise of power sounds promising but the outcome is business as usual.

A three-dimensional exercise of power provides the intellectual and political means of attaining even the most unambitious but nevertheless valuable objectives. The glimmer of such an exercise of power was apparent in the response of those groups who in solving their own problems enabled others to do likewise. Such thinking and practice was evident in the thoughts and activities of those who said, 'let's suspend our assumptions about the convenient ways of defining problems and producing solutions. Let's identify what would be the equitable solution and test the limits of what is possible to achieve it.'

Those ideas, 'testing the limits' and 'what is possible' do not mean that practitioners or volunteers ignore group concerns or the immediate pressure from colleagues in order to be seen to do something. It does mean that in addressing those concerns and pressures, they use their skills and political literacy to articulate alternatives. They do so out of a concern with equity and because it is socially, spiritually, artistically and politically stimulating to do so. The alternative consumes energy to defend old shibboleths and maintain familiar practices.

By contributing to their own and others' welfare, any citizen can achieve a creative sense of power, and this outcome can be linked to the events which caught international attention at the end of 1989 and the beginning of 1990. The goals and the connotation of policies of *glasnost* and *perestroika* produced conditions for breaking down borders and barriers in Eastern Europe. The release of Nelson Mandela after 27 years in prison at least produced optimism for change in an authoritarian, unjust system which had seemed unyielding.

The promise heralded in those initial changes can be kept only through a constant and widening dialogue about welfare through justice. That is a collective goal, but one which also requires different tasks to address competing priorities and thus an awareness of the politics of practice in any context. It is a goal to inspire practitioners and other citizens who want the chance to experience self-fulfilment because they have acquired skills to contribute in diverse ways to equity in relationships, and thereby to economic and social agendas which are ennobling and empowering.

References

1 The issues

Bitensky, R. (1973) 'The Influence of Political Power in Determining the Theoretical Development of Social Work' in *Journal of Social Policy,* vol. 2 no. 2 pp. 119–30

Hegar, R. (1989) 'Empowerment-based Practice with Children' in *Social Service Review,* Sept. pp. 372–383

Hirayama, H. and Cetingok, M. (1988) 'Empowerment: social work approach for Asian immigrants' in *Social Casework* vol. 69 no. 1 Jan.

McDermott, C. (1989) 'Empowering the elderly nursing home resident: the residential rights campaign' in *Social Work,* vol. 34 no. 2, March

Pinderhughes, E. (1983) 'Empowerment for our clients and ourselves' in *Social Casework* 64

Reisch, M., Wencour, S. and Sherman, W. (1983) 'Empowerment; conscientization and animation as core social work skills' in *Social Development Issues* vol. 5, Summer and Fall pp. 108–120.

Rose, S.M. and Black, B.L. (1985) *Advocacy and Empowerment* London: Routledge

Safilios-Rothschild, C. (1976) 'Disabled persons' self-definitions and their implications for rehabilitation' in Albrecht, G.L. (ed.) *The Sociology of Physical Disability and Rehabilitation* Univ. of Pittsburgh Press, pp. 39–56

Setterlund, D. (1988) 'Gender: a Neglected Dimension in Social Work with Elderly Women' in Chamberlain, E. (ed.) *Change and Continuity in Australian Social Work* Melbourne: Longman Cheshire

Smith M. (1975) *When I Say No I Feel Guilty* New York: Dial Press

Solomon, B. (1976) *Black Empowerment* New York: Columbia

2 The prospectus

Berger, P. (1974) *Pyramids of Sacrifice: Political Ethics and Social Change* New York: Basic Books

Berlin, S. and Kravetz, D. (1981) 'Women As Victims: A Feminist Social Work Perspective' in *Social Work* Nov pp. 447–449

Brook, E. and Davis, A. (1985) *Women, The Family and Social Work* London: Tavistock

Brown, C. (1988) 'Empowerment, Disadvantage and Social Justice as Guiding Themes for Social Work and Social Work Education' in Chamberlain, E. (ed.) *Change and Continuity in Australian Social Work* Melbourne: Longman Cheshire

Collins, B. (1986) 'Defining Feminist Social Work' in *Social Work* vol. 31, no. 3 pp 214–219

Curthoys, A. (1988) *For and Against Feminism* Sydney: Allen and Unwin
De Hoyos, G. (1989) 'Person in Environment: A Tri-Level Practice Model' in *Social Casework*, vol. 70. no. 2 March pp. 131–138
De Hoyos, G. and Jensen, C. (1985) 'The Systems Approach in American Social Work' in *Social Casework* 66 August pp. 490–97
Entwistle, H. (1979) *Antonio Gramsci, Conservative Schooling for Radical Politics* London: Routledge & Kegan Paul
Freire, P. (1972) *Pedagogy of the Oppressed* London: Penguin
Fromm, E. (1960) *Fear of Freedom* London: Routledge & Kegan Paul
Hegar, R. (1989) 'Empowerment-based Practice with Children' in *Social Service Review* Sept. pp. 372–383
Lukes, S. (1974) *Power, a radical view* London: Macmillan
McCleod, E. and Dominelli, C. (1982) 'The Personal and the Apolitical: feminism and moving beyond the integrated methods approach' in Bailey, R. and Lee, P. (eds) *Theory and Practice in Social Work* Oxford: Blackwell
Marquand, D. (1988) *The Unprincipled Society* London: Fontana Press
Milgram, S. (1974) *Obedience and Authority* London: Tavistock
Nes, J. and Iadicola, P. (1989) 'Toward a Definition of Feminist Social Work: a comparison of liberal, radical and socialist models' in *Social Work* Jan. pp. 12–21
Pinderhughes, E. (1983) 'Empowerment for our clients and ourselves' in *Social Casework* 64
Rapoport, J. (1981) 'In Praise of Paradox: A Social Policy of Empowerment over Prevention' in *American Journal of Community Psychology* 9 (Jan–Feb) pp. 1–25
Rubinoff, L. (1968) *The Pornography of Power* Chicago: Quadrangle Books
Setterlund, D. (1988) 'Gender: a Neglected Dimension in Social Work with Elderly Women' in Chamberlain, E. (ed.) *Change and Continuity in Australian Social Work* Melbourne: Longman Cheshire
Solomon, B. (1987) 'Empowerment: social work in oppressed communities' in *Journal of Social Work Practice* May pp. 79–91
Wearing, B. (1986) 'Feminist Theory and Social Work' in ch. 2 of Marchant, H. and Wearing, B. (eds) *Gender Reclaimed, Women in Social Work* Sydney: Hale and Iremonger

3 The promise of biography

Alinsky, S. (1969) *Reveille for Radicals* New York: Random House
Allott, R. (ed.) *The Penguin Book of Contemporary Verse,* Harmondsworth: Penguin 1959
Bayles, T. (1988) in Tokenism or Justice, proceedings of a seminar on land rights for Aboriginals, Univ. of Sydney, Nov.
Carr, D. (1986) *Time, Narrative and History* Bloomington: Indiana Press
Cox, D.R. (1989) *Welfare Practice in a Multicultural Society* New York: Prentice Hall
Department of Immigration and Ethnic Affairs (1984) *About migrant women* Canberra: AGPS
Desai, M. (1988) in Social Work and Social Change, Eileen Younghusband address to IASSW conference Vienna, July
England H. (1986) *Social Work as Art* London: Allen & Unwin
Freire, P. (1972) *Pedagogy of the Oppressed* London: Penguin

Gilbert, K. (ed.) (1988) *Inside Black Australia* Melbourne: Penguin

Hamilton I. (ed.) (1973) *Robert Frost Selected Poems* Harmondsworth: Penguin

Hawley, J. (1988) 'A poet dreams of freedom' *Sydney Morning Herald* 10 Sept. p. 71

Harlow, B. (1987) *Resistance Literature* London: Methuen

Hirayama, H. and Cetingok, M. (1988) 'Empowerment: social work approach for Asian immigrants' in *Social Casework* vol. 69, no. 1

Lerner, M. (1986) *Surplus Powerlessness* Oakland: Institute for Labor & Mental Health

McCaughey, J. and Chew, W. (1977) 'The family study' in McCaughey, J., Shaver, S. and Ferber, H. *Who cares?* Melbourne: Sun Books

McCaughey J. (1987) *A Bit of a Struggle* Melbourne: McPhee Gribble/Penguin

McGoldrick, M., Pearce, J.K. and Giordano, J. (eds) (1982) *Ethnicity and Family Therapy* New York: Guildford Press

Marris, P. (1974) *Loss and Change* London: Routledge and Kegan Paul

Moore, M. (1981) *The Complete Poems of Marianne Moore* Harmondsworth: Penguin

Nolan, C. (1988) *Under the Eye of the Clock* London: Pan

O'Connor, I, and Sweetapple, O. (1988) *Children in Justice* Melbourne: Longman Cheshire

Perlman, R. (1975) *Consumers and the Social Services* New York: John Wiley

Pinderhughes, E. (1983) 'Empowerment for Our Clients and for Ourselves' in *Social Casework* vol. 64, no. 6 June

Pinderhughes, E. (1982) 'Family Functioning of Afro-Americans' in *Social Work* 27, pp. 91–6

Rees, S. (1978) *Social Work Face to Face* London: Edward Arnold

Rees, S. and Emerson, A. (1984) *Disabled Children, Disabling Practices* Sydney: SWRC Monographs, no. 37

Rees, S. and Wallace, A. (1982) *Verdicts on Social Work,* London: Edward Arnold

Rose, S.M. and Black, B.L. (1985) *Advocacy and Empowerment* London: Routledge

Silverman, P.R. (1969), The Client Who Drops Out: a study of Spoiled Helping Relationships, PhD thesis, The Florence Heller Graduate School for Advanced Studies in Social Welfare, Brandeis University

Solomon, B. (1976) *Black Empowerment* New York: Columbia

Yevtushenko, Y. (1989) 'The Heart Went On Strike' first published in *Pravda* on 17 December 1989, Translation by Tania Shurova published in *Sydney Morning Herald,* 20 December 1989, p. 9

4   Power, politics and language

Altman, D. (1980) 'Redefining Politics' in ch. 4 of Altman, D. *Rehearsals for Change* Melbourne: Fontana Press

Anspach, R. (1983) 'From Stigma to Identity Politics' in *Journal of Social Science and Medicine* vol. 13, pp. 765–775

Banfield, E. (1961) *Political influence* New York: Free Press

Bell, D. (1979) *The Cultural Contradictions of Capitalism* 2nd edn, London: Heinemann

Blun, M.R. (1982) 'Animation and Social Work' in *New themes in social work education,* Proceedings of the XVI International Congress of Schools of Social Work, The Hague: pp. 60–71

Clarke, K.B. (1974) *Pathos of Power* New York: Harper & Row

Cohen, S. (1975) 'It's alright for you to talk' in Bailey, R. and Brake, M. (eds) *Radical Social Work* London: Edward Arnold

Collins, B.G. (1986) 'Defining feminist social work' in *Social Work* vol. 31, no. 3 pp. 214–219

Edelman, M. (1974) 'The Political Language of the Helping Professions' in *Politics and Society* vol. 4, no. 3, pp. 285–310

Etzioni, A. (1988) *The Moral Dimension: Toward a New Economics* New York and London: The Free Press

Foucault, M. (1974) 'The Order of Discourse' in Shapiro, M. (ed.) *Language and Politics* New York: N.Y. Univ. Press

—— (1986) 'Disciplinary Power and Subjection' in Lukes, S. (ed.) *Power* Oxford: Basil Blackwell

French, J. and Raven, B. (1959) 'The Basis of Social Power' in Cartwright, D. (ed.) *Studies in Social Power* Ann Arbor, Michigan: Research Centre for Group Dynamics, Institute for Social Research, University of Michigan, pp.150–165

Freire, P. (1972) *Pedagogy of the Oppressed* London: Penguin

Fromm, E. (1960) *Fear of Freedom* London: Routledge & Kegan Paul

Gilbert, L.A. (1980) 'Feminist Therapy' in Bradsky, A. and Hare-Mustin, R. *Women and Psychotherapy* New York: Guildford Press

Halleck, S.M. (1971) *The Politics of Therapy* New York: Harper and Row

Kotker, Z. (1980) 'The "Feminine" Behaviour of Powerless People' in *Savvy* March, pp. 36–42

Knott, B. (1974) 'Social Work as Symbolic Interaction' in *British Journal of Social Work* vol. 4, no. 1 pp. 5–12

Laing, R.D. (1967) *The Politics of Experience* London: Penguin

Lee, L. (1983) 'The Social Worker in the Political Environment of the School System' in *Social Work* vol. 28, no. 4, July

Lerner, M. (1979) 'Surplus Powerlessness' in *Journal of Social Policy* Jan/Feb pp. 19–27

—— (1986) *Surplus Powerlessness* Oakland: Institute for Labor and Mental Health

Lukes, S. (1974) *Power: a Radical View* London: Macmillan

Marquand, D. (1988) *The Unprincipled Society* London: Fontana Press

Murdach, A. (1982) 'A Political Perspective in Problem Solving' in *Social Work* Sept. pp. 417–421

Offe, C. (1984) *Contradictions of the Welfare State* London: Hutchinson

Rees, S. and Gibbons, L. (1986) *A Brutal Game* Sydney: Angus and Robertson

Reisch, M., Wencour, S. and Sherman, W. (1983) 'Empowerment; conscientization and animation as core social work skills' in *Social Development Issues* vol. 5 Summer & Fall, pp. 108–120

Rose, S.M. and Black, B.L. (1985) *Advocacy and Empowerment* Boston: Routledge

Solomon, B. (1987) 'Empowerment: social work in oppressed communities' in *Journal of Social Work Practice*

Usher, J. (1988), Taking Control: A study of low income families, Master's Thesis, University of Sydney, unpublished

5   Economic rationalism and social justice

Beilharz, P. and Watts, R. (1986) 'The Discourse of Labourism' in *Arena* no. 77 pp. 96—109

Beilharz, P. (1987) 'Reading Politics: Social Theory and Social Policy' in *Australian and New Zealand Journal of Sociology* November

—— (1989) 'Social Democracy and Social Justice' in *Australian and New Zealand Journal of Sociology* August

Beveridge, W. (1944) *Full Employment in a Free Society* London: Allen & Unwin

Brandt, W. (1980) *North-South*: The report of the independent commission on international development issues London: Pan Books

Brown, B. (1989) 'Our Common Purpose' in *Habitat Australia* August

Burton, C. (1989) 'Equal Employment Opportunity Policies' in *The Coming Out Show* ABC Radio, March 20

Centre for Popular Economics (1986) *Economic Report of the People* Boston: South End Press

Considine, M. (1988a) 'The Costs of Increased Control: Corporate Management and Australian Community Organizations' in *Australian Social Work* Sept. vol. 41, no. 3 pp. 17–25

—— (1988b) 'New Zealand's Lange Government and the Labour Tradition: Straying or Staying' in *Thesis Eleven*, no. 20, pp. 51–69

Crozier, M. (1964) *The Bureaucratic Phenomenon* London: Tavistock

Ehrlich, P., Holm, R. and Brown, I. (1976) *Biology and Society* New York: McGraw Hill

Galbraith, J. (1970) *The Affluent Society* London: Penguin 2nd ed.

Guardian (1988) 'Creation of wealth seen as a Christian duty' 12 May

Handa, M. (1985) 'Gandhi and Marx: An outline of Two Paradigms' in Ch XIII in Diwan, R. and Lutz, M. *Essays in Gandhian Economics* New Delhi: Gandhi Peace Foundation

Home Office/DHSS (1987) Report on the Practice of Supervision of Juvenile Offenders, London: HMSO

Ife, J. (1989), Can social work survive the decline of the welfare state? paper to Australian Association of Social Workers National Conference, July

Lekachman, R. (1982) *Greed is Not Enough: Reaganomics* New York: Pantheon Books

Lerner, M. (1986) *Surplus Powerlessness* Oakland: Institute for Labor and Mental Health

Macy, J. (1983) *Despair and Personal Power in the Nuclear Age* Philadelphia: New Society Publishers

Marquand, D. (1988) *The Unprincipled Society, new demands and old politics* London: Fontana Press

Pusey, M. (1991) *Economic Rationalism in Canberra* London: Cambridge University Press

Schumacher, E. (1973) *Small is Beautiful* London: Bland and Briggs

Stretton, H. (1987) 'The Cult of Selfishness' in *Political Essays,* Melbourne: Georgian House, pp. 184–194

Tawney (1931) *Equality* London: Allen & Unwin

Thomas, T. (1988) 'Hegemony of the Resolute Approach' in *Social Work Today* 3 Nov.

Thurow, L. (1988) *The Zero-Sum Society* London: Penguin

Titmuss, R. (1958) 'The Social Division of Welfare: some reflections on the search for equity' in *Essays on the Welfare State* London: Allen & Unwin, pp. 34–55

Watts, R. (1987) *The Foundations of the National Welfare State* Sydney: Allen & Unwin

Yeatman, A. (1990) *Bureaucrats, Technocrats, Femocrats* Sydney: Allen & Unwin

6 Explaining objectives

Berlin, I. (1969) *Four Essays on Liberty* London: Oxford University Press

De Bono, E. (1979) *The Happiness Purpose* London: Penguin

Goodin, R.E. (1985) *Protecting the Vulnerable* Chicago: University of Chicago Press

—— (1989) 'Markets: Their Morals and Ours' in *Social Justice in Australia*, Australian Society Supplement, Dec/Jan 88/89 pp. 7–9

Hughes, R. (1988) *The Fatal Shore* London: Pan Books

Jones, K. (ed.) (1978) 'Equality and Equity' in *Issues in Social Policy* London: Routledge and Kegan Paul

Land, H. and Rose, H. (1985) 'Compulsory Altruism for Some or an Altruistic Society for All' in Bean, P., Ferris, J. and Whynes, D. (eds) *In Defence of Welfare* London: Tavistock Publications, pp. 74–96

Mill, J.S. (1848) *Principles of Political Economy* London: Parker and Son

Moreau, M. (1979) 'A Structural Approach to Social Work Practice' in *Canadian Journal of Social Work Education* vol. 51, pp. 78–94

Orwell, G. (1965) *1984* London: Penguin

Rawls, J. (1972) *A Theory of Justice* London: Clarendon Press

Rubinoff, L. (1967) *The Pornography of Power* Chicago: Quadrangle

Russell, B. (1977) *Authority and the Individual* London: Unwin Paperbacks

7 Developing theory

Bailey, R. and Brake, M. (eds) (1975) *Radical Social Work* London: Edward Arnold

Carew, R. (1979) 'The Place of Knowledge in Social Work Activity' in *British Journal of Social Work* 9, pp. 349–364

Cingolani, J. (1984) 'Social Conflict Perspective in Work with Involuntary Clients' in *Social Work* Sept./Oct.

Corrigan, P. and Leonard, P. (1978) *Social Work Practice Under Capitalism* London: Macmillan

Curnock, K. and Hardiker, P. (1979) *Towards Practice Theory* London: Routledge and Kegan Paul

Davies, M. (1985) *The Essential Social Worker* Aldershot: Gower

De Hoyos, G. and Jensen, C. (1985) 'The Systems Approach in American Social Work' in *Social Casework* 66, no. 8, pp. 490–497

Deglau, E. (1985) 'A Critique to Social Welfare Theories: The Culture of Poverty and Learned Helplessness' in *Catalyst* no. 19, pp. 31–35

Findlay, R. (1978) 'Critical Theory and Social Work Practice' in *Catalyst* no. 3, pp. 53–68

Galper, J. (1980) *Social Work Practice: A Radical Perspective* New Jersey: Prentice Hall

Glaser, B. and Strauss, A. (1967) *The Discovery of Grounded Theory* London: Weidenfeld and Nicholson

Hendricks-Mathews, M. (1982) 'The Battered Woman: Is She Ready for Help?' in *Social Casework* 63, no. 4, pp. 131–137

Howe, D. (1987) *An Introduction to Social Work Theory* Aldershot: Wildwood

Leacock, E. (1971) *The Culture of Poverty: A Critique* New York: Simon and Schuster

Leonard, P. (1975) 'Toward a Paradigm for Radical Practice' in Bailey, R. and Brake, M. *Radical Social Work* London: Edward Arnold

Lewin, O. (1965) *La Vida: A Puerto Rican Family in the Culture of Poverty* New York: Random House

Liffman, M. (1979) *Power for the Poor* Melbourne: Allen & Unwin

McIntyre, D. (1982) 'On the Possibility of Radical Casework' in *Contemporary Social Work Education* vol. 5, no. 3

Marchant, H. and Wearing, B. (eds) (1988) *Gender Reclaimed, Women in Social Work* Sydney: Hale & Iremonger

Moreau, M. (1979) 'A Structural Approach to Social Work Practice' in *The Canadian Journal of Social Work Education* vol. 6, no. 8 pp. 490–497

Prottas, J. (1979) *People-Processing: The Street-level Bureaucrat in Public Service Bureaucracies* Lexington, DC: Heath and Company

Satyamurti, C. (1981) *Occupational Survival* Oxford: Basil Blackwell

Seligman, M. (1975) *Helplessness: On Depression, Development and Death* San Francisco: W.H. Freeman

Simpkin, N. (1979) *Trapped Within Welfare: Surviving Social Work* London: Macmillan

Smid, G. and van Krieken, R. (1984) 'Notes on theory and practice in social work: a comparative view' in *British Journal of Social Work* 14, pp. 11–22

Thorpe, R. (1983) 'Street Level Bureaucracy in Australian Community Welfare', Unpublished paper, Univ. of Sydney

Walker, A. (1988) *Revolutionary Petunias* London: The Womens' Press

Walker, H. and Beaumont, B. (1981) *Probation Work: Critical Theory and Socialist Practice* Oxford: Basil Blackwell

Young, P. (1979) 'Foreword' to Curnock, R. and Hardiker, P. *Toward Practice Theory* London: Routledge and Kegan Paul

8   Steps in empowerment

Berger, P. (1974) *Pyramids of Sacrifice: Political Ethics and Social Change* New York: Basic Books

Birmingham Women and Social Work Group '81 (1985) 'Women and Social Work in Birmingham' in Brook, E. and Davis, A. (eds) *Women, the Family and Social Work* London: Tavistock

d'Apps, P. (1982) *Social Support Networks: A Critical review of models and findings* Melbourne: Institute of Family Studies

Edelman, M. (1974) 'The Political Language of the Helping Professions' in *Politics and Society* 4, no. 3, pp. 285–310

Freire, P. (1972) *Pedagogy of the Oppressed* London: Penguin

Lerner, M. (1979) 'Surplus Powerlessness' in *Journal of Social Policy* Jan–Feb

Rees, S and Gibbons, L. (1986) *A Brutal Game* Sydney: Angus and Robertson

Rees, S. (1988) 'Empowerment, Disability and Development: the political theory for contemporary social work', paper to International Congress of

Schools of Social Work, Vienna, July
Rose, S. and Black, B. (1985) *Advocacy and Empowerment* London: Routledge & Kegan Paul
Rosenfeld, J.M. (1989) *Emergence from Extreme Poverty* Paris: Science and Service Fourth World Publications
Usher, J. (1988) Taking Control, A study of low income families, Master's Thesis, University of Sydney, unpublished
Whittaker, J. and Garbarino, J. (eds) (1983) *Social Support Networks* New York: Aldine

9 Politics of change in organisations
Feldman, S.P. (1988) 'Secrecy, information and politics: an essay on organizational decision making' in *Human Relations* vol. 41, no. 1, pp. 73–90
Hall, A. (1974) *Point of Entry* London: Allen & Unwin
Hashenfeld, Y.L. (1980) 'Implementation of Change in Human Service Organizations: A political economy perspective' in *Social Service Review* vol. 54, no. 4, pp. 508–520
Konrad, G. (1975) *The Case Worker* London: Hutchinson
Kramer, M. (1974) *Reality Shock: why nurses leave nursing* St Louis, Missouri: C.V. Mosby Co.
Lerner, M. (1986) *Surplus Powerlessness* Oakland: Institute for Labor and Mental Health
Rees, S. (1984) 'Authoritarianism in State Bureaucracies: the Psychology of Bureaucratic Conformity' in Martin, B., Baker, C., Manwell, C. and Pugh, C. *Intellectual Suppression* Sydney: Angus & Robertson
Schutz, A. (1982) Collected papers vol. 1, *The Problem of Social Reality* The Hague: Martinus Nighoff
Sherman, W. and Wenocur, S. (1983) 'Empowering public welfare workers through mutual support' in *Social Work* Sept.–Oct. pp. 375–379
Solzhenitsyn, A. (1971) *Cancer Ward* London: Penguin
Vickers, G. (1965) *The Art of Judgement: a study of policy making* New York: Basic Books
Zimrim, H. (1984) 'Do Nothing But Do Something: the Effect of Human Contact with the Parent on Abusive Behaviour' in *British Journal of Social Work* 14, pp. 475–485

10 Interactive and political skills
Argyris, C. and Schon, D. (1978) *Organizational Learning* Reading, Mass: Addison-Wesley
Bardach, C. (1972) *The Skill Factor in Politics* Berkeley: Univ. of California Press
Coles, R. (1984) *William Carlos Williams, The Doctor Stories* New York: New Directions
Desai, M. (1985) *An Anthology of Short Stories for Social Work Education* Bombay: Tata Institute of Social Sciences
Frost, R. (1973) 'The road not taken', in Hamilton, I. (ed.) *Robert Frost Selected Poems* London: Penguin
Jordan, W. (1987) 'Counselling, advocacy and negotiation' in *British Journal of Social Work* vol. 17, pp. 135–146
Lee, L. (1983) 'The Social Worker in the Political Environment of the School System' in *Social Work* vol. 28, no. 4

Marquand, D. (1988) *The Unprincipled Society* London: Fontana Press

Mathews, G. (1982) 'Social Workers and Political Influence' in *Social Service Review* vol. 56, no. 4, pp. 616–628

Murdach, A. (1982) 'A Political Perspective in Problem Solving' in *Social Work* September, pp. 417–421

Rose, S.M. & Black, B.L. (1985) *Advocacy and Empowerment* London: Routledge & Kegan Paul

11   Evaluation and preparation

Alfrero, L. (1972) 'Conscientization and Social Work', New Themes in Social Work Education: Proceedings of the XVI International Congress of Schools of Social Work, The Hague, Netherlands, August 8–11

Blaxter, M. (1976) *The Meaning of Disability* London: Heinemann

O'Connor, I. and Sweetapple, P. (1988) *Children in Justice* Melbourne: Longman Cheshire

Pirsig, R.M. (1976) *Zen and the Art of Motorcycle Maintenance* London: Corgi

Rees, S. (1978) *Social Work Face to Face* London: Edward Arnold

Rees, S. and Wallace, A. (1982) *Social Work Face to Face* London: Edward Arnold

Sheldon, B. (1987) 'Implementing Findings from Social Work Effectiveness Research' in *British Journal of Social Work* 17, no. 6 pp. 573–586

12   Assessment

Denzin, N. (1978) 'Triangulation and the Doing of Sociology', ch. 4 in *The Research Act* New York: McGraw Hill

Scheff, T.J. (1969) 'Negotiating Reality: Notes on Power in the Assessment of Responsibility' in *Social Problems* vol. 16, no. 1

14   Formal negotiations

Cohen, H. (1988) *You Can Negotiate Anything* Sydney: Eden Paperbacks

Fisher, R. and Ury, W. (1987) *Getting to Yes* London: Arrow

Mathews, G. (1982) 'Social Workers and Political Influence' in *Social Service Review* vol. 56, no. 4, pp. 616–628

15   Advocacy

Cameron, D. and Talavera, E. (1976) 'An Advocacy Program for Spanish-speaking People' in *Social Casework* vol. 57, no. 7, pp. 427–431

Hepworth, D. and Larsen, J. (1982) *Direct Social Work Practice* Homewood, Illinois: The Dorsey Press

Panitch, A. (1974) 'Advocacy in Practice' in *Social Work* 19, pp. 326–332

Rees, S. and Gibbons, L. (1986) *A Brutal Game* Sydney: Angus and Robertson

Rose, S. and Black, B. (1985) *Advocacy and Empowerment* London: Routledge

16   The interdependence of policy and practice

Berlin, I. (1958) *Two Concepts of Liberty* Oxford: Oxford University Press

Edwards, J. (1981) 'Subjectivist Approaches to the Study of Social Policy Making' in *Journal of Social Policy* vol. 10, no. 3, p. 289–310

Graycar, A. (1989) 'From Policy to Practice', paper to National Social Policy Conference, University of New South Wales, Sydney, July

Hall, P., Land, H., Parker, R. and Webb, A. (1975) *Change, Choice and Conflict in Social Policy* London: Heinemann

Heclo, H. and Wildavsky, A. (1974) *The Private Government of Public Money* London: Macmillan

Higgins, J. (1978) *The Poverty Business* Oxford: Blackwell

Hill, M. (1978) *Understanding Social Policy* London: Basil Blackwell and Martin Robertson

Lindblom, C. (1959) 'The Science of Muddling Through' in *Public Administration Review* 19, pp. 79–88

Mechanic, D. (1962) 'Sources of Power of Lower Participation in Complex Organizations' in *Administrative Science Quarterly*, vol. 7, pp. 344–64

Rees, S. and Emerson, A. (1985) *Disabled Children, Disabling Practices* Sydney: SWRC Monographs, no. 35

Rein, M. and White, S. (1981) 'Knowledge for Practice', in Gilbert, N. and Specht, H. (eds) *Handbook of the Social Service*, Englewood Cliffs, New Jersey: Prentice Hall pp. 620–637

Russell, B (a) (1918) *Mysticism and Logic* New York: Anchor Books

Russell, B. (b) (1977) *Authority and the Individual* London: Unwin Paperbacks

Sainsbury, E. (1977) *The Personal Social Services* London: Pitman

Schorr, A. (1985) 'Professional Practice as Policy' in *Social Service Review*, June

Stanton, E. (1973) *Clients Come Last* Beverly Hills: Sage

Titmuss, R. (1971) 'Welfare Rights, Law and Discretion' in *Political Quarterly* vol. 42, no. 1

Vickers, G. (1985) *The Art of Judgement: A Study of Policy Making* New York: Basic Books

17 Towards economic literacy

Barr, N. (1987) *The Economics of the Welfare State* London: Weidenfeld and Nicholson

Beeghley, L. (1983) *Living poorly in America* New York: Praeger

Boulding, K. (ed.) (1984) *The Economics of Human Betterment* London: Macmillan

Centre for Popular Economics (1986) *Economic Report of the People* Boston: South End Press

Collard, D. (1978) 'The Welfare State, economics and morality', in Boulding, K.E. (ed.) *The Economics of Human Betterment* London: Macmillan, 1984

Davies, B. and Challis, D. (1986) *Matching Resources to Needs in Community Care* Aldershot: Gower

Dixon, D. (1988) *Unemployment: the economic and social costs* Melbourne: Brotherhood of St Laurence

Edwards, M. (1984) 'The distribution of income within households' in Broom, D. (ed.) *Unfinished Business* Sydney: Allen & Unwin

Glennester, H. (1985) *Paying for Welfare* Oxford: Basil Blackwell

Guilder, G. (1978) *Visible Man* New York: Basic Books

Guardian, (1988) 'Creation of wealth seen as Christian duty' p. 12

Knapp, M. (1984), *Economics of Social Care* London: Macmillan

Korpi, W. (1985) 'Economic growth and the welfare state: leaky bucket or irrigation system' in *European Sociological Review* May, pp. 97–118

Kramer, R. (1981) *Voluntary Agencies in the Welfare State* Berkeley: University of California Press

Murray, C. (1984) *Amercian Social Policy, 1950–1980* New York: Basic Books

Nissell, M. and Bonnerjea, L. (1982) *Family Care of Handicapped Elderly: Who Pays?* London: Policy Studies Institute

Okun, A. (1975) *Equality and Efficiency the Big Tradeoff* Washington, DC: The Brookings Institution

Pemberton, J. (1988) 'The End of Economic Rationalism' in *The Australian Quarterly* Winter, 1988, p. 188–199

Pusey, M. (1988) 'The outlook is dry' in *Australian Society,* July

—— (1991) *Economic Rationalism in Canberra* London: Cambridge University Press

Saunders, P. (1988) 'Efficiency, Equality and the Welfare State' pp. 13–30 in Saunders, P. and Jamrozik, A. (eds) *Community Services Policy: Economic and Social Implications* Sydney: SWRC Proceedings, no. 75

Simpson, D. (1984) 'Technology, Communications, Economics and Progress' in Boulding, K. (ed.) *The Economics of Human Betterment* London: Macmillan

Szalai, A. (ed.) (1972) *The Use of Time* The Hague: Mouton

Trethewey, J. (1986) *When the Pressure is Really On,* A study of changes in income and expenditure among low income families, Melbourne: Brotherhood of St Laurence

Wolfenden Committee (1978) *The Future of Voluntary Organizations* London: Croom Helm

Select bibliography

Alinsky, S. (1969) *Reveille for Radicals* New York: Random House

Altman, D. (1980) 'Redefining Politics' in Altman, D. *Rehearsals for Change* Melbourne: Fontana Press, ch. 4

Anspach, R. (1983) 'From Stigma to Identity Politics' in *Journal of Social Science and Medicine* vol. 13, pp. 765–775

Argyris, C. and Schon, D. (1978) *Organizational Learning* Reading, Mass: Addison-Wesley

Bailey, R. and Brake, M. (eds) (1975) *Radical Social Work* London: Edward Arnold

Bardach, C. (1972) *The Skill Factor in Politics* Berkeley: Univ. of California Press

Barr, N. (1967) *The Economics of the Welfare State* London: Weidenfeld and Nicholson

Beeghley, L. (1983) *Living Poorly in America* New York: Praeger

Beilharz, P. (1987) 'Reading Politics: Social Theory and Social Policy' in *Australian and New Zealand Journal of Sociology,* November

—— (1989) 'Social Democracy and Social Justice' in *Australian and New Zealand Journal of Sociology,* August

Bell, D. (1979) *The Cultural Contradictions of Capitalism* 2nd edn, London: Heinemann

Berger, P. (1974) *Pyramids of Sacrifice: Political Ethics and Social Change* New York: Basic Books

Berlin, I. (1969) *Four Essays on Liberty* London: Oxford University Press

Berlin, S. and Kravetz, D. (1981) 'Women As Victims: A Feminist Social Work Perspective' in *Social Work* Nov., pp. 447–449

Bitensky, R. (1973) 'The Influence of Political Power in Determining the Theoretical Development of Social Work' in *Journal of Social Policy* vol. 2 no. 2, pp. 119–30

Blaxter, M. (1976) *The Meaning of Disability* London: Heinemann

Boulding, K. (ed.) (1984) *The Economics of Human Betterment* London: Macmillan

Brandt, W. (1980) *North-South: The report of the Independent Commission on International Development Issues* London: Pan Books

Brook, E. and Davis, A. (1985) *Women, The Family and Social Work* London: Tavistock

Brown, C. (1988) 'Empowerment, Disadvantage and Social Justice as Guiding Themes for Social Work amd Social Work Education' in Chamberlain, E. (ed.) (1988) *Change and Continuity in Australian Social Work* Melbourne: Longman Cheshire

Cameron, D. and Talavera, E. (1976) 'An Advocacy Program for Spanish-speaking People' in *Social Casework* vol. 57, no. 7, pp. 427–431

Carr, D. (1986) *Time, Narrative and History* Bloomington: Indiana Press

Centre for Popular Economics (1986) *Economic Report of the People* Boston: South End Press

Cingolani, J. (1984) 'Social Conflict Perspective in Work with Involuntary Clients' in *Social Work* Sept./Oct.

Clark, K.B. (1974) *Pathos of Power* New York: Harper & Row

Cohen, H. (1988) *You Can Negotiate Anything* Sydney: Eden Paperbacks

Coles, R. (1984) *William Carlos Williams, The Doctor Stories* New York: New Directions

Collins, B. (1986) 'Defining Feminist Social Work' in *Social Work* vol. 31, no. 3 pp. 214–219

Curthoys, A. (1988) *For and Against Feminism* Sydney: Allen and Unwin

Considine, M. (1988) 'The Costs of Increased Control: Corporate Management and Australian Community Organizations' in *Australian Social Work* Sept. vol. 41, no. 3 pp. 17–25

—— (1988) 'New Zealand's Lange Government and the Labour Tradition: Straying or Staying' in *Thesis Eleven* no. 20, pp. 51–69

Corrigan, P. and Leonard, P. (1978) *Social Work Practice Under Capitalism* London: Macmillan

Cox, D. (1987) *Migration and Welfare* New York: Prentice Hall

—— (1989) *Welfare Practice in a Multicultural Society* New York: Prentice Hall

Curnock, K. and Hardiker, P. (1979) *Towards Practice Theory* London: Routledge and Kegan Paul

d'Apps, P. (1982) *Social Support Networks: A Critical review of models and findings* Melbourne: Institute of Family Studies

Davies, B. and Challis, D. (1986) *Matching Resources to Needs in Community Care* Aldershot: Gower

De Bono, E. (1979) *The Happiness Purpose* London: Penguin

De Hoyos, G. and Jensen, C. (1985) 'The Systems Approach in American Social Work' in *Social Casework* 66, no. 8, pp. 490–497

De Hoyos, G. (1989) 'Person in Environment: A Tri-Level Practice Model' in *Social Casework,* vol. 70, no. 2, March pp. 131–138

Deglau, E. (1985) 'A Critique of Social Welfare Theories: The Culture of Poverty and Learned Helplessness' in *Catalyst* no. 19, pp. 31–35

Dixon, D. (1988) *Unemployment: the economic and social costs* Melbourne: Brotherhood of St. Laurence

Edelman, M. (1974) 'The Political Language of the Helping Professions' in *Politics and Society* 4, no. 3, pp. 285–310

Edwards, J. (1981) 'Subjectivist Approaches to the Study of Social Policy Making' in *Journal of Social Policy* vol. 10, no. 3, pp. 289–310

Edwards, M. (1984) 'The distribution of income within households' in Broom, D. (ed.) *Unfinished Business* Sydney: Allen & Unwin

England H. (1986) *Social Work as Art* London: Allen & Unwin

Entwistle, H. (1979) *Antonio Gramsci, Conservative Schooling for Radical Politics* London: Routledge & Kegan Paul

Etzioni, A. (1988) *The Moral Dimension: Toward a New Economics* New York and London: The Free Press

Feldman, S.P. (1988) 'Secrecy, information and politics: an essay on organizational decision making' in *Human Relations* vol. 41, no. 1, pp. 73–90

Findlay, R. (1978) 'Critical theory and social work practice' in *Catalyst* no. 3, pp. 53–68

Fisher, R. and Ury, M. (1987) *Getting to Yes* London: Arrow

Foucault, M. (1979) *Power, Truth, Strategy* Sydney: Feral Publications

—— (1986) 'Disciplinary Power and Subjection' in Lukes, S. (ed.) *Power* Oxford: Basil Blackwell

Freire, P. (1972) *Pedagogy of the Oppressed* London: Penguin

Fromm, E. (1960) Fear of Freedom London: Routledge & Kegan Paul

—— (1971) *Man for Himself* London: Routledge & Kegan Paul

Galbraith, J. (1970) *The Affluent Society* 2nd edn, London: Penguin

Galper, J. (1980) *Social Work Practice: A Radical Perspective* New Jersey: Prentice Hall

Gilbert, K. (ed.) (1988) *Inside Black Australia* Melbourne: Penguin

Gilbert, N. and Specht, H. (eds) (1981) *Handbook of the Social Services* Englewood Cliffs, NJ: Prentice Hall

Glaser, B. and Strauss, A. (1967) *The Discovery of Grounded Theory* London: Weidenfeld and Nicholson

Glennester, H. (1985) *Paying for Welfare* Oxford: Basil Blackwell

Goodin, R.E. (1985) *Protecting the Vulnerable, a reanalysis of our social responsibilities,* Chicago: University of Chicago Press

—— (1989) 'Markets: Their Morals and Ours' in *Social Justice in Australia,* Australian Society Supplement, Dec/Jan 88/89 pp. 7–9

Hall, P., Land, H., Parker, R. and Webb, A. (eds) (1975) *Change, Choice and Conflict in Social Policy* London: Heinemann

Halleck, S.M. (1971) *The Politics of Therapy* New York: Harper and Row

Handa, M. (1985) 'Gandhi and Marx: An outline of Two Paradigms' in ch XIII in Diwan, R. and Lutz, M. *Essays in Gandhian Economics* New Delhi: Gandhi Peace Foundation

Harlow, B. (1987) *Resistance Literature* London: Methuen

Hashenfeld, Y.L. (1980) 'Implementation of Change in Human Service Organizations: A political economy perspective' in *Social Service Review* vol. 54, no. 4, pp. 508–520

Heclo, H. and Wildavsky, A. (1974) *The Private Government of Public Money* London: Macmillan

Hegar, R. (1989) 'Empowerment-based Practice with Children' in *Social Service Review* Sept. pp. 372–383

Hill, M. (1983) *Understanding Social Policy* London: Basil Blackwell and Martin Robertson

Hirayama, H. and Cetingok, M. (1988) 'Empowerment: Social Work Approach for Asian Immigrants' in *Social Casework* vol. 69, no. 1 Jan.

Howe, D. (1987) *An Introduction to Social Work Theory* Aldershot: Wildwood

Jones, K. (ed.) (1978) 'Equality and Equity' in *Issues in Social Policy* London: Routledge and Kegan Paul

Jordan, W. (1979) *Helping in Social Work* London: Routledge and Kegan Paul

—— (1987) 'Counselling, Advocacy and Negotiation' in *British Journal of Social Work* vol. 17, pp. 135–146

Knapp, M. (1984) *Economics of Social Care* London: Macmillan

Knott, B. (1974) 'Social Work as Symbolic Interaction' in *British Journal of Social Work* vol. 4, no. 1, pp. 5–12

Konrad, G. (1975) *The Case Worker* London: Hutchinson

Korpi, W. (1985) 'Economic growth and the welfare state: leaky bucket or irrigation system' in *European Sociological Review* May, pp. 97–118

Kotker, Z. (1980) 'The "Feminine" Behaviour of Powerless People' in *Savvy* March, pp. 36–42

Land, H. and Rose, H. (1985) 'Compulsory Altruism for Some or an Altruistic Society for All' in Bean, P., Ferris, J. and Whynes, D. (eds) *In Defence of Welfare* London: Tavistock Publications, pp. 74–96

Lee, L. (1983) 'The Social Worker in the Political Environment of the School System' in *Social Work* vol. 28, no. 4

Lekachman, R. (1982) *Greed is Not Enough: Reaganomics*, New York: Pantheon Books

Leonard, P. (1975) 'Toward a Paradigm for Radical Practice' in Bailey, R. and Brake, M. *Radical Social Work* London: Edward Arnold

Lerner, M. (1986) *Surplus Powerlessness* Oakland: Institute for Labor and Mental Health

Liffman, M. (1979) *Power for the Poor* Melbourne: Allen & Unwin

Lindblom, C. (1959) 'The Science of Muddling Through' in *Public Administration Review* 19, pp. 79–88

Lukes, S. (1974) *Power: a Radical View* London: Macmillan

—— (1986) *Power: Readings in Social and Political Theory* Oxford: Blackwell

Macy, J. (1983) *Despair and Personal Power in the Nuclear Age* Philadelphia: New Society Publishers

Marchant, H. and Wearing, B. (eds) (1988) *Gender Reclaimed, Women in Social Work* Sydney: Hale & Iremonger

Marquand, D. (1988) *The Unprincipled Society* London: Fontana Press

Marris, P. (1974) *Loss and Change* London: Routledge and Kegan Paul

Martin, B., Baker, C., Manwell, C. and Pugh, C. (eds) (1986) *Intellectual Suppression* Sydney: Angus & Robertson

McCaughey J. (1987) *A Bit of a Struggle* Melbourne: McPhee Gribble/Penguin

McCaughey, J. and Chew, W. (1977) 'The family study' in McCaughey, J., Shaver, S. and Ferber, H. *Who cares?* Melbourne: Sun Books

McCleod, E. and Dominelli, C. (1982) 'The Personal and the Apolitical: feminism and moving beyond the integrated methods approach' in Bailey, R. and Lee, P. (eds) *Theory and Practice in Social Work* Oxford: Blackwell

McDermott, C. (1989) 'Empowering the elderly nursing home resident: the residential rights campaign' in *Social Work* vol. 34, no. 2, March

McIntyre, D. (1982) 'On the Possibility of Radical Casework' in *Contemporary Social Work Education* vol. 5, no. 3

Milgram, S. (1974) *Obedience and Authority* London: Tavistock

Moreau, M. (1979) 'A Structural Approach to Social Work Practice' in *The Canadian Journal of Social Work Education* vol. 6, no. 8 pp. 490–497

Murdach, A. (1982) 'A Political Perspective in Problem Solving' in *Social Work* September, pp. 417–421

Murray, C. (1984) *American Social Policy, 1950–1980* New York: Basic Books

Nissell, M. and Bonnerjea, L. (1982) *Family care of handicapped elderly: who pays?* London: Policy Studies Institute

Nolan, C. (1988) *Under the Eye of the Clock* London: Pan

O'Connor, I. and Sweetapple, O. (1988) *Children in Justice* Melbourne: Longman Cheshire

Offe, C. (1984) *Contradictions of the Welfare State* London: Hutchinson
Panitch, A. (1974) 'Advocacy in Practice' in *Social Work* 19, pp. 326–332
Pemberton, J. (1988) The "end" of economic rationalism' in *The Australian Quarterly* Winter, 1988, pp. 188–199
Perlman, R. (1975) *Consumers and the Social Services* New York: John Wiley
Petruchenia, J. and Thorpe, R. (eds) (1990) *Social Change and Social Welfare Practice* Sydney: Hale & Iremonger
Pinderhughes, E. (1982) 'Family Functioning of Afro-Americans' in *Social Work* 27, pp. 91–6
—— (1983) 'Empowerment for our Clients and for Ourselves, in *Social Casework* vol. 64, no. 6 June
Pirsig, R.M. (1976) *Zen and the Art of Motorcycle Maintenance* London: Corgi
Prottas, J. (1979) *People-Processing: The Street-level Bureaucrat in Public Service Bureaucracies* Lexington: D.C. Heath and Company
Pusey, M. (1988) 'The outlook is dry' in *Australian Society,* July
—— (1991) *Economic Rationalism in Canberra* London: Cambridge Univ. Press
Rapoport, J. (1981) 'In Praise of Paradox: A Social Policy of Empowerment over Prevention' in *American Journal of Community Psychology* 9, (Jan–Feb) pp. 1–25
Rawls, J. (1972) *A Theory of Justice* London: Clarendon Press
Rees, S. (1978) *Social Work Face to Face* London: Edward Arnold
Rees, S. and Wallace, A. (1982) *Verdicts on Social Work* London: Edward Arnold
Rees, S. and Gibbons, L. (1986) *A Brutal Game* Sydney: Angus and Robertson
Rein, M. and White, S. (1981) 'Knowledge for Practice' in Gilbert, N. and Specht, H. (eds) *Handbook of the Social Services* Englewood Cliffs, New Jersey: Prentice Hall pp. 620–637
Reisch, M., Wencour, S. and Sherman, W. (1983) 'Empowerment; conscientization and animation as core social work skills' in *Social Development Issues* vol. 5, Summer and Fall pp. 108–120
Rose, S.M. and Black, B.L. (1985) *Advocacy and Empowerment* London: Routledge
Rosenfeld, J.M. (1989) *Emergence from Extreme Poverty* Paris: Science and Service Fourth World Publications
Rubinoff, L. (1967) *The Pornography of Power* Chicago: Quadrangle
Russell, B. (1918) *Mysticism and Logic* New York: Anchor Books
—— (1977) *Authority and the Individual* London: Unwin Paperbacks
Safilios-Rothschild, C. (1976) 'Disabled Persons' Self-Definitions and their implications for rehabilitation' in Albrecht, G.L. (ed.) *The Sociology of Physical Disability and Rehabilitation* Univ. of Pittsburgh Press, pp. 39–56
Sainsbury, E. (1977) *The Personal Social Services* London: Pitman
Satyamurti, C. (1981) *Occupational Survival* Oxford: Basil Blackwell
Saunders, P. (1988) 'Efficiency, equality and the welfare state' in Saunders, P. and Jamrozik, A. (eds) *Community Services Policy: economic and social implications* Sydney: SWRC Proceedings, no. 75, pp.13–30
Scheff, T.J. (1969) 'Negotiating Reality: Notes on Power in the Assessment of Responsibility' in *Social Problems* vol. 16, no. 1
Schorr, A. (1985) 'Professional Practice as Policy' in *Social Service Review* June
Schumacher, E. (1973) *Small is Beautiful, a study of economics as if people mattered,* London: Bland and Briggs
Setterlund, D. (1988) 'Gender: a Neglected Dimension in Social Work with

Elderly Women' in Chamberlain, E. (ed.) *Change and Continuity in Australian Social Work* Melbourne: Longman Cheshire

Sheldon, B. (1987) 'Implementing Findings from Social Work Effectiveness Research' in *British Journal of Social Work* 17, no. 6, pp. 573–586

Sherman W. and Wenocur, S. (1983) 'Empowering public welfare workers through mutual support' *Social Work* Sept.–Oct. pp. 375–379

Simpkin, N. (1979) *Trapped Within Welfare: Surviving Social Work* London: Macmillan

Smid, G. and van Krieken, R. (1984) 'Notes on theory and practice in social work: a comparative view' in *British Journal of Social Work* 14, pp. 11–22

Solomon, B. (1976) *Black Empowerment* New York: Columbia

—— (1987) 'Empowerment: social work in oppressed communities' in *Journal of Social Work Practice* May, pp. 79–91

Stretton, H. (1987) 'The Cult of Selfishness' in *Political Essays* Melbourne: Georgian House, pp. 184–194

Szalai, A. (ed.) (1972) *The Use of Time* The Hague: Mouton

Tawney, R. (1931) *Equality* London: Allen & Unwin

Thorpe, R. (1983) 'Street Level Bureaucracy in Australian Community Welfare', Unpublished paper, Univ. of Sydney

Thurow, L. (1988) *The Zero-Sum Society* London: Penguin

Titmuss, R. (1971) 'Welfare Rights, Law and Discretion' in *Political Quarterly* vol. 42, no. 1

—— (1958) 'The Social Division of Welfare: some reflections on the search for equity' in *Essays on the Welfare State* London: Allen & Unwin, pp. 34–55

Trethewey, J. (1986) *When the pressure is really on, A study of changes in income and expenditure among low income families* Melbourne: Brotherhood of St Laurence

Usher, J. (1988) 'Taking Control: A study of low income families', Masters Thesis, University of Sydney, unpublished

Vickers, G. (1985) *The Art of Judgement: A Study of Policy Making* New York: Basic Books

Walker, H. and Beaumont, B. (1981) *Probation Work: Critical Theory and Socialist Practice* Oxford: Basil Blackwell

Watts, R. (1987) *The Foundations of the National Welfare State* Sydney: Allen & Unwin

Whittaker, J. and Garbarino, J. (eds) (1983) *Social Support Networks* New York: Aldine

Yeatman, A. (1990) *Bureaucrats, Technocrats, Femocrats* Sydney: Allen & Unwin

Zimrim, H. (1984) 'Do Nothing But Do Something: the Effect of Human Contact with the Parent on Abusive Behaviour' in *British Journal of Social Work* 14, pp. 475–485

Index